DOING BU

Writer and broadcaster Jeremy Beadle was born in York in 1956 and educated in York and Oxford. He now lives in East London. His previous work includes the murder mystery *Death Scene*, also published by GMP.

DOING BUSINESS

A Love Story
About Murder and the Free Market

Jeremy Beadle

◁◁◁‖‖GMP‖‖▷▷

First published in April 1990 by GMP Publishers Ltd
P O Box 247, London N17 9QR, England

©1990 Jeremy Beadle

British Library Cataloguing in Publication Data

Beadle, Jeremy, 1956–
Doing business.
I. Title
823'.914 [F]

ISBN 0–85449–110–4

Cover art: *El Don de la Palabra (The Gift of Speech)* by
Roberto Gonzalez Fernandez
Taken from the book *Journeys* (GMP)

Distributed in North America by Alyson Publications Inc.
40 Plympton St, Boston. MA 02118, USA

Distributed in Australia by Stilone Pty Ltd
P O Box 155, Broadway, NSW 2007, Australia

Printed and bound in the EC on environment–friendly paper
by Norhaven A/S, Viborg, Denmark

For Michael Connors & Keith Bradley, the guides and mentors

Facilis descensus Averno:
Noctes atque dies patet atri ianua Ditis;
Sed revocare gradum superasque evadere ad auras,
Hoc opus, hic labor est.

It's easy to drop into Hell: the doors of the dark
Underworld are open all night and all day; but
retracing your step and escaping back to the fresh
air — well, that's hard work, bloody hard work.

(Virgil, *Aeneid VI*)

1

Later, when I found myself staring down the business end of the gun, I realised what a complete fool I'd been.

Hindsight. I'm a master of it. I can always tell when I've gone wrong or when I've made the wrong decision. Actually, I suspect I often know when I'm in the process of going wrong or making a wrong decision. Another brilliant gift of mine. But don't expect me to explain why I've managed to go wrong quite so often, quite so unerringly. If there is a reason, it's too tediously autobiographical to be worth the investment of anyone's valuable time. Anyway, when I actually found myself staring down the business end of the gun, I found myself ditching careful historical analysis in favour of more elementary and basic pastimes. Like sphincter control, pathetic pleading, random superstition - all the manifestations of true naked yellow Fear.

It's easy enough to see it now. That night I saw the guy get stabbed in the Magpie I should have gone straight to the Police. Looking back, I think they'd have believed me after all. Not many months do go by without some act of violence or other going on in the Magpie. I once saw one boy knock another half-way across the upstairs bar and through the banister, so he fell practically to the bottom of the stairs. Mind you, that looked more dramatic than it really was. It's not such a steep staircase and the 'victim' (who'd really been asking for it) was too pissed and stoned to hurt himself. The worst thing that happened was that my table got knocked over and my drink – or, knowing me, drinks – went west. Irritating, very. But in all a mild incident in Magpie terms.

The stabbing was more what you'd expect. But I found it a bit upsetting, never having seen a stabbing at first hand before. I mean, you see worse things on TV every night. I've paid good money to see films where infinitely more grotesque acts of violence have been lovingly and lavishly depicted. Pinned to my wall right in front of me now are some very nasty events given the full works by the great Italian masters – like that woman saint getting her tits chopped off or that bloodthirsty bitch in the Old Testament hacking off some poor sod's head. God knows, when I was a Biology 'A-Student' (to use a hideous but convenient unEnglish phrase) I regularly did more horrid and graphic things myself.

OK, I know, I'm digressing. You spotted. Well, I do. I was renowned in the Magpie for it. I got completely on Aidan's tits digressing. In fact, none of the boys in the Magpie found it too endearing a habit. Digressions, you see, aren't good for business. You don't close a deal by digressing. In fact, conversation of any kind isn't really the Magpie's forte, and certainly not its raison d'être. And the Fourth Magpie, just off Shaftesbury Avenue on the edge of Soho, is a pub with a purpose.

That particular night in November I'd sworn I'd go straight home. Work had been the usual piss-off – so much so that I shan't waste time describing it. Not anywhere, so don't hold your breath if you're looking for an exhaustive account of office life. The chances were, though, that if I did go straight home then I'd get a 'phone call I really didn't want and I've never been able not to answer a ringing telephone. So it was either risk a heavy conversation with Alec or get slammed out of my brain. No contest. Mind you, I have an uneasy suspicion that this is a bit of an after the event justification.

So I went out, straight from work – on my own, naturally. Most people I know are too conservative to set foot in the Magpie. I've forced all my 'nice' friends in there once, but they all got very sniffy about the experience afterwards. 'That terrible place, Gordon, it can't do you any good, why on earth do you go there, surely there are more salubrious places, et cetera, et cetera.' The lecture usually runs along those lines. Well, of course there are more respectable places – that's the point, I tell them. The Magpie's tacky and squalid. And I suppose it was a love of the tacky that led me there once upon a time. God, those glorious innocent days when I used to think the Magpie was just 'tacky'. I hadn't even heard of the Adonis Club then, let alone been there. I think those days must have belonged to another century. Anyway, by last November they were well past and gone forever and I was long out of that naivety.

Getting to the Magpie from work usually involved the Underground, unfortunately, unless I was feeling energetic enough to walk the mile and a half or so. And who feels energetic in November? Also at that time of year I prefer to avoid shops as much as possible. Christmas is usually spreading among them like a tenacious and rampant epidemic of syphilis – one of those strains which isn't fatal but lasts for months and is a bugger to get rid of. Actually, give me clap rather than Christmas any day. There's usually fun somewhere along the line with clap, which is more than you can say for Christmas. And clap doesn't twinkle in with a forced smile on its stupid face and urge you to consume, consume, consume. As I was due to hit my first Christmas party the next night I wanted to avoid any reference to the dread season if I could, and that would be possible, with a bit of luck, if I took the Tube and then cut through Chinatown.

I left work about half five, so – because the Northern Line was involved – I covered the whole six station journey by quarter past six. The Northern Line was on great form, not just because they'd managed to run the occasional train, but because they'd come up with a whole rash of excuses. I used the kind gift of this unscheduled leisure time to calculate some probabilities. Whatever an 'incident at London Bridge' really is, there's a one in four chance one happened today.

When I finally got where I was going, I applied my infallible Gordon McKenzie Rule of the Underground – 'The quickest way out is always marked "No Exit"' – and pushed my way into the stale London drizzle. Shaftesbury Avenue was a mess of aimlessly milling people, several of whom seemed to be after my money in one way or another, and totally immobile traffic.

The cars were easily dealt with, but the beggars touched my conscience. But it's unwise to give money away before you get into the Magpie. It's also pretty bloody daft to give it away afterwards, if you haven't been stupid enough to spend it all in there.

The door to the place is on a corner of two side roads. It's a pretty small pub with fairly ordinary decor. Nobody's bothered with more than the slightest lick of paint in years. Every so often, I've heard, the brewery who run the place – and God knows what they actually think about it – stick in a new landlord or landlady who tries to revamp it and change its essential self. It never works. It couldn't. Physically and spiritually the Magpie is immutable. Physically, in fact, it would be bloody impossible to mutate it, because it's a small square place and must contain the basic requirements – an entrance, a staircase to the upper bar, a bar (fairly essential), a door to subterranean toilets and stock rooms and a side door leading to an alternative staircase. Try arranging that lot over a small area and see how much room for fancy manoeuvre and subtle permutations of decor you've got left. Throw in minimal bar furniture and a couple of fruit machines and you're even more hampered. The upstairs bar is smaller.

A pretty typical Magpie scene greeted me. Right by the door were a couple of dubious looking scruffs, both a bit old by now. They weren't amongst my range of acquaintance. Over at the far side of the bar, Jackie McTavish was alternately sucking a bottle of lager and holding forth to an old drunk slumped neatly in a corner. Two teenage boys in tight blotchy jeans were playing on a fruit machine in a way that mystifyingly combined boredom with absorption. Every now and again one would hit it, the other would yell a curse or a whoop of delight and then they'd lapse into apathy. These noises seemed totally unrelated to whether or not the thing paid out any money. Wandering to the bar to order a drink I noted a fair number in already, mainly boys so far; there were one or two older men reading the evening paper, but not many as yet.

Of the boys I knew, there were the two Jasons, Paul (who was really called Patrick) and Patrick (who was really called Paul). Little Phil, whom I didn't like, was there too with some pretty little piece. Not my type. The usual Irish clique was over by Jackie McTavish; two of the endless, limitless Murphy clan, including the demonically handsome Paul who'd kissed me once in the Adonis Club. His erstwhile boyfriend Dermot, a lovely, large, plumpish bottle blond with a charming nature and a hopeless memory (mainly because he was always stoned) was standing deferentially behind them. He waved at me vaguely. Paul Murphy gave him a sharp look. Jackie McTavish treated me to a stage hostile glare.

As I ordered my drink, Paul (who was really called Patrick) came across and engaged me in innocent chit-chat.

'Gordon. How's it going? Ain't seen you for ages.' He had a rather fetching type of gap-toothed lisp which meant he aspirated his sibilants, or, as he would have put it himself if he'd had the vocabulary, ashpirated hish shibilantsh. His accent was pure London, his tone rather high-pitched, occasionally cracking, as if his voice was taking out an option on a second break. Aidan does a killingly funny impression of him.

'I was in on Friday. Today's only Monday.'

'Yeah, well, that's days innit? Can you buy us a drink, please?'

I was impressed. He'd managed three sentences before asking. And he'd said please. It must have been National Politeness Day. 'For you, Paul, certainly. How are you?'

'Oh, don't ask, don't ask.' He named a drink and I added it to my order. The barman, an incredibly ennui-struck youth with spiky peroxide locks, nodded wearily. Not exactly the Labours of fucking Hercules, I thought to myself, the opening of a bottle of German lager. I turned back to Paul and smiled, or did what passes for smiling with me. He was a nice looking youth, rangy, longish fair-brown hair, a good dress sense, rather a beaky nose and a deeply impressive criminal record. Picking up his bottle of pseudo-Teutonic gutrot he leaned down to me confidentially and murmured, 'Guess what? I've got clap.' He straightened up again and giggled. 'That stupid bitch Jackie,' he explained.

'Sorry to hear it,' I said. I never like to think of anyone's livelihood being threatened. 'You're out of action, then?'

'You must be joking. A boy's got to earn a living, ain't he? No, I've got to naff off to Maida Vale in a minute or two, see a punter there. 'Ow long d'you reckon it'd take me to get there?'

'Fifteen minutes for the journey. Add seven for the wait. Another five for stops in tunnels and five for the doors opening and shutting six times at Baker Street. Call it thirty-five to be on the safe side.'

'Aw fuck it, I'll get a cab.' He eyed me speculatively. 'You wouldn't happen to - '

I was about to resign myself to the inevitable when a hand descended on my shoulder and Paul stopped. A friendly gesture, you might think, a hand on the shoulder. Innocent, chummy, protective even. Well, not in this case. I recognised the sleeve, the hand, the touch and waited for the awful voice – that slimy mid-Atlantic Scots twang which I hadn't heard for some while now.

'Hey, man, how're you doing? You buying us a drink?'

'Fuck off, Gray,' Paul said, 'can't you see the man's talking to me?'

'Did anybody ask you – little boy.' A statement, not a question. In fact Paul was about the same height as Gray (real name Gary), but Gray had about him a substance of flesh and a sheer ability to menace which made Paul seem flimsy. I turned to face Gray, who only now removed his hand. Tall, quite muscular, dark – a handsome devil – he would have been stunning if he hadn't always been unshaven and drug-eyed. He tickled me under the chin like I was a pet or something. He must have been about eight inches taller than me, around six-two, but I always felt I was half his height or less. 'Hello, Gordon baby,' he said, 'long time, no see.'

'You – er – you haven't been – um – around,' I said. 'Have you been – well – away?' Behind me, Paul snorted.

'Oh yeah, man, I've been away for a while. You see, I accidentally stabbed someone. Where's my drink, then?'

Put like that, how could I refuse? The barman looked at Gray dubiously; every so often he got himself barred, but he always seemed to worm his way back in again. Whatever the barman's doubts, though, an elaborately-capped bottle of something was produced. Gray flicked back the cap and started drinking. He paused and waved his bottle at me.

'Man, you get thinner every time I see you. You ill or something?' I shook my head. 'You sure of that? I reckon you've used too many needles. Or too many pricks maybe.' He laughed at his own wit.

I looked round uneasily. Paul made an urgent gesture with his head, indicating that he was desirous of private conference. I shrugged gently. I didn't want to stand talking to Gray, but I didn't really want to have to shell out Paul's taxi fare to Maida Vale. Gray, meanwhile, was rambling on ominously about how he was 'totally skint, man,' and we both knew where that conversational route led. Somebody selected a song on the juke box, a bloody awful song I'd heard hundreds of times at the cinema, designed to flog fizzy drinks as either a substitute for or a companion to early sexual experience. Aidan did tell me what it was called, but I'm fucked if I can remember. Not my sort of tune. Things took on an even darker hue as my one line of retreat was cut off by the advance of the Jasons. They were long-standing cronies of Gray's - I think he pimped for them from time to time - so it was a pretty inevitable advance.

'Will you buy me a drink, please, Gordon?' asked the taller of the two, Lewisham Jason.

'Yeah, come on, Gords, I'm thirsty.' You may be getting a sense by now of why I regard Paul as a model of tact and courtesy. The second request came from Mile End Jason, quite short, in a dark spivvy suit, polecat handsome with a reptile smile. Gray turned to them and greeted them enthusiastically.

'Christ, I don't know why you put up with it,' Paul said as I turned back to the bar. 'Why don't you just tell them to fuck off?'

'Because they're bigger than me, I suppose. Do you need another one while I'm at it?'

'Well – oh, all right then.' It was a concession meant as a favour. 'You shouldn't let them push you around like that. Hello, Bob's got trouble.' I made one of those querying noises. Paul leaned against the bar and explained to me quietly. 'That bloke Bob's just coming down the stairs with, he's some rep for the brewery. Some new geezer. I heard Bob and Doreen talking about it this lunchtime. This new geezer's dead straight. Not like the last one. Could cause a few problems.'

I turned discreetly. Bob, the landlord, and his guest had reached the foot of the stairs. The brewery man was a classic faceless bureaucrat type, reminding me rather of a Labour MP I'd once bumped into in the Adonis Club. Bob, amiable but none too bright, with the look of an ex-Navy boxing champion, was definitely worried. He guided his guest to a table in the far corner, one often used by the boys as a point of rest when they got sick of trying to attract the attention of punters. The brewery man was carrying some ledgers which looked like props from a low-budget TV programme. A couple of boys who had been lounging at the table scuttled out of the corner. Paul Murphy strolled over to the juke box and selected some tunes so dreadful that my brain refuses to remember them. He then turned to the 'phone and began to make a call.

All four of my drinking acquaintances seemed to have been distracted by this not very enthralling chain of events and, with an eye to the main chance, I slipped out of the cordon. One of the rare advantages of being short and skeletal (tall and skeletal seems to make you sexy these days, though I've never seen it myself). Unobtrusively I perched myself on the low window ledge by the foot of the stairs. Gray and Mile End Jason wandered off in the other direction, sinking deep into a conversation which I was glad I couldn't hear. Paul was accosted by his friend Patrick (who was really called Paul). This left Lewisham Jason at a loose end and I was the lucky beneficiary.

'Things are really bad,' he offered, shaking his spiky-topped head. He drew back his lips momentarily, baring his feral teeth. When I first met Lewisham Jason, I'd rather fancied him, but a brief spell away, on much the same terms as Gray, had aged him in an indefinable way. I didn't object to that as a matter of principle, but he'd also picked up a hostile, edgy manner, a sense of something nasty lurking beneath the surface which added a harsh gruffness to his South London accent. Before, he'd been a pretty working-class boy in a red baseball jacket and tight jeans; now he was recognisably an ex-convict. I'd gathered from hints he'd dropped that he now found business hard to come by, although most boys would say that as a matter of course. 'I don't know how I'm gonna get through the week, I really don't,' he went on. 'Have you got a – oh, you don't smoke, do you?'

'The one vice I'm saving for my old age.'

'Well, if you're after any other vice tonight –' I cut him off by laughing and shaking my head. 'You never do, do you? Buy us a packet of fags, would you?'

'I'll give you the money. I always get the wrong sort. How much are they?'

'About two quid.'

'Nice try, Jason, nice try.' I started to count out one pound fifty, but as I was about to hand it over, the door burst open and a thin hyper-active blond with large ice-blue eyes burst in. He spotted me immediately and knew exactly what was going on.

'God, Jason, are you on the scrounge again? If you give him one penny, Gordon, I'll belt you.' The rich Lancastrian burr warmed up the bare language. Darren tended to watch me – after a few drinks I'd start handing cash out on enormous scales, and for various reasons Darren thought this should be discouraged. I'd say that at that juncture Darren was the boy I knew best – I even knew his real name and where he came from – and he could certainly have corrected Jason's theory that I 'never did.' I think Darren tended to look at me as one of his regulars, but that wasn't right either.

'Fuck off, Darren, what's it to you? It's the man's money, innit?' Jason's air of menace was real enough to me, but it failed to impress Darren.

'You after an early night's sleep, Jason?' He put his left hand into the pocket of his leather jacket. 'I think your mate wants you, so why don't you go and talk to him? And stop – scrounging – from – my – mates.' Each of these words was accompanied by a little right-handed prod into Jason's chest. The sentence ended with a gesture across to the bar where Gray stood by the fruit machine with Mile End Jason and Paul Murphy. Gray crooked his finger and beckoned Lewisham Jason.

'You've got a very high opinion of yourself, Darren,' Jason said with another feral scowl. But he tamely turned away and went to join his friends. Darren gave a manic laugh, briefly bent his body double – I think you'd call him wiry rather than muscular – and then playfully punched me on the shoulder.

'He's right – I've got an exceedingly high opinion of myself.' He rolled the adverb around his mouth, obviously proud of his command of it. 'Nah then, you old bag of bones, you. You nearly hurt me then,' he said, examining his knuckles for bruises. 'I rang you up a few minutes ago.'

'Was I there?'

'That's a question we all ask, Gordon. Hey – talking of people who aren't all there, that fucking moron Billy was back in the Adonis last night. Followed me around like Mary's fucking little lamb. I had to find him a punter to get rid of him. Fucking embarrassing. I was trying to buy some stuff off Nigel – about five people waiting to buy it from me as well, all had to be done last night – and fucking Billy hanging around going "Darren" like some kid who's lost his way to the toilet.'

'Knowing Billy, that might well have been the case.'

Darren laughed again. I can't describe his laugh, it doesn't translate; like his accent, really. He took up his narrative. 'In the end I had to get rid of him on some punter I don't know too well, and I don't like recommending a fucking cretin like Billy to anyone. I mean, it doesn't do my reputation any good if he turns funny and starts nicking again and I recommended him.'

'I didn't realise he was a thief.'

'Oh, I don't know that he does. You know Billy, he's a bit wrong up here – ' Darren touched his temple – 'doesn't always know what he's doing.'

'Sad. I nearly took him back once – I felt sorry for him.'

Darren shook his head vigorously and pushed a stray lock of blond hair back from his eyes. 'Never, Gordon. Never. He doesn't even nick things he wants or things he can sell. If he's nicking, he just nicks and carries things round in his bag for weeks.' He looked round quickly. 'Not much doing here as bloody usual.'

'That little mob over there look busy.'

'Oh, I know what they're up to. They'll be off down to t' toilet in a minute. I sold Gray some stuff last night. Complete shit it was. I wouldn't waste good stuff on that shithead.' He looked over and smiled graphically and insincerely at Gray, who gave an equally trustworthy salute back. However, rather than heading for the loo, he picked up the 'phone; his cronies gathered round him, Paul Murphy staying with them. I looked back at Darren, who was eyeing me appraisingly. 'What're you up to tonight then, Gordon? Are you down the Adonis later? Nigel said he'd have some of them tabs tonight.'

'Ah. That sounds interesting. Basically my plan was to get slammed. I'm avoiding someone.'

'Anyone I know?'

'You know I don't talk about my private life to anyone. Not here, not at work, not to my friends – nowhere.'

'Don't worry – I just meant would it stop you going down the Adonis?' He paused to take out and light a cigarette. 'I mean – I'm looking for somewhere to stay tonight.'

'You've still not found anywhere?'

He nodded and exhaled smoke. 'No bastard where to go. So I was wondering – '

'Ah. Well. I am working tomorrow. Supposedly.'

'Well, we can talk about that later, after we've had a few – ' Darren carried on, but at that exact moment the door to the

Magpie opened and my universe changed its shape.

I can give you all the details about Aidan you'd ever need, if you want; his height, his gentle brown eyes, that thin, long, curved nose, the elastic neck, the light brown hair, the thin frame (unusual that, my ideals are always rather macho as a rule) – all that and more I could give you over and over again in various nauseatingly periphrastic manners, like Barbara Cartland after twelve lines of sulphate. But none of it could ever convey that first moment, that first impression. In the end, it's always the ears I come back to, the Clark Gable 'don't give a damn' ears. And later, that nearly-dimpled, rubber-necked smile. The initial attraction wasn't crude. Aidan doesn't go in for crotch-hugging, bulge-enhancing jeans or torso-revealing T-shirts. He was well, but not eye-catchingly trendily dressed; his hair was stylishly, but not modishly cut. But before I ever got to speak to him, I think I lost my heart and, most crucially in this context, my mind to his ears.

Aidan has a cautious manner. He hangs back after walking through a door. That night he gave an impression of not being obviously familiar with anyone there. He told me later that he saw me staring at him as he walked carefully to the bar. 'Gawping you were, like your eyes was on stalks.' Darren noticed too, and commented at the time.

'Hello? Hello? God, he's somewhere else again. Gordon – do be just a little more subtle. Could you? Like put your tongue back in your mouth?'

'Who is he?' I managed to articulate.

'His name's Aidan. Sort of everybody knows him but nobody does really, if you know what I mean. He doesn't go down the Adonis or that. I'm surprised you've not seen him before.' I was still transfixed. 'He's only another rent boy, Gordon, like the rest of us.' This pragmatic approach elicited no response either. 'Look, seeing how you're a mate, and you've done us favours and all that, and I like you even if you are a difficult bastard, I'll introduce you. I know him; he bought some stuff off us once. But I don't know what he's like, if you can trust him or owt like that. So if he does turn out nasty, don't blame me.'

Darren turned and looked. Aidan was still alone, apparently. Darren turned back to me. He extinguished his current cigarette. 'I'll go and have a word. But just bear one thing in mind, Gordon. I'm never quite sure what you're doing in here half the time. I'm never that sure you know what you're up to yourself. But whatever it is you're looking for, or whatever you think you're looking for, the answer won't – it fucking won't –

be a rent boy. Not for a minute. Not me, not Jason, not Billy, and not Aidan. Just remember that.'

'Rent boys are people, Darren. People are all different. That's their great redeeming feature.'

'Rent boys aren't people when they're after punters, Gordon. And punters aren't people either. It's just meat and customers. Goods and consumers. That's all. You might think we're all different, but we don't give a fuck what you think. 'Cos we don't think you're all different.'

I smiled. 'Well, everything you've been saying shows that neither side of that equation is true with you and me.'

'Maybe. But that doesn't make Aidan your Dream Prince.'

'Unless you introduce me, I'll never be able to find that out for myself.'

Darren shrugged, raised his eyebrows and started to move off. I called him back and slipped him a fiver. 'Get the three of us a drink,' I said.

An agonised eternity of waiting followed for about two minutes. Darren had a way with bar staff, which mainly consisted of yelling perpetually until he got served. I suppose it's a trick you learn as a baby. I watched him insinuate himself next to Aidan at the bar and initiate conversation. What about, I don't know. Aidan pointed to his glass, obviously indicating what he wanted to drink, so that was OK. Both boys looked over to where I was sitting. Aidan smiled – was it to me or at me? Whichever, it was devastating. Darren gave Aidan a glass, then turned back to the bar and grabbed two more.

'Aidan, this is Gordon, a very good friend of mine.' Darren handed me a glass which I quickly switched to the left hand and thrust my right towards Aidan. He raised his eyebrows in salutation and took my little paw in his long slim elegant hand. The handshake was soft and allowed to linger.

'Pleased to meet you. Ta for the drink.'

'Pleasure. Are you from Liverpool? No, not quite.'

'Not bad.' He smiled again. 'Manchester. Most of them down here seem to think I'm from Glasgow, you know.'

I laughed. 'People down here are stupid.'

'You're not from London, then?'

'No – I'm the original hick from the sticks.' I looked at him as I said this. He was definitely different from the others; he had a gentle look I'd never seen in any of them. Darren coughed at this point to drag my attention back.

'I'll – er – just go for a wander, Gordon. See who's around.' I raised my hand in benedictive dismissal. Darren moved away. I looked back to Aidan and smiled again.

'You're not going for a wander just yet?'

'I never wander round here if I can help it.'

'Ah. That may be why I've never seen you before.'

'Haven't you? I can't claim to be exactly a stranger round here. Actually, I think I've seen you once or twice. You was talking to someone.' The accent was strong, but the voice was very gentle. Listening to him required concentration, particularly when there was a high level of noise around. Paul passed by on his way out – presumably off to Maida Vale at last – and gave me a wave. He also gave a calculating look at Aidan and made a gesture with his head which could have meant several things, none of them very savoury.

'You know all the bad lads, do you?' Aidan said to me.

'Oh, I'll talk to anyone.'

'Ta very much.' Aidan smiled. 'I bet you say that to all the boys.'

'No, I – well, I'm always talking. I even talk to myself.'

'Well, you know what they say about that.' He looked at me, amused. 'Is it true? You off your chump, Gordon?'

'Oh, completely. Ask any of my friends. My real friends. Not the people in here. Or the Adonis Club.'

'Oh God, you don't go in there, do you? I never go in there. Shithole, that place.'

'So where do you go?'

'Oh, I go to the Blue Parrot, me.'

'That's quite nice, isn't it?'

'It's all right. I think that's where I've seen you, actually. You was sitting round the piano talking to some kid or other. I think it was you.'

By now you may be tiring of this high-level quickfire banter worthy of Noel Coward at his best. My problem was that I just hadn't drunk enough. I didn't want to subject Aidan to a barrage of personal questions – they always find that uncomfortable – and I don't like talking about myself. What I wanted was to hear him talk about himself on his own terms; but I had to find a way in first. With the other boys there was always hostility if you pushed the personal questions.

I wasn't afraid of that with Aidan. I was more afraid of upsetting him, of embarrassing him. There was something a bit fragile about his manner, an air of vulnerability. I wanted to hold him as much to protect him as for the sexual thrill. Something about him tapped feelings in me I'd forgotten I had. As we went on in a gentle, meaningless question and answer session about London and Manchester, I felt these feelings deepen at an uncomfortable pace. I became aware of quite how deep they'd already become when for some reason I raised the subject of biology experiments I'd done at school. I think Aidan was complaining about a muscular twinge in one of his calves brought on by too much swimming, and I was drawing some pointless analogy with a dead bunny I'd mutilated once. Rather gleefully I was going into detail when Aidan shuddered.

'Gordo, shurrup, please. If you don't mind. I think that's horrible, doing that to an animal. You wouldn't do it to a person, would you?'

'Of course I wouldn't. I physically couldn't. Anyway, the rabbit was dead.'

'I don't know that makes it any better. I mean, anyway, it couldn't fight back, could it? It's not like a rabbit could come at you with a knife and cut you up even if it wanted to.'

'You mean you think it's worse to do that to a dead rabbit than a live human being?'

'In some ways I do, yes. It's certainly more – you know – cruel.' I laughed, and Aidan looked at me quite sorrowfully. 'I hope you're not cruel to animals, Gordon.'

How could I resist this soft-hearted boy? 'Of course I'm not,' I said gently. 'But I do value people more than animals. Other animals, I should say. Basically, I suppose because I'm a human being myself and I happen to value the things human beings have done. I mean, name one major opera composed by a Giant Panda. Show me a great painting by a Blue Whale. Expound me a mathematical conjecture posited by a Great White Rhino.'

Aidan laughed uncertainly. 'Could you talk English, do you think? Actually, Gordon, I couldn't name you an opera by anyone, so I don't really know what you're on about.'

'It's all right. I'm not going to talk about opera to you. Unless you want me to. Do you know Mile End Jason? The one over there in the suit?'

'Him? He's a mate of that Gary, isn't he? I keep well away from him.' There it was again. I wanted to look after him and keep him safe from this harsh world he was so obviously at sea and lost in.

'He's not a bosom pal of mine. He just keeps trying to scrounge drinks off me.' I hoped that this gave the impression he didn't succeed. 'No, I once tried to explain about opera to him. Ridiculous. He said to me – ' I put on a thin, wheedling

19

East London accent – ' "Gordon, I don't know fuck all about fuckin' op'ra and I don't want to know fuck all about fuckin' op'ra. Except that guys that go to op'ra usually have plenty of handbag. Now that I do find interestin'." So I learnt my lesson from that.'

Aidan smiled – a conventional smile, he still hadn't used his killer yet. 'That sounds dead like Jason, actually,' he said. The compliment made my day.

At that moment we were interrupted – infuriatingly and surprisingly – by Paul Murphy. I thought it unlikely he wanted me and I was right.

'Aidan. Come over here a minute. I need to talk to you.'

'I can hear you just as well over here, thanks, Paul.'

'It's urgent. Private.' He put his hand on Aidan's arm and let it rest there.

'Oh God. All right. I'll see you over there in a minute.'

Paul smiled. He was very handsome, but had appalling teeth. 'Am I interrupting something?' He hadn't withdrawn his arm yet and I was beginning to wonder if I could hit him somehow. My punch packs the power of a lettuce leaf, but even so I have my passions.

'Actually, yes,' Aidan said. 'Look, I'll talk to you in a bit.'

Paul squeezed Aidan's arm. 'You'd better.' It wasn't just a question of physique here; Aidan was about as tall as Paul and similarly built. But Paul seemed invested with seniority, both in age and in Magpie experience; his twenty-five or so easily outranked Aidan's – well, I didn't know, but I guessed around twenty. And also Paul was confident, while Aidan seemed so lost. Paul was so sure of himself that he allowed me a malicious grin of triumph before leaving us together.

'Sorry about that,' Aidan said. 'He's one of the reasons I don't come here much. He fancies me, you see, and expects it free. Well, sort of free, anyway.' He shrugged. 'Fancies himself as a fixer. The only thing he fixes is heroin.'

'Does he fix that for you?'

'You are joking, I hope. No, a little bit of dope's my limit. That's how I know Darren. Shit. Looks like our trip to the Parrot's off.'

'Were we having one?' I asked disingenuously. Aidan gave me my first taste of his special smile; a coy, dimpled look on his face and a rubbery forward dart of his long slender neck. I think I sighed audibly. 'Do you have to do what he wants?'

An earnest look appeared on Aidan's face. 'Look. I like you. You're obviously a nice guy, on the level and that. Why don't you meet me later in the week? What about Wednesday?'

In my excitement I grabbed his arm for a moment. 'Sorry.' I let it go, blushing furiously beneath my acne. 'It must be a bit awful for you, I mean, here I am, more than ten years older than you and – '

'I'm twenty-one.' He gave another rubber-necked smile. 'Something like that, anyway. You're thirty – what? Five? Not so much, is it?'

'Thirty-three. But it is ten years. A bit over, actually.'

'Brilliant, Gordo. Mental arithmetic must be your thing.'

'Actually, I've got a doctorate in pure mathematics. For what that's worth.'

'What is it worth? You free Wednesday night, then?' I nodded happily. 'Half seven in here. OK?' He took hold of my right arm, leaned down and kissed me on the cheek. If you'd seen the state of my acne, you'd know what an amazing tribute to his bravery that action was. 'Don't forget now,' he said. 'I get fucked off by wind-up merchants.'

'I'll be there.' I stared with amazement at him. 'I swear it.'

Aidan moved away, giving me a little wave with his fingers. I watched him go over to Paul Murphy's little group. Jackie McTavish wasn't with them now, he was slumped next to the old drunk. Darren was nowhere to be seen, presumably upstairs. As Aidan reached Paul, Gray and the Jasons moved away towards the door. All three glanced at me, but only Mile End Jason was feeling friendly enough to offer a malevolent smile in my direction. They left, and through the slowly closing door I could see the clinical light of a burger bar, a thin and muggy drizzle lit up by it. The door closed again, sealing us back in our hermetic nether world. Paul was obviously explaining something to Aidan, using gestures I couldn't follow, like a bookie at a racetrack; Aidan, as far as I could tell, looked as puzzled as I was. I gazed at him lovingly, wishing I had the means to rescue him. A sleepy Irish brogue accosted my attention.

'Hello Gordon.'

I started. It was handsome big puppy Dermot, looking fairly casual in faded denim this evening. 'Hello, Dermot.'

'So when are you taking me out to dinner?'

'I kept trying to. You kept forgetting.' I wondered if the implication of the past tense would be lost on him.

'What about this week?' It was.

'Not sure. I'm a bit busy. You know Aidan, do you?' I asked, just for the pleasure of saying the name aloud.

'Not really. What're you looking at?'

I was looking at Paul Murphy escorting Aidan to the door. Before they left, Aidan half turned and looked right at me. He raised his left hand and pointed a finger. That made it definite. I had made a sort of bargain with the Fates, the Powers that Most Certainly Be, that if he went without some kind of farewell sign or if I left and he didn't see me going, then he wasn't serious and so I shouldn't keep the date. However much he'd staggered me, however beautiful et cetera I found him, I wasn't a complete fool. Rent boys break and forget dates as easily as they make them – and so do punters. And, being sensible (which was rather hard for me), did I really need, right now, at this point in my life, to get involved with a rent boy, however devastatingly charming? Sense – financial, common and sixth – argued against it. As always in a doubtful case, I submitted the matter to a higher authority. Sorry if that sounds a bit cosmological, but without getting over-confessional, you'll get to see that I have a view on this kind of thing.

'Nothing,' I said to Dermot. 'Just staring. I think I need another drink. Presumably you do.' At this point we were joined by Darren, bouncing downstairs. So I bought a round and then I bought another round or three, trudging the short space across the faded, drink-smeared carpet, following the subtle and ever-increasing trail of fag-ends, while the three of us sustained a conversation of such intense fascination that I can scarcely remember it. You'd think I'd remember every part of that evening in the smallest detail since it turned out to be so crucial. But there you are. Even when life is at its most intensely thrilling, it's crammed to the gills with deadly dull bits. I recall Dermot bemoaning the boredom of the office temping jobs he kept getting fired from (as I rather uncharitably assumed; he called it 'walking out'). Darren was explaining how he'd be going to America next week to make his fortune running video arcades. Darren had been explaining this ever since I'd met him nearly a year earlier. I kept my own counsel to a remarkable extent, managing only one slight digression on the topic of perspective in fourteenth and fifteenth century Italian painting. I won't repeat it now. Darren rather squashed this by suggesting that a bit of perspective in the twentieth century about certain people who hang around the Magpie wouldn't come amiss. Dermot then assumed he was being got at and they started to prod each other. I decided that the best diplomatic tactic was to relieve my bladder so I left them to get on with it.

The door to the loo in the Magpie opens onto a steep flight of stairs leading downwards which turn a sharply right-angled corner. The gents then lies dead ahead of you (the ladies is somewhere on the first floor and anyway only gets used by men). On the right and left are different kinds of stock room, cellar, tube room, whatever. All I know is that the bar staff move barrels and crates from one to the other for arcane purposes of their trade. Quite often during an evening either or both of these doors will be open. There's no real reason, then, why the awareness as I reached the turn in the stairs that the right hand door was open should have made me pause. I mean, I must have been treading softly anyway; no-one heard me coming. OK, I'm a skinny runt, but I'm usually quite noisy. Anyway, I stopped. And I heard that voice.

'Right boys. Hold him carefully. This has got to be clever. You poor bastard. You shouldn't have bothered snooping round here, man.'

I flattened myself against the wall and sidled down two of the four steps left in front of me. Another brilliant mistake. I was getting involved here.

The door wasn't wide open. It was more ajar on a grandiose scale, if you see what I mean, creating in its own way a line of perspective that could have come straight out of an early Uccello or Piero. My eye was led along the line of the door to a shaft of light, throwing in a touch of Caravaggio, which lit up that arm, that sleeve, that hand – and in the hand a knife of the kind strenuously denounced by Government Ministers and easily bought from the nearest sweetshop. Seeing Gray standing there wielding the thing prompted a bizarre thought: didn't he go out? And how did he get back in again? Was I imagining things? Cautiously, I gave my eyes a quick rub.

No, he was still there. He made a quick jabbing motion with his hand and I could just make out the knife hitting something. White fabric. No, it was red and white. There was a deep resistance against believing what I was seeing here. Gray was at an angle to me that allowed me to see the man's face. Bespectacled and, the only time I'd noticed it earlier that evening, stern and austere. Well, he didn't seem too austere now. In fact, he didn't seem anything much now, except maybe in pain. He let out a low winded moan. Gray laughed.

'Hey, man, don't make too much noise. We don't want anyone gatecrashing our little party, do we boys?' This was met by muffled giggling. I hadn't taken in the earlier hint that Gray had accomplices; I couldn't actually see them and I was now too terrified to shift myself so I might be able to. I was too terrified even to make an immediate break for it.

'Right, man, it's time to make a move. Can you hear me? Let's go.' Panic seized me. What now? Up or down? Another giggle bought me a moment's planning time. 'Aw, for fuck's sake, man, are you so stoned?' I took it that this wasn't addressed to the victim. 'Oh, all fuckin' right, I'll do it myself.' He stepped forward so that all I could see was his back. This had to be my moment. Any second's delay and I'd be facing at least him and God knew how many others. Clinging to the wall, I moved stealthily back, all this time wondering why no-one else was coming down to the loo on a busy night. Well, you do wonder odd things under pressure. It seemed so unlikely that I became unsure again whether I was really seeing all this. Perhaps I was still talking to Dermot and Darren or still at work or in bed or dead or something. Round the corner, quietly up the stairs, I was now only two from the top. I'd made it. I reached for the door handle.

And then, just before I could push it open, in the half-light of the stairs I saw Gray appear in the turn at the bottom with the brewery rep's arm draped around his shoulder. He pulled his victim up with near contemptuous ease. He turned his head back and called softly, 'Didn't need you guys anyway,' then he looked ahead of him straight up the stairs.

I was trying to hide, I really was. I'm quite good at going unnoticed as a rule. But it didn't work. Gray looked straight up at me. 'Hey man.' He laughed. For a moment we both stood, frozen – then I sprang, through the door, into the bar, pushing people aside. One of them was Darren. He and Dermot were standing together doing – well, I can't remotely remember what they were doing. For all I'd have registered it they could have been giving each other blowjobs.

'Quick,' I said to Darren, 'quick.'

'Gordon? What's up? What's – ?' He looked at me. I grabbed him with a strength you wouldn't associate with me and dragged him out into the street. I imagine this attracted some attention, but I had other preoccupations.

'No time,' I said. 'Please. Run. Tube. Twenty quid if you see me safe onto train.' I galloped off. I wasn't bothering to look round and see if Gray was following. I just assumed. Across Shaftesbury Avenue and into Chinatown, I realised that Darren had stuck with me. He seemed capable of speech.

'Who're we running from? Do you want me to see you home? I need somewhere to stay tonight, anyway.'

'Explain. Later.' I swerved round some people, ran across

the road to the less busy entrance to the station. Through the barrier, down the escalator. On the Southbound platform I stopped, panting heavily. 'Was anyone chasing us?'

Darren panted too, overdoing it a bit. 'Now you bloody ask.'

The train was due in one minute. That could mean anything up to half an hour. I looked at Darren, his pop eyes bulging with curiosity. Did I tell him? I wasn't sure now what I had seen. 'Gray,' I said eventually, breathing heavily. 'Wanted my money. He had a knife.'

'Oh, that pillock. You shouldn't take any notice of him.'

'It wasn't him I took notice of, it was his knife.'

'You should have told Bob or Doreen. They'd have thrown him out. You should have – '

'Please. Darren. Don't.' The wind of the incoming train brought a stale refreshment to my sweaty face. 'I don't want to talk. Not now. Do you want to come back?'

'Yeah, I don't mind. I've not got anywhere for tonight. If you can do us that favour too. The score.'

Money. Who needs it? Well, I do, for one. Still, I'd promised. 'I promised, didn't I?' We got on the train and it pulled away. Safe. After all, Gray didn't know where I lived, where I worked and there wasn't anyone to tell him, was there? Then it struck me. I didn't know who his partners in crime had been. Supposing I'd taken one of them home once. Although I was well known for not doing business as a rule, every rule has its exceptions and there were three or four boys apart from Darren who knew where my flat was. Still, if I didn't go near the Magpie again, maybe they wouldn't bother, they'd just leave me alone. So all I had to do was stay out of the Magpie.

But I couldn't do that, could I? Of course not. I'd promised Aidan I'd meet him there on the Wednesday. And underneath all the fear and terror I was certain of one thing. I had to see Aidan again. I simply had to. Whatever the risk.

2

Simon Green poured a packet of sumptuous World Snacks into a tasteful dish with an Asian design. 'Well, if that's what you saw, you should go to the Police.' He handed the dish to me. I took it across his sitting room and deposited it on the spotless tablecloth calculatedly draped over his sturdy oak table in the bay window.

'It is what I saw. I wonder why you don't believe me.' Actually, I knew bloody well why he didn't believe me. I picked out a World Snack and bit it. The only flavour I could detect was Artificial. Official Artificial flavoured crisps. Just what the world needs. 'And you know why I can't go to the Police.'

Simon fixed me with his fair vulpine features. 'I'm not sure I do. After all, they didn't actually charge you.'

'No. But they did arrest me. It'll be somewhere on their records, on one of their green screens. So I go and see them, tell them what's happened – what's the first thing they do? Run a check on me. Let's play Police Bingo. Then they hit the jackpot.'

'I think you're exaggerating really.' Simon views me as a fantastical child, which is his right. I really don't mind. The fact that he's four years younger really doesn't matter. He gets his moral superiority from a horribly cool mind and, most important, the fact that he earns a good fifteen thousand a year more than me. I can't argue against his rights over me in the face of that. 'Anyway,' he said, pulling open a packet of Round The Globe Mexican Beef Flavoured Cookies to fill the three expectant bowls sitting in front of him, 'at least you'll keep away from that awful pub now.'

'Ah.' I smiled.

'Oh God. The coy smile. That's bad.'

I'm not aware of how my coy smile differs from any other smile I possess. Simon's never been at all illuminating on this point.

'You are going to stay away from there, then?' For a moment he set his exotic titbits aside. 'I mean, if you saw what you say you saw then you're hardly going to want to go back there again. Not if that peculiarly unpleasant thug actually saw you.' Simon had once encountered Gray when I was conducting sight-seeing tour of London's low-life. 'I mean, if you go back there – ' he paused and returned his attention to his crunchy

26

bits, making this pregnant with symbolism.

I tried smiling again, uncertain whether it would be seen as coy. 'Simon, I think you don't believe me.'

'Well – that's not exactly it, but – sometimes you – well, you have been under some strain, haven't you?'

'Have I?'

'Well, you know, what with – '

'Simon.' I interrupted him. I didn't want to follow where this conversation looked like running off to. 'None of us can pretend that I'm the most reliably balanced person around, but I haven't suddenly developed a tendency to hallucinate. Particularly not to hallucinate murders.'

'You don't know it was a murder.'

'Well, I don't think it was a historical tableau. After all, Gray's never struck me as the amateur dramatics type. Do you think I could possibly have a drink? Or do you think that's part of the trouble?'

'I think you sometimes drink too much. But you know that.'

'Drink too much?' The interjection came from a female voice. Through the door came Simon's girlfriend Sally, carefully portering a couple of jugs of a punch which would inevitably be weak, spineless and sickly. Even though she was intensely concentrated on her task, her small pale face evinced its usual air of complete surprise. Sally always looked as though the world had just made her some fascinating, lucrative but slightly shocking offer. This evening she'd tied her shoulder-length fine blonde hair back into a pigtail. Sally was a much sought after woman; not only beautiful in a distinctive way, but intelligent and on a higher salary than Simon.

She took her burden to the table in the window and deposited it carefully. 'Can anyone drink too much?' she asked with a light girlish laugh. I bet the girlish laugh had made her a fortune in the City. As I'd never seen her drink more than a glass of white wine and soda, her espousal of extreme indulgence didn't strike me as exactly convincing.

'Gordon's just been telling me about a murder he saw.' If I'd been at all uncertain of Simon's attitude, I had it crystal clear there.

'Oh really? How exciting. I must say, Gordon, you always make me feel I lead such a boring life.'

'Another day, another drama, that's me. Even if it's only a new zit.'

'So witnessing a murder is like getting a zit?' Simon asked. 'Interesting perspective.'

'He doesn't believe me,' I explained to Sally.

'What did the Police say?' she asked.

'Oh, I haven't bothered them with it. Not their kind of thing, really. Anyway, I'm allergic to policepersons.'

'Oh, I see.' Well, that was that. Sally didn't believe me either.

'Whatever you saw,' Simon said, returning to a favourite theme, 'maybe you'll stay out of that bloody awful pub now. Any chance of that?'

'Any chance of a drink? A real drink?' Simon gave a shrug of exasperation, reached into a cupboard nearby and pulled out a can of lager. He threw it at me. It was lukewarm to the touch. I don't care about these things very much. I only drink lager because it's fattening. Toying with the ring pull I smiled again.

'One more coy smile and you're on orange juice for the rest of the night.'

'I have a very important appointment there tomorrow night. At the Magpie, I mean.'

'Oh yes?' Sally said. 'Is this with what's his name? Alec?'

'I said your little tiff wouldn't last,' Simon took up. 'You're just embarrassed because you tried to make out it was definitely the end, aren't you?'

'It was definitely the end. I'm not meeting Alec. I'm meeting a charming young man with Clark Gable ears and a killer smile who impressed me greatly yesterday. In fact, more than impressed me, I think.'

'Oh God. Not lurve. I can stand anything but lurve.' Simon thrust two bowls of ersatz-flavoured dainties at me. I took them for a walk around the room while he harangued me. 'The great thing about Alec, as far as I could see, was that you weren't completely besotted with him. Apart from the fact that he struck me as a reasonably intelligent person and the kind you could take home to meet your — I mean, the kind of person you could introduce to your friends. So who's this charming young man with jug handle ears?'

I was torn between an anxiety not to be subjected to one of Simon's moralistic tirades and an intense desire to talk about Aidan. 'He's called Aidan.' You can see which side won. 'He's got a beautiful Mancunian accent and rather a neat sense of humour and —'

'Where did you actually meet him?'

I raised my eyebrows. 'Does that matter?'

'I suppose that means in the Magpie. And does this Adrian have a job? Can I possibly guess what it is?'

'Oh, don't be horrible to him,' said Sally. 'It must be nice to be besotted with someone. Just because you're incapable of it –'

'He's called Aidan,' I said. 'Yes, I did meet him in the Magpie. Yes, you probably can guess how he makes his living. It's hardly his fault, is it?'

'No, of course not. After all, being a rent boy's compulsory now, isn't it? I mean, there aren't any other jobs going in the South East, are there? There aren't any training schemes or sponsored courses, are there?'

'Don't be childish, Simon. You know you born-again Tories are always the worst.'

'Now, now,' Sally interjected. There was always a danger of this argument turning bitterly personal. I had known Simon when he had been a left-wing activist, before he had taken the Road to Damascus and faced the historical inevitability of the New Realism of the Free Market. Sally had heard this all before, and she was one of those people who believe that politics shouldn't be discussed in a decent home.

'Don't worry.' I gave her a weary smile. 'I shan't start pleading the cause of the runaways and dispossessed or any of that stuff. But it is possible to be compassionate without advocating prostitution, you know. Simon knows the arguments as well as I do. He used to put them across a lot better than I ever could.'

'We seem to have got a long way from your murder,' she replied with a plastic laugh.

'Don't we?' Simon said. 'Well, I don't give people advice, Gordon. You know me. But if you saw what you say you saw, then I think you should go to the Police. And even if you don't, I wouldn't risk going back there and getting entangled with this Aids-boy or whatever he's called. After all, I don't really think you want to get beaten up, either by Gray or this big-eared beauty of yours.'

'Aidan didn't strike me as the type who beats people up,' I said.

'Maybe not. But I bet he knows a man who does.'

'Didn't you know someone who got murdered?' Sally said to Simon.

'Mmm,' he said absently, not following that one up. Then, as if by magic, the doorbell rang. Simon went to admit the first real guest – I don't think I earned enough to count as a guest. This left Sally with the awkward task of trying to find something to talk to me about. I could tell her heart wasn't in it when she asked me about my work. I gently deflected her on to something I knew she'd prefer, like telling me about the state of the Euro-Yen or whatever. People began to arrive, most of them known to me, most of them people I'd introduced Simon to years ago, people he'd refused to know then because they were all 'Right-Wing City Whizz Kids'.

I could, of course – maybe I should – give you all the biographical details of Simon, Sally, Dougie, Horst and all the others. I know these facts; they're solid, sure, the kind of commodity not really available when dealing with the Jasons, Darrens and Pauls in the Magpie. But however many facts I might give you, you'd not really be any wiser at the end of the day (and other assorted cliches). At the time I'm talking about I thought I knew these people. I thought they were as rock solid predictable as the boys in the Magpie and the Adonis Club were impulsive, shadowy and fictitious. Perhaps I was right to think that. Perhaps the reason I don't think that any more is just me.

It soon transpired that Simon was immensely amused by my 'anecdote'. Not too far into the evening, Dougie Simpson came floating – if someone of six feet two with the build of an ex-rugby player could ever be said to float – over to where I was giving protection to a few innocent, vulnerable half bottles of gin. These days Dougie sported trendy gelled hair, which I couldn't quite get used to, perched on top of his long, large face. 'Really, Gordon,' he launched in, as though we'd seen each other a few minutes before, 'what's this preposterous rubbish about you seeing a murder?'

'My latest joke. Ha ha. Not so much a punch line as a stab line.'

'You are joking then? Simon wasn't sure.'

'He seemed sure enough just now. Where's Horst?' I needn't have asked. A tall willowy figure with conspicuously natural Aryan blond hair cut in the recommended Hitler Youth style drifted languidly along.

'Good evening Gordon. Nice to see you.' He bowed slightly. Horst is Dougie's other half. They've been together something like three years now. Before Horst hove into view Dougie was a well known cock about town, spending ten hours a night hanging round pubs and clubs lowering his standards minute by minute until he got a fuck. Since Horst he liked to behave like an advert for *Good Housekeeping*. I was actually genuinely pleased that they had a good relationship, but I rather resented their pretence that their solution to the riddle posed by life's shit-heap was the only real one. I needn't really add that both of them earned a great deal more money than me. You can usually take that as read; in fact, I've a nasty suspicion that you can take that as read not just for Dougie and Horst but for Mile End Jason, Paul and even Barmy Billy.

'We were just talking about Gordon's murder,' Dougie said, affably indicating the risibility of the concept.

'Oh yes. You must tell me of it.'

'I can't imagine it caused much comment in the Magpie,' Dougie said. 'It was the Magpie wasn't it? Or was it in that frightful club you took us to?'

'Oh yes. The one like a lavatory.' Horst's English was impeccably pronounced.

'Do you mind?' I riposted. 'Most lavatories are much cleaner.'

'You should know,' Dougie said, 'you spend enough time in them.'

'Dougie, I think you should be less unpleasant,' Horst said. 'You have no position from which to speak.'

While I was trying to fathom out that idiomatical masterstroke, Dougie gave me a reassuring peck on the cheek and asked me how Alec was.

'Gone. History. I used him and cast him aside and left him weeping in Soho. Took him to the Magpie and broke his heart. I wouldn't mind but I did offer to fix him up with someone else, so I can't see what he'd got to complain about.' Looking up at them, I could see they weren't amused. 'No,' I said, in what I think they call a reasonable tone, 'we did split up in the Magpie and it was my idea to finish it. That much is true.'

'That, I think, is most sad.'

Dougie put his hands on my shoulders. It was a nice gesture, but I felt pretty insecure about the glass full of punch in his right hand and its likelihood of going down my back. Wearing the stuff was probably preferable to drinking it, but I wasn't really keen to do either.

'Are you sure that was the right move, after everything else?' Dougie asked tenderly. 'And why are you still going to the Magpie? You should come and see us more often, we're always in, aren't we love?' A fond lovers' look passed between them. I felt faintly sick. Despite this I managed some word of thanks for the pointless invitation. It was well-meant, after all. By way of a gesture of thanks, I asked them both about their flat and their jobs. Dougie explained to me that whilst the inflation rate was generally disastrous for him personally in his line of work it was very useful as high interest rates did something or other, but by this time I'd turned off.

Horst, as always, was much better value. He had landed

some kind of prestigious writing contract with the BBC, doubtless because the Austrian perspective on most subjects is of such pressing importance. Apparently he was occupied now on part of a glamorous epic – you know the sort of thing, three generations over nine decades (or vice versa), a story of love, treachery, pride, wealth, ambition, passion and perfect skin. This one was intended to reflect the whole of twentieth century life and give the production team a lot of large meals in a lot of exotic locations. Naturally, it was a family epic where eight children are scattered across the globe and through all the different social strata; their fates were diverse enough to catch the San Francisco earthquake, the revolt of the Young Turks and the Chinese Revolution, whilst the Jewish branch of the family felt an overwhelming urge to move to Czechoslovakia or Holland in 1937. All good, realistic stuff. I assumed that Horst was writing some stuff about decadent Imperial Vienna or the Anschluss, but it turned out that he was doing the bits about Liverpool and China, neither of which he had ever visited. Listening to him unfolding the story line was somewhat galling; can someone employed to write this kind of thing really keep a straight face when accusing me of exaggerating about a common or garden little murder? When I tentatively suggested that the product might be a little more reliable if they cut back on their travelling and eating expenses and shelled out the copyright fee for a worthwhile novel and made a film of that, Horst turned decidedly Middle European on me and Dougie glared horribly. I let Horst drivel on and switched myself off again.

My eyes drifted around the assembled well-heeled company and fell to rest on an extremely handsome young man (well, it wasn't so much that he was young in a boyish sense, merely that he looked to be untouched by time), dark-haired, blue-eyed, impeccably smart in an unflashy way and apparently the escort of a dark, strikingly individual woman wearing clothes which would have looked tarty on anyone else but on her seemed demure and proper. I'd seen her at Simon's before – just as I'd seen the couple of semi-discreet queens she and the man were talking to. I couldn't remember any of their names. All I could remember was that the older of the two queens was the only person I'd ever met who wanted to talk about tennis in the middle of winter. I mean, tennis is boring enough at the best of times when it's supposed to be there, but in winter – well, for fuck's sake.

I began to calculate the chances of sliding off and finding

where Simon had hidden the telly. I suppose that just leaving would have been more polite, but I'd run out of drink at home and I didn't want to buy any more because Darren had cleaned me out of cash (sort of by mutual consent, I hasten to add) and I always feel that writing cheques at the off-licence is somehow immoral (and so does my account manager). Also the more I spent that day, the less I'd have to spend on Aidan the next night. But anyway, I didn't want to be on my own quite yet. Not for a fortnight or so. Maybe longer.

Let me set your mind at rest. Darren in no way overstepped the mark. I had invited him back for protection and company on an entirely financial basis. We had watched some amazingly bad Australian TV programmes – if you choose your channel carefully these days you'll always find a dreadful Australian soap on somewhere – mainly about dykes in prison having trouble around the steam press. Then we'd drunk all my drink. By that time, as Darren enterprisingly pointed out with all the skill of an insurance salesman on commission, it seemed point-less not to go the whole hog. Well, he had a living to make and otherwise he might have had a case against me for loss of earn-ings. And I needed the diversion to take my mind off what I'd seen and to relieve some of the desires Aidan had provoked. Anyway, in my limited experience, Darren comes as close as anyone to constituting value for money. He didn't even comp-lain when I murmured 'Aidan' at some highly-charged moment. He also gave me some tablets as a present, which I call thoughtful.

Inevitably I decided against going to work, not least because Darren flatly refused to get up and I'm not prepared to leave people alone in the dingy, poky three-roomed shoebox I laughingly call home. Not that the average rent boy is likely to find much there to tempt him; reproductions of Giotto, Uccello and Piero hardly command vast market prices in the West End and my thesis on probability structures arising from Mandelbrot's chaos theories and their potential applications in the field of quantum mechanics (they haven't got any) is not as yet a red hot property. Nor is my collection of opera libretti. The only thing anyone left alone in my flat could realistically do would be to decorate it. But I'm afraid I'm old-fashioned. So, I'd had to stay in until three in the afternoon to shift Dar-ren. I'd not told him about the stabbing, sticking instead to my original story of why I'd been scared the night before. Darren had gone off vowing vengeance on Gray, but that wasn't my problem. He'd also gone away distinctly peeved on the topic of

Aidan, about whom I'd proved incapable of not waxing lyrical.

'Don't trust him, Gordon.' The Lancastrian burr, so different from Aidan's urban Mancunian, was firm in urging me. 'Something about him makes me feel bad.'

'Something about him can feel me any time.'

'Don't be daft. I know you know what I mean. A pretty face is one thing, but I'm convinced there's something – I'll find out for you.'

On issues such as this, Darren took himself so seriously it was hard not to laugh. I took his warnings, he took my money (but on a much more engaged basis) and I saw him to the Tube. Then I rang Simon, knowing he'd taken the afternoon off to get his party ready, and asked him if he wanted any help. What I actually wanted was a free drink and a chance to discuss my ordeal seriously with someone I could trust. That turned out to be a bloody funny joke.

You may remember before this digression took hold that I was listening, so to speak, to Horst. Quite out of the blue he addressed a direct question to me which I managed to miss. Fortunately I was saved by a tall patrician figure with sharp features and slightly manic eyes. Despite the drink in one hand he gesticulated wildly at the sight of us. Toby Castle was someone I was actually pleased to see.

'Ah.' Toby's exclamations are Wagnerian. 'Ah yes,' he said, veering into the pseudo-sepulchral, 'the famous murder. Simon has told me everything.' Listening to Toby you can hear centuries of patrician country dynasties suppressing their peasants with small kindnesses and enormous brutalities. When you hear his laugh, you can understand why not a few people think he's vaguely insane in an acceptably English way. This view is not one I like to comment on – after all, very few of my acquaintance would swear to my sanity. Toby gave me one of his best laughs. 'I must say, Gordon, I'm surprised that you'd be surprised. At a murder in that terrible pub. Hello, Dougie, Horst. Has Gordon ever taken you there?'

'I have been there myself,' Horst said gravely.

'Really?' Toby said. 'I hope this doesn't mean you're living off immoral earnings, Douglas.' He laughed again. 'Did Gordon introduce you to that peculiar and sinister creature who practically had needles sticking out of his arm? What was his name – Red?'

Dougie waved the index finger of his drinkless hand. 'That tall one? Scottish, doesn't shave? Yes, I know the one you mean.'

'Gray,' I explained. 'Actually, you're all so fascinated by it, even though you do all think I'm making it up, that you'll be thrilled to know that he's the one who did it.'

'No, Gordon, I'm sorry,' Dougie said, 'any convincing murder has got to be done by someone unlikely.'

'The last person you'd suspect,' Toby confirmed.

'I remember this person Gray you speak of,' Horst said suddenly, obviously having at last got over Toby's joke at his expense, 'I am surprised that you would wish to keep his company.'

'Ah now,' Toby interjected, 'I'm not surprised at all. I understand it perfectly. It's all to do with Gordon being deeply religious.'

'Do you want me to go away while you talk about me?'

'Where's the fun in that?' Dougie asked. 'But I can see what Toby's getting at. I mean, what about that month you claimed you kept meeting angels?'

'You seemed to think at the time that that proved I was deeply mad rather than deeply religious.'

'I am sorry,' Horst said, 'but what is this to do with angels?'

'Oh, nothing special,' I replied airily. 'Last May, I was out late in Soho a couple of times feeling miserable, lonely and broke, and each time I bumped into young men – different young men, I should add – who took me round amusement arcades winning lots of money for me, then saw me to my night bus, and they wouldn't take anything, not money, not food, not coffee. Just saw me off and then disappeared.'

'So, yes?' Horst asked.

'Well, my assumption is that they were angels. You know, real angels from somewhere else and not here. I mean, ordinary young men in London don't behave like that. They mug you, scrounge, try and sell themselves to you, but they don't behave generously and courteously. It's just not fashionable. More tellingly, they don't disappear.'

'I find I cannot understand this story.'

'It's Gordon's religious sense again,' Toby said sepulchrally. 'He wants to believe in angels and so he finds them. Do you believe in devils, Gordon?'

'Oh, most certainly. We were just talking about one.'

'How about The Devil?' Dougie asked, distinctly amused.

'Since you ask, yes. But I know that for you this is all good sport. Never mind. Excuse me.' I decided to walk through the cordon the three of them formed around me. Toby took my arm before I could escape.

'Gordon, I'm sorry. I didn't mean to offend you.'

'No, I know. You didn't really. I'm just a bit jumpy.'

'Shall we get another drink?' Toby suggested. He was over-looking my private gin lake and merely asking the question his natural breeding prompted.

'Tobes, I've got all the drink I want here. Let's take this gin for a walk and go and have a look at the World Snacks.'

'Look,' Dougie said before we could move, 'how about lunch or dinner some time? We are very concerned about you, Gordon, the last thing we'd want to do is to upset you.'

'Stop worrying,' I said. I found the concern more alarming than the cynicism. 'Call me. Please. I'd like that.'

'And pardon me for mentioning it,' Dougie went on, 'but if you wanted to bring Alec round – well, I know what you said, but we really liked him and I do think you ought to think it over before you – '

'I wouldn't bring Alec,' I smiled. 'Can I bring Aidan, though?' This provoked an interrogative look. 'I met him last night and I'm spellbound. He's gorgeous, amusing and a rent boy. Come on, Tobes. See you two later.' There's no point in hanging around when you've shocked someone deliberately, I thought. And Dougie was obviously shocked to his middle class core. Toby is at heart unshockable. Breeding again.

'Aidan,' he said as we moved through the crowded room, 'rather an unfortunate name in his line of business.'

'Well, I'm sure he's got plenty of others. Names, I mean. They usually have.'

As we crossed the room – not so very large – I heard observa-tions on: (a) the likelihood that the Swedish tennis team was too shagged out at the end of the year to win something or other; (b) the US Budget deficit; (c) the illness of a Tory MP in a safe seat; (d) the US Budget deficit; (e) a dead cert on the markets not yet known to the public; (f) the US Budget deficit.

Over at the World Snacks, where the punch was being ignored, the first thing to register was that there was music drivelling on. At the risk of being confessional I should explain that music – opera apart – doesn't do too much for me. I can spot a tune, because I usually reduce tunes to mathematical progressions (which is all they are anyway), but without that additional visual engagement it tends to strike me as just so much tinkling. And of no music is this more true than all that limp self-important Baroque stuff. Which was just what we were getting. Vivaldi on Compact Disc, one of the great cul-tural emblems of our time, along with that 'cello piece everyone goes mad about because the woman who used to play it well died. Simon plays both of these CDs repeatedly, and when it isn't them it's Pachelbel's fucking *Canon* or, probably worst of the lot, Dvorak's abysmal *New World*. He considers these pieces tasteful. When I first knew him, Simon didn't have, want, or care about 'taste'. Nor was he ambitious to work in the City and make money.

So Vivaldi tinkled away, played on authentic instruments made in 1986 (a self-contradiction the purists seem to have overlooked), and Toby and I leaned on the table and surveyed the mob. I pointed discreetly to the handsome man and his consort. 'I know I know her,' I said, 'but I can't remember her name.'

'God, isn't she beautiful?' Toby said. 'Fascinating woman. I keep asking her out to dinner and she keeps putting me off.'

'Well, if he's the reason why, I'm afraid I can understand Why, Tobes.'

'Ah now. Is he? That's the interesting part. It's beginning to look more and more as if he is. But I'm not sure.'

'Well, who are they, then? You're brilliant at not letting on sometimes.'

'You ought to remember Katy Goldsmith from our University days. She was very close to Simon then.'

'Yes, of course, that's who she is. No, I never really met her. Simon used to keep a lot of his friends from me. Or vice-versa. But I, being generous, donated all of mine to the cause, which is why I'm talking to you here now. Katy Goldsmith. Is she clever?'

'Diabolically. She's in the legal department of that man's bank. He, by the way, is currently the youngest Vice-President in the City. Probably. He's weathered early whispers of scandal and still has, I'm reliably informed, an enormous income quite apart from his vast salary. He's something of a legend, as you can imagine. It was the Crash which made him, really. He managed to make a fortune out of it by selling practially his entire portfolio just before it happened. Then he bought back in when everything was dirt cheap.' Toby laughed. 'In effect, he's made the same fortune twice. Simple but brilliant. So all the early scandals were forgotten and he was hailed as a hero.'

'It must help to be quite that good-looking.'

'It certainly won't hurt. But I don't think he's slept his way to the top. Well, I'm fairly sure he hasn't. Well – now you come to mention it, there used to be stories that he's of your persuasion. And I don't know – well, this is rather up your street. You said

37

you saw a murder. Do you remember a couple of years ago there was a gay murder scandal – a weekend's wonder? Some boy was killed. They found his body outside a club. Anyway, that boy was a friend of Katy Goldsmith's, and I did hear a story that he was living with Michael when he was killed.'

'Who's Michael?'

'That's his name. Michael Hamilton. Anyway, no-one really knows about that, and Michael certainly never says anything. And now he's always seen around with Katy.'

'Which could mean everything or nothing.'

'Yes.' Toby looked at me. 'I think I'll introduce you. In fact, I ought to, because Michael and I were talking about you only the other day.'

'Highly likely,' I replied drily.

'Strange – but true.' Toby raised his hand theatrically. 'We were having a drink together. We're trying to interest his bank in a business proposition, you see.' I recognised the second 'we' as the corporate pronoun. 'Michael suddenly started talking about advanced mathematics and chaos and all that highly bogus stuff you've specialised in. I had to explain to him that I don't sully myself with things like that, but I happened to know someone who was so far ahead of the field that he can't get a university post in this country. You, in other words. He looked most intrigued. He has a rather strange view that it may be useful in the world of finance. So I ought to introduce you to him. And then you can use your instinct and tell me whether my suspicions are justified. After all, you people have such an instinct. It never ceases to amaze me.'

' "We people?" Do you mean gays or mathematicians? Anyway, why are you so keen to know?'

Toby laughed. 'No reason. Except some friends of mine in the Party are. Apparently Michael Hamilton's been making significant but discreet gestures of a monetary kind which can mean only one thing.'

'He wants to enter politics?'

'Exactly.'

'From what you've told me and from where I stand he seems ideal for the modern Tory Party.'

'I'm not so sure. He strikes me as the type who only joins winning sides. Twenty-five years ago he'd have been making these advances to the Labour Party.'

Perhaps I should explain that Toby's uncle had been a very right-wing MP in the late '60s and early '70s when being a reactionary old fart didn't carry the glamour and cachet it does these days. Hence, probably, his resentment at the thought of an opportunist and parvenu who was handsome to boot. At that moment the handsome parvenu looked in our direction and gave Toby a formal wave. Toby smiled and waved back, rather eagerly I thought.

'While I remember.' Toby raised one finger and stared at me intently. 'You mentioned *Parsifal* when we were having dinner with Clive. I've got the tickets.'

I looked at him, amazed. 'Great man, Tobes. Great man. I didn't think you were taking my hint at all seriously. I certainly didn't mean you to. So how much do I owe you?'

'I seem to remember that I owe you some cash, in fact, from a meal a few months ago. So we'll call it quits. As far as I'm concerned.'

'Fine.' I had no recollection of this debt, but seats at Covent Garden would easily wipe it out.

'Of course, being deeply religious you will enjoy *Parsifal*.'

'Great theory of yours, this. Of course, you know that Wagner's not a favourite of mine.'

'I shall have to change that. At least, I must encourage you to give more time to Wagner and less to Gray and his ilk. If Gray has an ilk, which I sincerely hope not.' He laughed at me suddenly. 'I take it Aidan won't want to come with us.'

'You shouldn't prejudge people's tastes, Toby. Actually, from what I gathered last night I rather doubt it. He didn't express a specific view of Wagner, but I imagine if I took him to Covent Garden he'd only try and pick up punters in the bar.'

'He'd probably do very good business. Perhaps you should become a *maquereau*, Gordon.'

'Are you too middle class to say "pimp", Tobes? Actually, chance would be a fine thing.' I asked him about the date of the opera. It turned out to be rather short notice, but I keep an uncluttered social calendar. 'Tobes,' I went on, 'don't think me rude, but I have a yen to watch the TV if I can find it. Terrible, I know, but there it is. I'm going on a hunt. Speak to you before I go.'

'You mustn't go yet. I haven't introduced you to Michael. He seriously was interested in meeting you.'

'Don't bother. I'd only be a sad let-down.' I laughed, picked up my drink, pocketed the lonely spare bottle I'd brought across the room with us and edged towards the door, being careful to avoid hearing any references to the US Budget Deficit or Mats Wilander.

My hunch turned out to be right and the TV was in the bedroom. The TV spent more time in the bedroom than the sitting room anyway, largely because Simon, being puritanical about it as an object, liked to keep it out of sight. It didn't really fit in with his concepts of 'taste'. Sure enough, in the corner of the scrupulously tidy room stood his modest TV plugged in and ready to go. I turned it on and sat down on the bed.

' – and this photograph of the grassy knoll was taken at precisely the time the hypothetical third shot could be distinctly heard across Dealey Plaza. It shows a distinct blur which, after enhancement, when an outline is placed around it, clearly shows a shadowy figure firing a gun and wearing an official badge of some kind. Several bystanders – '

I sat transfixed as the American voice led me ever more deeply into increasingly implausible layers of conspiracy. But this was all much more plausible, much cosier, than what I'd seen the previous night. In fact, I was beginning to take the same view of the 'incident' as everyone else. My eyes stayed glued to the eternally rerun flying brain, the woman scrambling over the car boot to get it back. All too soon the programme finished, having laid the blame fair and square at the door of the entire American establishment under the directions of Dwight Eisenhower and Walt Disney. Very sad, I fell back onto the neat pile of expensive coats belonging to Simon's guests. Disrupting their order, I found myself in possession of a copy of the evening paper which had evidently slipped from a pocket.

I hate all evening papers. They're invariably dreary, parochial and right-wing. However, I'll read anything. I'm famous for it. I have no discrimination in my reading habits whatsoever.

It was all the usual stuff. Hysterical outbursts against left-wing councils. Government initiatives to change the face of the world. I laughed at a blurred photo, thinking how it would have constituted conclusive evidence in the documentary I'd just watched. Then I looked at it properly. 'EXPRESS TRAIN VICTIM NAMED' read the medium type headline above it.

'Mr Anthony Parkins, travelling representative for' – here the paper named the brewery – 'was today named as the man killed by an express train near Vauxhall Station last night. The Police say they are satisfied that there are no suspicious circumstances surrounding Mr Parkins's death.'

So that was it, was it? Two sentences. No mention whether he'd had a family, a wife, a lover, children. Nothing about the man. No memorial. Just a bad photograph and an untruth.

And reading that untruth I knew that I hadn't been hallucinating. I had seen what happened and it had happened. Bearing my proof, I rejoined the party, to try and persuade my friends of my sanity. But, of course, they weren't having any of it. It wasn't the kind of thing that fitted in. So I gave up and went home, all too aware that my personal safety was now very much at risk because I knew what I knew.

3

Imagine you're hanging around a dive in fear for your life. Add the complication of 'first date' nerves. What you really need, as I'm sure you'll agree, on top of all that is a snivelling little git telling you a dreary anecdote. Quite how snivelling and little this git is can easily be deduced; I mean, I'm five feet six, I can't afford to go around calling that many people 'little'.

So there I was in the Magpie, terrified shitless from sheer fear and terrified shitless about seeing Aidan again. It was a long time since the bright elusive butterflies of love had infested my digestive system and in my thirties the business seemed to carry with it some distinctly unromantic side effects. Or was that the simple fear? Anyway, I sidled into the Magpie, and it turned out I was early. This was a blow. I'd been hoping to go in, pick Aidan up and drag him away somewhere else quickly. That was about as far ahead as I'd got in my campaign plan of love. Once I'd got him away to one of the pubs round the corner – I was pretty certain that Gray was still barred from every other pub in Soho – then I could start to try and think coherently. But I hadn't been planning for ten to twenty minutes' nervous dread. Why I'd been so incompetent as to be early, I don't know. It's odd, too, that I was so certain that Aidan would show up. But I hadn't been counting, whatever else was going on around me, on Little Phil.

Although I'd met the rodent-faced, dyed blond, self-loving little git on a couple of occasions, he wasn't one of the regulars I drank with or talked to. I'm pretty certain he disliked me or despised me or both, at least partly because of a lack of interest in commercial transaction with him that I'd once exhibited, and I'd heard that he used to tell the other boys that I was just a wind-up merchant. Not entirely an inexplicable point of view on his part, I suppose; he preferred regulars who wanted to take the systematic approach to the menu on offer, with a view to eventually sampling everything on it. Anyway, all I usually warranted from Little Phil was a scowl of recognition at best. I don't think he got back any more than he gave. Quite why this evening was different wasn't immediately apparent. I think I'd smiled at him as I ordered my drink, pleased not at seeing him but at not seeing Gray anywhere. Instead of scowling, Phil gave me a thin-lipped smile, showing off his ratty little teeth. A burst of largesse made me mime the offer of a drink. After all, apart from Jackie McTavish he was the only person in there I knew even by sight. It wasn't exactly a record-breaking night. So Little Phil came over and asked for some implausible concoction with Southern Comfort in it. I think it included lemonade, blackcurrant and other sweet things. I really can't recall – thus, by the way, disproving a theory of Aidan's.

'A lot of the lads drink really daft drinks,' he once said, ''cause then you'll remember the boy for the drink even if you don't remember his name.'

Little Phil raised the glass containing the pernicious and dubious sub-alchemical formula. 'Your health.' The accent was South Coast meets South London, the tone as thin as his smile. I'd encountered a similar accent once in a hunky young man from Brighton, Martin by name, whom I'd taken home one afternoon and who had taken his clothes off and fallen into a drunken stupor. Another Fun Incident from History.

I raised my definitely stodgy, dreary pint of lager. 'And yours.'

'You been keepin' all right then?'

I shrugged. 'The usual complaints. Work. Money. The weather. Et cetera. How about you? It seems an age since we last talked.'

'Yeh, well, I've been havin' some problems, you see. Lot on me mind.' He eyed me up suspiciously. As nearly everyone is taller than me, it was almost unnerving to be looking down at someone who was appraising me. 'You're quite posh, aren't you?' he said. 'I mean, you must know some posh people, right?'

'Depends how you define "posh",' I answered defensively.

'Well, you know any lawyers? I mean, it's really lawyers I'm lookin' for.'

'I do know some lawyers – in fact, I know one really rather good one – but I don't think any of them are looking to meet anyone in your – well, how shall I put it exactly? – anyone in your line of work. Unless of course it's career advice you're after or something, in which case – '

'Christ, you don't half yack on. No, I just want a fuckin' lawyer. I used to live down in Brighton, right? Well, I got done for TDA and – '

'Sorry, you'll think I'm awfully stupid, but what's TDA?' To my ignorant ear it sounded glamorous and pregnant with untold evil.

'Takin' and Drivin' Away.' Such a let-down. It had even happened on The Archers, I now recalled. Little Phil resumed what I knew was going to be a sensational story. 'Anyway, I got sentenced to eighty days' community service. Fuckin' mugs' game. So I did thirty-seven days and then skipped up 'ere. Well, I was all right for a couple of months, but then I got arrested for fightin'. I mean, I tried to give them a false name, but I'd got ID on me – fuckin' stupid that was – so anyway, they didn't just charge me or what have you, they've got me now where I've got to report to the fuckin' police station every fuckin' day or I get banged up on fuckin' remand.' He paused for a drink and I offered a sympathetic comment.

'That's such bad luck. Could happen to anyone. And a terrible bore.'

'Too fuckin' right. Well, they gave me this lawyer on legal aid, but he was fuckin' useless. That's why I asked you. 'Cause there's this punter of mine, a couple of days ago he offered me two thousand quid to go with him to Marbella for a fortnight. Says to me, "You can have anyone you like while we're there, so long as you spends the nights with me." All that and two thousand quid, right. So I goes to this lawyer they gave me and I says, "Look, I got some urgent things come up, work, chance of a job like, can you get us off signin' on at the fuckin' police station for a couple of weeks while I get it all sorted?" and the fuckin' bastard cunt says he can't or won't. So I want a fuckin' good lawyer who will.' He paused to drink again and to sigh at the injustice of it all.

'I mean,' he went on eventually, 'two thousand fuckin' quid. I could get two fuckin' enterprise allowance grants for that.'

'You want to start a business?' I asked, perhaps a shade too incredulously to be polite.

'Yeh, well – ' he became slightly defensive. 'Well, I 'aven't made me mind up yet, but I don't see how I can ever fuckin' start anythin' at this rate. I mean, you don't get that many fuckin' punters wavin' two thousand fuckin' quid around, do you?' I had to agree with this, limited though my experience of being offered money by punters was. 'Anyway, you can see why I need another fuckin' lawyer. Any of your mates be any good, you reckon?'

'The thing is,' I said, desperately trying to sound as if I cared, 'that my friends in the legal profession mainly do contract work. Not criminal law. So they wouldn't be a great deal of use to you. If I were you, I'd write to your MP and explain that your attempts to use your business and enterprise initiative are being stifled by bureaucratic red tape. As long as it's a Tory MP.'

Little Phil looked at me, his expression restored to what I normally expected from him. 'Thanks. I'll bear it in mind. Excuse me, I'm just goin' for a wander.'

I raised my hand in a parting benediction. I was glad to be rid of him. Aidan was due any minute now.

'Hey, man. I've been looking for you.'

Gordon McKenzie's Tips for a Long and Healthy Life, Number 417. If you're avoiding a mad knifeman, don't stand in lowlife pubs with your back to the door. I felt myself possessed by complete immobility. I couldn't run. I couldn't turn round. I couldn't even lift up my drink to give myself that small comfort.

'Hey, man. What's the matter?' I could tell that Gray was now right in front of me, but I couldn't look up. 'You don't seem pleased to see me. Is that any way to treat an old friend, baby?' He thumped something, presumably the bar. 'Joey, can we have some service here? Give my friend Gordon another drink. Same again? Something stronger? Get the man a Bloody Mary, Joey. And a double Malibou and Orange for me.'

So what was this, the condemned man's Happy Hour? I managed to raise my eyes. I also found enough release from fear to wonder who was paying. Gray slammed a fiver casually on the bar. The only fivers I'd ever seen him with before were the ones he'd bullied out of me.

'Make the vodka in the Bloody Mary a large one, Joey.'

'Um, Gray,' I began nervously.

'Relax, baby, it's payday. You've been sweet to me, so now I'm sweet to you. That's fair, isn't it?' He put an arm round me and squeezed. 'You old bag of bones, you.' This is it, I thought, this is where he breaks an arm or a spine or two. But he let me go more or less intact. 'So, Gordon baby, what brings you in here tonight? You at a loose end? You looking for someone? We don't want you to get bored, that just wouldn't do.' And as he said this, a light began to flash very dimly in my head.

'I'd arranged to meet someone here, actually.' I raised my preternaturally large Bloody Mary to his health.

'Oh – one of your posh friends, is it? Off to the theatre? The movies?'

I shook my head. 'Just a young man I met in here the other night. Did you see me talking to him?'

'What, that stupid cunt Darren? He's just a crazy dealer, man, you want to steer clear – '

'No, not Darren. The boy with the ears. Aidan.'

Gray sipped his drink. Then he smiled and nodded slowly. 'I know the one you mean. Yeah, man, he's cute. Those ears – like that fucking elephant in that cartoon film. So what're you up to with Aidan? Straight back to your place, I'll bet.'

I shook my head. 'I thought I'd take him out for dinner, actually.'

'Oh, man, that's sweet. You actually like this guy? Dinner. Fucking hell.' He laughed. I couldn't see what was quite so amusing. He reached into his pocket and I tensed up again. But instead of the knife I was anticipating, he pulled out a roll of banknotes. 'Listen man, I owe you some cash.'

'I don't really think you do, I mean – '

He thrust some notes into the top pocket of my jacket, pushing them down so I couldn't get to them without taking the jacket off. 'Don't argue about it, man, I told you, it's payday. Hey. Is this your Aidan coming in now?'

I turned, all immobility gone at the thought of Aidan. There he stood, cautiously hanging back at the door. I waved. He raised his hand and gave me a killer smile. Gray leaned down and whispered to me.

'How much is he charging you?'

'Well, I haven't, we haven't really – '

'Don't give him more than twenty-five. Let me have a word with him.'

'No, look, I'm not sure that – '

'You want him, don't you, man? Have him, then. He's selling, you want to buy. It's simple. Just let me fix the price as a favour.'

Gray moved off before I could say another word and intercepted Aidan. Despite Aidan's height, he looked puny and feeble next to Gray. I wasn't entirely happy at the thought that he might be somehow susceptible to Gray's influence, either. I took a large swig of Bloody Mary and felt slightly giddy. Someone put a record on the juke box. An etiolated Australian teenager began to bemoan her devotion, resorting to the occasional line of ill-pronounced French. Total crap, but better than Vivaldi on authentic instruments. Gray and Aidan joined me. I gave Aidan my hand and he held it for long enough to make me feel special. Gray gave me another of his threatening claps on the shoulder.

'Let me get you both a drink, man,' he said. 'Same again, Gordon.' This was an instruction, not a question.

'Thank you very much, I'll have a lager.' There was something quaintly old-fashioned about Aidan's manner as he said this. Gray slammed his hand down on the bar and leaned down to me, whispering so that Aidan wouldn't hear.

'I've fixed it for you, Gordon baby. I've told the man the score.' He straightened up again, procured us our drinks, took his and backed away, pausing only to prod Aidan delicately in the chest. 'Remember what I said, man.' He moved off towards the telephone; as he picked it up, Paul Murphy came in. Gray put down the 'phone and called him over. I looked up at Aidan, embarrassed.

'I'm terribly sorry,' I said, 'that had nothing to do with me at all, honestly.'

Aidan gave me a rueful half-smile. 'Well, I was going to say. You've got some nice friends, Gordo. I reckon you must be one of those men me mam warned us about.'

'That might be true, actually. But Gray's no friend of mine. I really don't know what he was up to just then.'

'He's a complete prat. I mean, he thinks he's some big man or something, just because he gets hold of a few hard drugs every so often, but he's nothing.'

'I wouldn't quite say that myself – '

'Yeah, but you're only three feet tall, Gordo. It's easy for him to scare you.'

'He's not a friend of yours then? The way he was talking, I thought – '

'Don't be daft. Honest to God, Gordon, I can't stand him. I don't have nothing to do with him. I've not really got any friends in here, I told you. I mean, that lad who introduced us, I'm not sure who he is. David, is he? Daryl?'

'Darren.'

'Darren, right. Most of the ones I know are in the Blue Parrot.'

'Do you fancy going there later? What do you fancy doing before? Just say. I'm not rich, but, well – '

'I don't mind. It's your money, Gordo.'

Which reminded me. 'Could you do me a favour?' I asked.

Aidan grinned. 'As long as it's not disgusting. Disgusting costs money.'

'It's not meant to be disgusting. Could you feel in my top pocket – '

'Are you sure it's not disgusting?'

'Top jacket pocket. There's some money there, but I don't know how much.' Really I should have been ashamed of myself. It wasn't my money and it was almost certainly a bribe. But I had no intention of giving it back to anyone. Aidan fished in and pulled out the catch.

'I could palm this, you know,' he said, casually flicking his fingers and then opening the palm of his hand to reveal it empty. He did his rubber-necked smile again. It gave him a look of absurd innocence, made him seem younger than the years he'd laid claim to on our first meeting. Then he reached down, touched my ears and made the tightly rolled notes reappear. 'It's all there,' he said. 'I do tell a few lies now and again, but I don't steal.' He gave me a full laugh. I was surprised to see how large his teeth were. 'Actually, I tell a lot of lies.'

I took the money from him. 'Like your name, I suppose.'

'No-one uses their right name round here. I bet you don't all the time. No, seriously, I do use Aidan most of the time if I'm not with me family. People say it suits me. I got it from a film actor I saw on telly once. So I'd like it if you did call me Aidan. D'you mind if I say something?'

'Fire away.'

'Don't you think you ought to put that money away? I mean here isn't really the right place to wave your cash around. And if it's all a stunt to impress me, don't bother. Takes a lot more than that to impress me.'

'Sorry. No. Someone gave it to me. I just hadn't counted it yet.'

'Someone gave it to you? You couldn't introduce them to me, could you? I could do with a few friends like that.' He said something else, but I didn't really catch it. His voice was soft, his accent strong, and my counting had surprised me. I'd anticipated twenty, maybe twenty-five. I'd got seventy. Not, I'll admit, riches beyond the dreams of avarice, but quite a pleasant amount to have foisted upon you for no good reason. Well, in fact for a very bad reason.

'Seventy,' I said aloud, not particularly to Aidan.

'Might just see us to ten o'clock,' he said, giving me a playful cuff on the arm.

'Or not. Well. Another drink.'

'Thank you very much. Will you just excuse me a minute, please, Gordon? There's someone I have to give a message to.'

'Bring him over. Let me get him a drink.' Mister Magnanimous was definitely in town tonight.

'No, it's just a message. Really. I don't like him very much.' Aidan gave my arm a reassuring pat and darted off. I followed him with my eyes; he'd gone up to a spindly frail creature with a blond mop top haircut, wearing jeans so tight it seemed physically impossible he'd ever be able to take them off or put them back on again. I knew him vaguely; another Jason, this time from Tottenham. He had an encyclopaedic knowledge of horror and sci-fi films and no other topic of conversation.

'Gordon. Buy us a drink, please.' I awoke from my Aidan-centric reverie to find Paul and Mile End Jason presenting themselves. I wasn't really in the mood for them, but I'm not very good at saying no, so I bought them a drink. It seemed the easiest way out.

'You 'aven't seen that fuckin' bitch Carol, 'ave you?' Mile End Jason asked. I shook my head, as if I would have known her if I'd seen her. I had met her once, when she'd pursued Jason into the pub while he'd been trying to do a punter; her cry of 'Leave him alone you dirty old man' had rather nullified all Jason's hard work. 'Good,' he said. 'She's tearin' around after me in a strop and I don't want to 'ave to 'it 'er. Just 'cause I left some knock-off in 'er flat. God, she's a stupid bitch. I mean, she gets in a strop if I do Norman 'Unters, so I've got to try and make a fuckin' livin' some'ow. Fuckin' typical. Just 'cause she 'ad my kid, she reckons I owe 'er one.'

'You got a kid?' Paul asked. 'I never knew that, Jason. What is it, boy or a girl?'

'Little girl. Samantha.'

'Really? You got any pictures?' Jason shook his head. Paul fished inside his capacious leather jacket, the swallow tattooed on the back of his hand seeming to take flight, and pulled out a wallet from which he took a photograph. 'This is my little boy. David. Only the daft bitch of a mother never lets me see him any more just 'cause I got in trouble that time.'

I took the photo as Jason didn't seem too interested. It depicted Paul, obviously proud, holding an astonishingly wide-eyed baby which was looking at the camera with bemused innocence. A lump crept into my throat for what I had missed and for what Paul had lost. Jason gave a me a sly and scornful smile.

'Wouldn't have thought you'd be too interested in kids, some'ow, seein' you're a bender.'

I handed Paul back his photograph. 'Beautiful,' I said, softly as I could. I had learnt something.

'Know what?' Jason said. 'Our Gord's an old softy.'

Paul laughed. Normal service was resumed. He whispered to Jason, who nodded. 'I'll see you over there,' Paul said out loud, evidently for emphasis. Jason, weasel-like, smiled a fearful smile, picked up his drink and moved off. Paul leaned down close. 'Can I have a word, Gordon?'

'I am with someone,' I said brusquely. Paul looked round.

'Let me guess. Aidan. Yeah, everyone noticed you was taken with him the other night. You want to watch him, Gordon. He don't do Christmas discounts or January sales. He does do runners, though. Two or three of my punters have had a bad time with him.'

'Thanks for the warning. I'll bear it in mind.'

'Yeah, well. Listen, Gordon, I was in court today. They nicked me for fighting. Fuckin' hundred quid fine. I was just wondering if you could – '

'Paul. I'm very sorry, but there's no way I could possibly afford to.'

'Just thirty would be a help – '

'Really. I can't afford it.'

'Oh, come on, man. I bet you've got more than thirty on you.'

'What I've got on me is my business. I need it. I'm taking Aidan out.'

On cue, as if by magic, Aidan rejoined us.

'I'm afraid that's right, Paul,' he said. 'Afraid for you, that is.'

'You never took me out, Gordon, and you did say you would.'

'Whose fault was that? Who didn't turn up?'

'That wasn't my fault. I'd been jacking up all afternoon.'

'And that wasn't your fault?' Aidan asked as he leaned in to grab the pint of lager waiting for him. 'Sounds to me like you blew it, Paul. Sorry and that.'

Paul ignored him. 'Look, Gordon, I know you've got thirty on you – '

'Listen.' Aidan very gently prodded Paul in the chest. 'The man can't help you. The man doesn't want to help you. Do us a favour, Paul. Fuck off. The man's arranged to meet me. He's busy tonight. All right?'

'Gordon,' Paul whined, but Aidan's face took on a shape I wasn't keen to see again in a hurry. 'OK, I'm going, I'm going.'

Aidan turned to me. 'You've got to get rid of these scroungers, Gordo. I mean, I quite like that Paul, but he doesn't half talk a lot of shit. What was he on at you about?'

'Court fine.' I explained the scant details. Aidan gave a slurping sucking sound at the back of his teeth and treated me, for the first time, to his accurate and cruel impersonation.

'Give ush shome cash. Couple o' shcore or shomefing.' The switch to the London accent was perfectly achieved and I wondered if Aidan's voice was as elastic as his face seemed to be.

'How was Jason?' I asked.

'Oh – boring cunt,' he answered, back to the Mancunian now. 'Still, that's not news, is it? No, I had to fix him up with a customer, one of mine who did me a bad turn. Jason's a complete rip-off, he just falls asleep the minute they get him back, unless he throws one of those fits of his – '

'He's epileptic, isn't he?'

'You been eating dictionaries again?'

'Customer.'

'What?'

'You said "customer". Not punter.'

'Yeah, well – I just think it sounds nicer. More respectable. And more honest. Right, Gordo.' He drained his lager and replaced the glass on the bar. 'Where are we off, then?'

I finished whatever it was I was drinking. I felt a bit unsteady on my feet. I'd had a lot to drink in a very short space of time and I couldn't honestly recall eating much during the day. A couple of bars of chocolate aimed at putting back the two pounds I'd lost since Monday, but no real food. 'Um, yes. What don't you eat?'

'Oh, I'll eat anything. Except I don't like Paki food and that Greek muck makes me sick.'

'How liberal and cosmopolitan. I take it you mean Indian food.'

'Same difference.'

'Pizza OK? I mean real pizza, not that Pizza Shack rubbish.' I knew a cheapish but smart pizzeria just off Regent Street.

'Fine. I really don't mind.'

The usual light dank drizzle was on the go outside. My clothes hung from me, slowly absorbing the moisture. The tawdry light of Old Compton Street played in Aidan's hair and I could see that he had almost finished growing out some rather cheap blond highlights. This didn't strike me as very in character. Aidan looked down at me and smiled.

'What're you looking at?'

'Your hair.'

'Oh that. It's terrible, isn't it? I must get it cut again.'

'It's a nice style. Leave it. You look very smart.' He did; a distinguishedly worn leather jacket, brown, over a green and white sweater with some kind of compass design on it and a pair of light brown chino's. It was obvious that Aidan cared about clothes.

'Thank you very much.' He smiled again, but this time to himself. Dodging drunks, punks, cars, invitations into strip joints and lost Japanese tourists, we crossed a road and passed the Revuebar. Aidan laughed. 'I had a job there once.'

'I didn't think you were the kind of stripper they wanted.'

'No, you daft – I was a bouncer. Well, an usher they called it. I had to throw people out if they got heavy with the girls. They never did, mind. Just a lot of tourists, really. The pay was rotten. I mean, honest to God, Gordo, I can make more in half an hour selling me arse than I could in a week there. We were supposed to get commission on dirty books we sold as well, but you had to sell the whole lot to get more than a couple of quid. So I chucked it in.'

I was torn by this. I could see his side of it, but I felt I ought to be encouraging him to go in for steady, reliable employment. 'So how long did you work there?'

'Just the one night.' He gave me the rubber-necked smile together with an imbecilic laugh. 'The novelty wore off after that. It usually does with me with jobs and that.'

'Is there anything you'd actually like to do? I mean if you had the choice of anything at all.'

'Down the job centre I told them I wanted a job as an astronaut. I don't think they believed me. Are we nearly there yet, Gordo? I'm starving.'

I led him through a deserted square, where various elements of the British film industry lived, moved and had their very tenuous being. 'Nearly there, now,' I said, 'just round the corner,' rather as one would talk to a petulant child.

The restaurant was half full, but quite noisy. We sat in a corner, by a window looking up the narrow fringe of a Soho street. Piped bland jazz blared out and then stopped suddenly. At the other side of the large room three figures were arranging themselves on a small stage. 'Oh great,' I said, 'it's the Mexican harp trio. We've really hit lucky tonight.'

Aidan turned to look. 'Bloody hell,' he said, 'are they serious?' His question was answered by the plaintive twang of a Spanish guitar, a quick arpeggio on the harp and then – ludicrously – an irritating tinkle from the portable electric keyboard. A rather handsome dark-haired waiter who recognised me as a semi-regular customer came to take our order. He looked vaguely puzzled at the conjunction of myself and Aidan; the spotty skinny runt with very thinning straw-like hair, looking so much older than the handsome well-dressed youth who still managed to give off a whiff of 'the game.' I ordered some food and a lot of drink. Beer, wine, spirits. Gray's blood money had removed any sense of financial caution (and you may have noticed I haven't got any such sense to start with) and I realised I was about to get stinking drunk. Fortunately the waiter brought the drink before the food. I smiled.

'All right, then. Tell me everything.'

'What about?'

'About you. Like why did Paul tell me to watch myself with you? Why does that moron Gray think he can order you around, which I'm sure he can't? And what the hell are you doing hanging around the Magpie?'

'Well, that one's pretty obvious, isn't it? And why are you there, Gordon? Is that obvious too?'

'Not usually. I've been with rent boys about five or six times and no more. That's the truth.'

'Actually, I believe you. Thousands wouldn't. But I can tell. Even if that stupid bastard Gary – that's his real name, you know, that Gray – does come on like a mate of yours. He's nowt to do with me. None of them are. I mean, I sell my arse, it's an easy way of making money and that's what I come down to London for. There wasn't room for seven of us up in Manchester and they didn't seem that bothered whether I learnt owt at school and that, they just let me sit there. I can just about read now, I had to learn when I was on remand, it was something to do. So after they let us out, I come down to London, 'cause I knew that the rent scene was good for a few bob here. I'd been stuck up in Crewe one day when I were about thirteen, no money to get back, no money to get food and that and I were hanging around in the station when this old geezer started talking to us. I told him what the situation was and he said he'd give me enough for a ticket home and something to eat if I'd give him a wank. Well, that seemed all right to me. That's how it started. Then there weren't any jobs in Manchester, not when you'd been away and that, so I come down here and got a few new names. I still go home, see me mam and the family, our Bren, our Teresa, our Damian, our Mary – '

'Irish Catholics, right? How did I guess?'

'Our mam's dead keen on all that stuff. She wanted us all to be nice, respectable and all that. Not like her family. They're travellers. I ran off with them when I was a kid, but they got fed up with me and sent me back after a bit. 'Cause I was a little bastard, basically. That's where I learnt to palm things and do tricks.'

He picked up a small card – the kind restaurants leave out for customers to take away so they'll remember where they had their unique, charming culinary experience. Aidan made the card disappear and reappear from the top pocket of my jacket. As he did this, he let his hand linger against my chest just long enough for my body to react. 'You like that, Gordo?' He smiled. I blushed. He took his hand back. 'I can't figure you out.'

'We were talking about you. Running away with the Gypsies.' How much of this should I believe? The colouring was wrong for an Irish Gypsy boy; but I tend to believe what I'm told. Aidan sensed what I was thinking.

'Honest to God, Gordon, I swear on me mam's life this is all true. I tell a lot of fibs and that, but this is God's truth. And I haven't told anyone else, either. 'Cept this bloke that's lent me his flat. And he's in America.'

'He's lent you a flat? He's a – customer?'

'Not really. He just looks after me when I'm down here. He's a lot older. I mean, he's very old. He keeps some stuff of mine and he knows me real name and me mam's address, so if I did skip off with owt of his he'd know how to cause trouble. It's all right. It's a nice flat. Bloomsbury. Baths when I want. No bills to pay. I don't have sex with him – well, I do once in a while. I think he'd like it if I did a bit more, but it's not as though he's giving me money as well. He lets me take customers back there, though.' I raised my eyebrows. 'Oh, Laurence doesn't mind as long as I don't let them stay the night. You'll have to meet him when he gets back again.'

I wasn't sure about all this. 'Well, if you've got a more or less settled place, why don't you try and get a proper job? Do some training or something?'

'I tell you. I wouldn't mind training as a plumber or something. Plenty of money in that. But I don't fancy it just yet. Time for all that later, maybe.'

'So, no responsibilities? No kids, no girlfriend – '

'None of that. I don't go with girls now. I used to.'

'But you are straight?'

'Bisexual.'

'A lot of rent boys – if you don't mind me using the term – say that. It usually means they're really straight but they know punters like to think the boys they go with are gay.'

Aidan nodded at me. 'You know more than you let on, Gordo, don't you?' He poured us some more wine. 'Isn't it time we heard about you a bit?'

Although well over half-pissed now, I was still on guard. 'I'm not a very interesting topic of conversation. Let's talk about you. I thought most of you boys preferred talking about yourselves, anyway, when you talk at all. And I get the impression you quite like talking.'

'Depends who I'm with. You're easy to talk to. Too easy. I mean, look at the other side of it, Gordon. The customers and the other old guys who hang round the Magpie, they usually just talk about themselves. Like the boys, it's all who they know, how much they earn, how important they are. The other night I thought you was going to turn out the same for a minute. All that stuff about being a doctor in – what did you call it? Pure mathematics? Whatever that is. But that's all you've told me so far. That daft bastard Gary tells me how much I ought to ask you for, that pathetic prat Paul asked you for cash. You know Darren. I've not got much else to go on. I can guess a bit. Like I can guess you're a kind bloke who likes to do a few favours. I can guess you'd like to go to bed with me. I can guess you'd like more than just a quick wank and more than just the bed or we wouldn't be here now. I can guess you earn fuck all, or you wouldn't start wetting yourself when someone drops seventy quid on you. But I don't like guessing – it's a kid's game. What about your folks? You said you weren't from London. You told me the other night.'

He smiled. I laughed. Some food arrived. Aidan began stuffing himself methodically, cutting his food carefully into polite-sized lumps, feeding himself discreetly as though actually being caught eating would bring terrible reprisals on his head. I watched him, the tawdry highlights at the very edges of his hair glinting in the light of the candle between us on the table. I felt drunk and weak from love and alcohol. My stomach felt far too peculiar to take food in.

'Look, Aidan. I don't like talking about myself. That's all.' Well, it was part of it, but it wasn't all. How do you say, casually over the dinner table, my family was wiped out in an accident last February? It's hard enough talking to close, long-standing friends about grief; what reaction was I going to get from a rent boy, however charming, sensitive and lovable?

'Family, Gordo. Everyone's got some. Blood's the most important thing. Blood counts.'

'I haven't.' Stupid memories crowded in. 'Mine were all kil-led. Earlier this year.' Well, I'd said it. 'My parents, my brother, his wife, their seven month old kid. A stupid bloody car acci-dent. I don't talk about it usually because I can't really handle it. Most of my friends think I've gone a bit mad since then. I probably wasn't all that sane anyway.'

Aidan stopped eating and reached across the table. He pat-ted my hand which was fiddling nervously with the wrapped sugar cubes. 'That's dreadful. I mean that. Really dreadful.'

I looked at him. The restaurant candlelight, the wine, the awful music, his ears, his accent, his unexpected compassion. 'Oh God, I think I love you,' I said very quietly.

'Thank you very much. That's nice.' He started eating again. 'We could say thirty quid as a favour. That's cheap, special for you. Or tell you what, you could buy us some new clothes. I could do with some.' He smiled at me. 'That's a much nicer way of doing it than just handing over cash, isn't it? Why do your mates think you're mad? You don't seem very mad to me.'

'They think I make things up.' Response seemed the easiest way through this emotional minefield. 'Like yesterday. I went to this posh party a friend of mine gave. Lots of people I was at University with. And I told them about something I'd seen the other night – the night I met you, in fact – and they all thought I was making it up.'

'Why, what was it? Virgins in Soho?'

'I saw Gray – Gary – stab a guy – a brewery man in the cellar room at the Magpie.'

'What, that – ? You mean the one who jumped under a train? It was in last night's paper that was.'

'Yes. That one. Only I saw Gray stab him. I saw the stuff in the paper yesterday. I know all that. But I know what I saw. And the thing is that Gray saw me. That must be why he's being nice to me, buying me drinks, giving me money –'

'Trying to fix me up for you.' Aidan wiped his mouth with the red paper napkin provided. 'You're sure about this, Gor-don? I mean, if your mates think you make things up – but I know some barmpot liars and you're not like any of them.'

'Oh, I don't know. Maybe I did imagine it. Maybe I got a glimpse of another Universe. Maybe I just see blood where I shouldn't. You tell me.' And suddenly I started off about rudimentary quantum theory, telling Aidan about Schrodinger's cat – the cat with a fifty-fifty chance of being gas-sed in a sealed box depending on the fission of a particle. He rested his chin on his left hand and looked at me with mock severity.

'I don't know what all this is about cats in fucking boxes, Gordon. Not strictly relevant, I think that's the phrase. It's what they said to me down the job centre when I was explaining me qualifications for being an astronaut. Stick to the point. You been to the Police, have you?'

'No. They once took me in for cottaging. Didn't charge me, but gave me a hard time. So I'm bound to be on some computer record somewhere. So if I go in and say, excuse me I'm Gordon McKenzie and I was having a drink in the Fourth Magpie when I – well, they'll just stop me there, look me up, find they once nearly had me for gross indecency and start asking me about rent boys. No, thank you. I'll give the Active Citizen bit a rest.'

Aidan nodded. Some more food arrived. I ordered another vat or six of wine. 'You know that's no answer,' Aidan said when the waiter had gone. 'I mean, I don't know how well you can handle your booze, but I wouldn't have thought – a bloke your size and that.'

'Look, Aidan, I don't have a drink problem. I have a drink solution.' It wasn't original, but he wasn't to know that. However, he didn't show any recognisable sign of pleasure or appreciation at this poached epigram.

'So you saw prat Gary stab someone,' Aidan recapped, stuffing his mouth full of Pizza Fiorentina (twenty-five pence of every one sold goes to the upkeep of the Uffizi galleries. I can't stand spinach – far too healthy – but I love pictures, so I always plug the pizza heavily to friends when I'm eating there). 'And you don't want to go to the cops. And prat Gary knows you saw him, and suddenly he's being as nice as pie. Or was he always nice to you?'

'Well, it's all relative,' I said. 'He once borrowed some money from me at knife point. Only about a fiver, it was all I had on me at the time. And until this evening his use of the term "borrow" was open to semantic dispute.'

'Is that right? What does "semantic" mean? Do you mean he waved a knife at you and asked for cash and you gave it to him? God, Gordo, you might be bright but you're fucking brainless sometimes. Now, look, I don't know much about all this and I don't want to get involved, but have you thought about something?'

'I've thought about lots of things in my time, principally probability theory – '

'Stick to the point. How much money has Gray usually got on him?'

'Well, he always tells me he's skint, but I suppose he could be lying.'

'No, he's always skint. Blows it all on drugs and crap like that. That's why he's so weird, he fucked his mind up with heavy stuff years ago. So where's he suddenly got the money to give you cash, buy you drinks, give me twenty to drop me price?'

'He gave you twenty to –'

'I wasn't going to tell you, but I – well, some things are worth being honest about. So where's Gary got cash from?'

'Done a punter? Pimped a bit? I know he used to. Sold some drugs?'

'You can forget the first two. He lost all his customers years ago. The word's been out on him since ages before he went away. And no punter's going to take anyone he tries to pimp for. No classy punter, anyway, and we're looking at a cash injection of well over a ton here.' I was fascinated to listen. Aidan had absorbed his vocabulary from the oddest sources. Any minutes now he'd be on about shots in the arm of the economy. 'As for selling drugs, he doesn't usually have the money to buy enough to sell for that kind of cash. Fifty's his top whack on any one deal. And anyway, Gordo, if sweet little Gaz thought you was likely to squeal on him, then left to himself he'd settle for a cheaper answer than throwing a pile of money at you. Think about it, you effing intellectual moron, Doctor – what's your other name?'

'McKenzie.'

'Gordon McKenzie. You must be a Jock then.'

'No. English, Irish, a bit of French thrown in.'

'Great. You figured it out yet?'

'Someone gave him the money?'

'Brilliant. Look, Gordo. Was Gary alone when he stabbed this geezer?'

'Ah. No. But whoever was with him was stoned. That's what he said, anyway, because they weren't doing what he told them.'

'You do realise it could have been me? I mean, it wasn't, but –'

'No. No. I saw you go out with Paul Thing, the Irish one.'

'And Gary didn't go out? He did, didn't he?'

'Ah. Yes.' Fear and panic returned, making a very strange and unpleasant addition to alcohol. 'Aidan, you weren't, I mean –'

'Relax, Gordo. But remember. You've learnt two things now. One, don't go round the Magpie blabbing your head off. Two,

Gary and his mates may have stabbed this bloke, but they're not the ones in charge. And whoever is in charge doesn't want you got rid of. Not yet, anyway.'

'This is all a bit deep for me,' I said. I began to suck my thumb reflectively. 'I'm like you. I'm not going to get involved.' I drank some gin, some wine, some more gin, some beer, poured some more wine out and drank that. Aidan took my glass from me.

'It's a bit late to decide you're not getting involved.'

'Aidan, darling,' I said, 'give me my glass back. No, I've taken my bribe. I'm a coward. I'm a nervous wreck. Don't forget that you're the only person who's believed me so far. So we can't talk about something else, something simple like politics or religion?'

Aidan gave me my glass back. 'Remember what I'm telling you now,' he said. 'You're only not involved as long as other people let you stay that way. Once they decide you are involved, that's it. And the way you're playing it, I don't fancy much for your chances. Which is a shame. You and me could get on all right, I reckon, even if you do talk Double fucking Dutch half the time.'

I sat up and gawped. 'Do you mean that? Aidan, do you really? Because you know how I feel – '

'I'd worked that one out. Think about it. You must have been shitting yourself before you come into the Magpie tonight, and I bet when Gary come up to you, you thought that was it. So why did you show up?'

'I promised you I would.'

'Right. Any bloke who risks something to keep a promise has to be worth knowing.' He stuck his hand across the table and took hold of mine again. 'You're all right, Gordon.' He fixed me with a serious stare. Then he let go, sat back and smiled.

At last, a vote for my sanity. Admittedly it came from a self-confessed workshy liar rent boy who hadn't told me his real name, but in a democracy they all count. 'Aidan, I adore you,' I breathed.

'Very nice, Gordo. Thank you. But I'd better be honest. Adoring doesn't get you a discount.' He laughed. 'Actually, it'd be hard to treat you like a customer after all this.' His fork hovered over my plate. 'You not eating that?' I shook my head and he speared a slice of Pizza Quattro Formaggi. 'Are we having a pudding?'

'Your wish is my command.' From my alcoholic infatuated daze I watched him eating. Dreamily I waved at the waiter.

Plates were cleared, other plates brought. More drink was provided. Coffee came. The conversation meandered on, with me trying to steer it away from myself or things I'd seen. Aidan illuminated me with his views on politics and world affairs.

'Oh, I'd vote for Maggie,' said this apparently textbook specimen of disaffected alienated youth. 'I mean, she's what I'm used to. She's the Prime Minister, isn't she? The others aren't, are they?' A quick run through governmental policy both existing and potential showed he didn't agree with a single item. 'The Yanks, they're all crap,' he said, as horizons broadened, 'except Reagan, he's all right. Why can't he stay on as President? I tell you, though, that election they had the other week, I couldn't have voted for that one who looked like he sold kebabs in his spare time. No, that Reagan was all right – like when he bombed that pillock – you know that mad one, the Libyan one – or that barmy old Ayatollah git. I reckon he must have been dead for years really, they're just keeping him alive on a machine or something.' The names Mitterrand, Craxi, Kohl, Haughey rang no bells. 'That one the Russians have got now, he's all right, I reckon. Well, he's all right for a Russian.' It was clear that for someone in his line of business, Aidan was unusually highly attuned to world events.

The arts proved a less fruitful field. Music was a non-starter, as our previous conversation had rather suggested. I mentioned a few relatively popular films, but was turned aside with a disarming smile. 'The last film I saw at the pictures was that one about the rabbits. You know, Bright Eyes and that. I liked that. Isn't there one coming out about a rabbit soon, a cartoon or something? I wouldn't mind seeing that.' Painting was a disaster too, even when I tried to explain my geometric theories of art. 'Sorry, Gordo, I've never hard of Umbrella or whatever you called him.' He interrupted my views on perspective in Piero. 'Very nice. Have you got a pen?' I fished in my pocket and pulled out a black pentel. He took an unused paper serviette from the next table and drew a few quick lines, then gave it to me. It was a nearly perfectly proportioned line drawing of a horse seen in three-quarter profile. I looked across at him, puzzled.

'You mean, you can do something as good as this without any real effort?'

'Is it good?'

'Don't be disingenuous.'

'What's "disingenuous" mean?'

'Don't pretend you don't know if it's good.'

'I don't know if it's good or not.'

This circular argument held threats of tedium beyond my theories of art. 'You could train, you should train, use your talents.'

'Oh yeah. Training. Like school, isn't it? Well, look what happened in school. I told you. They just let me sit there and didn't bother. What's the point of going through all that again?'

'If it's something you're good at, if you get on the right kind of course, they'll help you, give you special attention, make sure you benefit – '

'Christ, Gordo, you sound like one of them fucking adverts. I've seen them all. Had them all down the job centre.'

'Look, I know people in that Department, I could have a word, find out what – '

'You may be bright, our kid, but you live on another fucking planet. Those courses – they're to fool people like you that someone's doing something.'

'And there speaks a Conservative voter.'

'Well, what good'd the other lot do? At least foreigners take notice of Maggie.' We had now finished our coffee. I wrote out a distressingly large cheque, being superstitious about parting with hard cash. Aidan craned over the table to see how much his company had cost me. 'Thanks very much, Gordon,' he said humbly. He looked at his watch. 'D'you fancy going to the Blue Parrot?'

I nodded. I was intoxicated in several senses. When we got outside, the impact of the drizzle made me unsteady. Aidan held on to me to stop me falling. His touch gave me a stirring sensation which the drink ought to have prevented. I grinned childishly up at him.

'You've got a smile like a little kid. You know that? Clear up those zits and you'd look really sweet.'

'Can't. The zits are my hobby. I'm growing them for research.'

Aidan laughed. 'You're sure you're all right?'

I took a deep breath. 'Never better. Lead on.' We retrod some of our earlier course, until we were quite close to Aidan's former place of employment. At the door of the Blue Parrot two relatively elderly bouncers greeted us.

'Good evening, gentlemen, you do realise this is a gay – ' Then they saw Aidan. 'Right. Do come in.' Aidan exchanged a few pleasantries while I paid an entrance fee which was comparatively paltry. No more than the Adonis Club, but an altogether plusher location.

Immediately to the right of the entrance stood a large grand piano surrounded by stools. Beyond this, in a hollowed out dell, were the loos. The bar was straight ahead of us, facing back down the room. Plush red couch seats lined the walls on either side, with prettily made-up tables dotted along them. The bar was already busy, staffed by a synthetically handsome youth and a plump boy in drag. Amidst the generally ordinary clientele, which included quite a few real women of the opposite sex, three or four glamorous drag queens drifted around. One of these, very tall, in a huge blonde wig and striking red evening dress, was the proprietor. The others were appearing in a show at the adjoining, more expensive bar. Aidan and I made our way across to buy drink. Chords rang out from the piano, where a blond gnome, a well known accompanist on the drag circuit, had ensconced himself at the keyboard. He was sharing a few jokes with camp followers sitting around him.

'Are you sure you ought to drink any more?' Aidan asked.

'This concern, this concern. Just getting second wind, dear.'

'I'm not a deer,' Aidan replied. 'Different animal altogether.'

'That's what I'm hoping.' I paid for a couple of impausible doubles and we sat down. I sat next to him and stared at him deeply. 'God, you're beautiful.'

He laughed. 'Thank you. But actually I'm not. I'm plug ugly with funny teeth and daft ears. And listen, Gordon, don't forget I'm a real bastard sometimes.'

I put my hand on his shoulder. 'Do you mind?'

'No. I babysit.' I didn't get this at the time. 'Gordon, don't have any daft ideas about me. I do bad things. I've done runners on punters. One thing I do is get them in a taxi, ask them to pay me there, then do a runner. Dead easy. Even my best customers don't get much. I know ways of making a bloke come in less than five minutes. And that's their lot, just a wank, I never do owt else. I learnt some tricks in the massage trade, you see.'

'You're a qualified masseur?' I asked dreamily.

'Don't be soft.' I could have sworn I heard affection in this. He began to stroke the back of my neck. 'Don't be soft,' he repeated.

'All right. You're the big bad wolf. So what?'

'Look, Gordon, I'll stick with you here tonight, but we're not doing business. Not now, anyway. We'll talk about it another day when your head's a bit clearer.' He leaned over and kissed me on the lips. I pulled him back, but no repeat was forthcoming. I let go.

'Sorry.'

'Don't worry about it.'

'You know what we were talking about earlier?'

'We've talked about just about everything, haven't we?'

'Gray. Gary.'

'Oh yeah. What're you going to do about that?'

'Fuck knows. I can't go to the Police. Why should you care?'

Aidan laughed. 'I just hate Gary so much. I'd like to see him go away for good.'

'What's he done to you?'

Aidan pulled back the sleeve of his jacket, then the sleeve of his sweater. A long scar ran down his arm, not quite reaching the wrist. 'Nothing much,' he said with a smile. I ran my hand up and down the scar.

'I'll finish him.'

Aidan shook his head. 'You wouldn't know how to start.' He replaced his sleeves. As he did so, a drag queen slipped from a door alongside the bar and made his/her way to the piano. An old favourite on the circuit, and I use the word 'old' advisedly. Norma Jean Bakelite had an easy manner, a strong voice and a good line in foul-mouthed repartee. The choice of songs was amazingly obvious and each one struck me as profound, deep, sentiment-laden and commemorative of Aidan. When the first interval came, I teetered over to Norma Jean and congratulated him/her on another brilliant performance. If you've ever seen Norma Jean perform, you'll know what this says about my drunkenness or my sanity or both. I then asked for a particularly nauseating song from a show especially for Aidan. Back at our table, Aidan was talking to a small thin woman wearing a red suit with a very short skirt and a lesbian haircut. I recognised her from previous visits here as one of the handful sitting around the piano who would be called upon by the cabaret turn to sing later in the evening. She always sang 'September In The Rain' and 'Blue Moon' in a key too low for the human ear to detect.

'Kelly, this is Gordon,' Aidan said. We shook hands.

'Darling, your lovely boyfriend was just saying the sweetest things. I must sing a song for the two of you. Oh, it's my lucky week. There was a very important agent in here on Monday and, fingers crossed, little Kelly may be going places at last.'

'Fingers crossed,' I said. 'And please sing Aidan a song. Is there one you like?' I asked him.

'I love Kelly singing "September In The Rain".' As though there was any chance of her singing very much else. Kelly blew us both a kiss and went back to the piano. The second half of the show began.

'Now,' Norma Jean said, 'I've been asked to sing a song for a young man called Aidan with lots of love from Gordon.' A word was whispered to the keyboard gnome. Chords were strummed. 'As long as he needs me,' Norma Jean belted out, 'I know where I shall be.' Aidan kissed me on the cheek.

'Thanks,' he said. 'Thanks a lot.' He laughed and shook his head.

'Gordon. Can I have a word?' The voice was familiar. Very familiar. I looked up and there was Darren, blue eyes bulging, a severe look on his face. I looked up stupidly, still clutching Aidan's arm.

'Hello, Darren,' I said. 'A drink?'

'I'm not really – oh, all right.' He named his improbable concoction.

'I'll get them,' Aidan said, springing to his feet. I gave him a tenner.

'You'll be wanting change from that, won't you, Gordon?' Darren said.

'You'll be getting change, won't you, Gordon?' Aidan gave Darren a sweet smile and moved off to the bar.

'Darren,' I said. 'Dazza. Please be a little more polite. After all – '

'Oh, I heard that bloody daft dedication,' he said. 'Gordon, you're pissed. Look, I've got to talk to you. And you've got to get away from fucking Aidan. He's poison. Absolute poison.'

'Well, I'm not actually fucking Aidan. Yet.'

'I've been asking some of my punters. It's not a pretty picture, Gordon.'

'He's told me himself about his tricks. I doubt whether you can tell me worse than he has already.'

'If anything happens to you, I'll kill him.'

'Darren, I'm touched. Really. But I know what I'm doing.'

'I don't think you do, I really don't. I've heard your name mentioned by some very strange people recently.'

'Are we still talking about Aidan?'

'Well – not so far as I know.' Darren sat down next to me. 'What have you been up to? It was something that night I came back with you. That night you had that run-in with pillockface Gary.'

I was about to tell Darren a brief version of the truth, but then I remembered what Aidan had said. But, I argued to myself, Darren was upstairs when it was going on. Yes, but Darren was brighter than the others. He'd get himself an alibi. And he was involved in some pretty strong druggy business. So I said nothing. 'What do people say I've been up to?'

'God knows. I just heard them mentioning your name. Mainly Gary and mainly on the 'phone.' He covered his face with his hands. 'God, I'm knackered. What're you doing later?'

Aidan returned with the drinks. 'You look tired,' he said to Darren.

'Too long in the Magpie and the Adonis,' I said.

'There's some heavy stuff going on there,' he said. 'Very heavy.'

'Well,' Aidan said, sitting down on the other side of me, 'I try not to get involved.'

'Gordon,' Darren said, 'can you meet me tomorrow?'

'Well –' I turned to Aidan. 'Any chance of seeing you tomorrow?'

'Oh. I'm sorry. I've got two customers tomorrow. I'll be in here late on, though. Still, I tell you what. How about Friday? Maybe you can show me your place. That'd be nice.'

I tried to hide my disappointment and turned back to Darren. 'OK. Tomorrow.' We made an arrangement. Norma Jean began to belt through 'I Am What I Am'. Darren got up and wandered round, looking for business. Aidan and I started an inane conversation parodying everything else we'd talked about. Aidan did an impression of Darren, quite good, and then resumed being Paul, which was hilarious. I laughed loudly. Kelly sang 'September In The Rain' and 'Blue Moon' but a deluge of agents with contracts did not materialise. Norma Jean sang 'New York, New York' and then we were all thrown out because it was closing time. Darren was now deep in conversation with a middle-aged man in a suit. Well, that was him settled for the night. A fat man in glasses kept trying to smile at Aidan, only to get me scowling at him. By now I was very drunk and the night air made me feel sick. My eyes were trying to stay closed and my body had some very strange ideas.

'Gordo. You coming down the 'Dilly for a coffee?' I nodded and Aidan steered me round a few corners. When we reached the all night coffee and kebab shop, Piccadilly Circus was already flooded with boys crowded around the shop, sitting brazenly on railings, whilst middle-aged men skulked in the shadows of the National Westminster Bank. By this time of night on the 'Dilly you could see every Jason in the world, Paul, Patrick, a young computer buff called Robert who was rather cute and whom I'd taken home once. Robert made a beeline for me, but Aidan saw him off before he'd really arrived. I paid for two coffees. Blurredly I made out Little Phil, talking to a punter, telling his tale of woe – the magic words 'Marbella' and 'Enterprise Allowance Grant' came floating across the night air. I was now so drunk that I felt dizzy if I looked higher than pavement level. I was trying to think of a love song to Aidan's shoes.

'Gordon. Get a cab.' This was Aidan being authoritative. 'I'll see you on Friday, same time, same place. And don't listen to Darren. He doesn't know fuck all. Can you lend us a tenner? Two'd be nicer.' I pulled out three from somewhere. 'Hey, be careful, they film all this.' I could see no cameras, but then I don't suppose they embed them in the pavement. Aidan took the cash in the style of one of his palming tricks. Then he stuck out his arm and a cab arrived. I told the driver my address. He looked dubious but allowed me in.

'Friday,' I said. 'Thanks. I love you.' Then I lurched the rest of the way into the cab and slumped down. As it drove off, I looked back. Aidan had already wandered over and started talking to the fat man in glasses, who had evidently followed us. I thought about crying at first. But then I realised I was being unfair. After all, the boy had a living to make.

4

As it turned out, it was a good idea to stop the cab a few times so I could throw up. After a bout of serial vomiting and a few cups of sugared tea (my recommended hangover cure) I was fit and raring to go, ready to take on the brand new day. I roamed around my little flat in the dawn light like a caged tiger – well, maybe guinea pig or hamster would be a better analogy. People don't usually think of me and tigers in the same breath. The point is that getting drunk makes me restive when I come round a bit. Sleep and I aren't particularly well acquainted anyway, not these days. A few more gallons of sweet tea and some sweet sherry I found under the sink and it was more or less time to hit the office. Luckily, I'd got quite a few of Darren's much vaunted tablets, so there was no danger of me suddenly nodding off at work. The office is the only place where sleep ever tends to find me.

Not long into the working day, it transpired that I was the prime social attraction of the era. The telephone rang incessantly. I kept hoping it might be Aidan, but it wasn't. Had I given him my number? I couldn't remember. This was faintly chilling; I'd spent the whole night awake and I still couldn't remember what I'd done. This could be bad; I could have got a lot of money out of the cash machine at the bank and forgotten about it. That had been known to happen. Obviously I could sling a broad narrative outline together, as you have seen: but there were a lot of gaps. And don't hold your breath − I still haven't filled them.

Anyway, before I could worry too much about all that Simon rang me. This wasn't so notable. He usually called me at least twice a week, and conscientiously kept at least one evening a fortnight free for seeing me. In his own way, he cared. They all did, in their different ways and for their markedly different reasons. About a week (or a month or a day or something like that) before this whole escapade had begun, I'd been having lunch with Alicia, a dear, beautiful, clever, sexy woman, wife to my up-market lawyer friend (and slightly more successful than him in her own right), and I'd been confiding to her that I was probably round the twist and spending far too much time in (and too much money on) what used to be called 'low company.'

'But Gordon,' she said, 'you should see more of us. More of all your real friends.'

I patted her hands and thanked her. But how do you say politely, 'You're all such couples, all you so-called "real" friends − all so fucking domestic and I just can't fit into that?' How do you explain that 'real' friends are just a vain illusion, somewhere lower on the scale of comfort than your moth-eaten old teddy bear?

Simon spent what seemed like centuries telling me about some film he'd seen the previous night. It was one of those about a kid let loose in an adult body − there was a big vogue for them round then. The concept, very popular here in the 1870s, had just reached the Americans. Late as usual. Something to do with their infantile politics, I suppose. What Simon's excuse was, fuck knows. I listened politely to a precis of all the hilarious misunderstandings and puerile double entendres while my brain read an article in the morning paper headed 'WHY DID JOHNSON GO TO DEALEY PLAZA?' Just as I'd got to a really interesting bit about Lee Harvey Oswald's hitherto unknown journey to Albania in 1958, Simon finished his film critic stint and started asking me about me.

'So did you go out last night, then?'

'Too right. I had a date, mate.' For some reason I was being Australian.

'He turned up, then, did he?'

'Too true, blue.' This had to stop. 'Yes, he did, actually. An excellent time was had by all. Well, by me.'

'So this – what was he called, Bug-a-Lugs? – oh, sorry, Aidan – this Aidan's the proverbial tart with the heart, is he?'

'He's a very charming young man who isn't at all typical of his – oh, what's the word?'

'Profession? Calling? Vocation?' Simon giggled smuttily to himself. 'And was the charming Gray around? I take it that he didn't murder you.'

'Gray was around, yes. Actually, he was punctiliously courte-ous. Insisted on buying me a couple of drinks.' I had decided not to reveal any more of Gray's generosity as my conscience was still doing quirky contortions.

The change in Simon's tone of voice was perceptible even via a medium managed by British Telecom. 'That's the most suspi-cious thing you've told me yet.'

'I don't see why someone buying me a drink is so suspicious. I'm not completely beyond the social pale yet, am I?'

'Don't be stupid. You know what I mean as well as I do.'

I did. But I didn't really want to. So I said nothing.

'Hello? You still there?' I gurgled. 'Look, were you serious about what you said the other night? And about that bloke in the paper? Because if you were, I really think you should go to the Police.'

'So you said the other night,' I replied. 'Which was your polite way of saying you didn't really believe me.'

'I think we've had that conversation. Can we try another one instead? Look, I think you should do something. Report it. Even if you did imagine it, it wouldn't do any harm to get the cops into that pub.'

'You report it.' I waved the receiver round and stared at it, vaguely annoyed and rather guilty. 'I don't want to get involved. If I did see anything, I've got away with it. Let's leave it there, shall we?'

'Well.' Simon went very serious. 'At least you're still alive. Still infatuated, too?'

'More than that.'

'Oh God. Well I hope he's not exploiting the situation and overcharging you.'

'Nothing like that happened. No business. We just had dinner and a few drinks.'

'For which you presumably paid. So he let you wine him and dine him. Very generous.' Simon rambled on like this for a while. I was touched in a way, but I didn't want to get into a dreary explanation. Eventually, to cut him short, and because my work colleagues were beginning to look askance at the length of the call, I interrupted.

'Well, at least he believes me when I tell him things.'

'You told him about – ? Christ, you're bloody mad. He could be involved, for all you know.'

'Don't be silly. Well, OK, I know what you mean, but I happen to know you're wrong.' My eyes had strayed back to the newspaper article in any case. Simon waffled on. We made an arrangement to meet. I put the 'phone down, full of praise for myself because I hadn't got stroppy with him. Darren's tablets had a tendency to make me aggressive and the brief spasms of being Australian were a fairly reliable early warning sign. Still reading the paper, I used a minimal portion of my brain to make a few negative recommendations on pieces of work lying around on my desk. I was just reading the sentence 'incontrovertibly proving Lyndon Johnson's membership of a Texan cartel of arms dealers, gang bosses, Cuban subversives and Grand Wizards of the KKK' when the 'phone rang again. It was Dougie wanting to know if I could meet him for lunch.

'Well, I had to check you were still alive,' he said, 'after everything you were telling us the other night. Horst gave me a real telling-off, you know. He was very worried about you.'

'What, worried I was being stalked by gangs of marauding knifemen or worried I was completely bonkers or both?'

'Nobody thinks you're mad, Gordon.'

'Oh, but I do.' I looked at the dreary crap on my desk. 'I must be mad to keep wandering into this place every day. Lunch today, you mean?'

'I know it's short notice, but – I think I owe you a meal. Our bet, if you remember. The American thing.'

I didn't, but so what? 'If you say so. I know I was right and you were wrong. And if you want to buy me lunch, I'm delighted.'

'Well, someone's got to make you eat something. I'm sure you never eat. So we'd better have a steak at the Leather Room. Laugh at the Brit dealers sinking deeper into their misery.' He meant Brit-bond dealers, I think. He reminded me where the Leather Room was exactly and I promised to be there on the dot of twelve thirty. This was all well and good. Free expensive food, which meant, of course, free expensive drink. I rattled the newspaper with glee and the 'phone rang again.

'Gordon. Excellent.' Fruity tones and a quiet but manic laugh.

'Toby. Good to hear from you.' Or was it? Did this mean that *Parsifal* had fallen through? 'Everybody's ringing me today,' I prattled on, 'mainly to find out whether I'm still alive.'

Toby laughed. 'Oh yes, of course. Last night was the night you braved the jaws of death for the sake of true love, wasn't it? And how was the sinister Red?'

'Gray. As nice as pie. I'll tell you when I see you.'

'Good. Then you can tell me this evening, if you could manage a quickish drink after work. There's something I want to talk about. It could prove helpful. I – er – I can't really say any more.' He gave another spluttering laugh which (I think) was meant to indicate confidentiality.

'It all sounds terribly exciting.' I thought. Wasn't I supposed to be meeting someone? Oh yes, Darren. Well, that wasn't until quite late, or so I seemed to remember. He'd mentioned going to the Adonis Club, so it must have been later rather than sooner.

'How can you resist?' Toby pressed.

'Tobes, why are you always so mysterious?' A mutual friend of ours, Clive, always complained about this. 'Is this some other bizarre job you're chasing?'

'Ah – ah – ah – ah - not exactly.'

'Where shall I see you?' I laughed. 'How about the Magpie?'

'Gordon!' Toby gave an audible shudder. 'No, what about that rather baroque camp place near Piccadilly you once introduced me to? That would seem eminently suitable. I should be free by half six. Is that all right?'

It certainly was. Suddenly it was raining social events. 'Isn't life like that?' I said aloud to my colleagues as I replaced the receiver. They all looked at me with pity and annoyance, as they generally preferred the atmosphere in the office to be like a reference library. I sighed, picked up some work, read it and threw it at my in-tray. Too boring for contemplation. My body, egged on by amphetamines, wanted movement. The 'phone rang again. Who was after me now? I grabbed it eagerly.

'Hello, can I help you?'

There was a silence. Then a laugh. Then that voice. 'Hey, man. Gordon, baby.'

'Sorry, who is – ?'

'You know who it is, man. You have a good time last night? Was your friend co-operative?' He laughed again.

'How did you get this number?'

'Contacts, Gordon, contacts.'

'What do you want, anyway?'

'Relax, man. I don't want anything. I'm just asking after your health. A lot of us are very concerned about your health. We want you to stay healthy, Gordon. We want you to look after yourself. Not take any risks. Give your body lots of exercise and give your voice a nice long holiday. No risks.' He laughed again. 'I'm sure you read me, man, I'm sure you read me.'

'Like a book, Gray, like a book.'

'Very good. You around tonight, man? When you seeing that Aidan again? Or you want to see some other boy? You want me to fix you up with someone?'

'Thanks – but no thanks. I said I'd meet Darren tonight.' Immediately I'd said this I kicked myself, bit my tongue, cursed my hyperactive mouth.

'Oh, Darren. An old friend of yours, isn't he, man? It's good to meet old friends. Just remember, Gordon baby. Keep yourself healthy. And that way your friends stay healthy. Your old friends. And your new friend. That's what we all want, isn't it? 'Bye, man. See you around.' The 'phone went down. I sat, holding the receiver, staring blankly at my desk.

Passengers on Eastbound services on the District Line were experiencing delays to all destinations due to an 'earlier incident', I was gleefully informed by the District Line Information Service from the Control Room at Earl's Court. As usual, by some law of Underground perversity, an Eastbound District Line train arrived before the announcement was quite over. As the half empty train lurched chaotically towards the City, I shuffled edgily around, too speeded up to sit down, too terrified to stand still. The overriding question was boringly simple. Where had he got my 'phone number from? My work number. He didn't know where I worked and, anyway, when I was in the Magpie I always lied about my job. Had I given the number to Aidan? I didn't think I had. No, this all suggested something that didn't really bear thinking about. But it was hard to think about much else.

I tried to avoid thinking about it by listening to Dougie in his most zealously reforming mood. Fortunately the food and the drink were excellent, although one of the side effects of Darren's tablets was (supposedly) suppression of the appetite. I tend to be biologically perverse, so it didn't seem to make too much difference. Much more effective as appetite suppressants were (a) the obsessional fear caused by Gray's 'phone call, (b) Dougie's conversation and (c) the other people in the Leather Room.

The Leather Room resembles, in its shape, a long and wide corridor. This general effect isn't helped by the lay-out of the tables, which had obviously been done by someone normally employed by British Rail. Leather-backed two-seater banquettes faced each other in quasi-compartments down either side of the place. Waitresses, like guards, parade up and down the middle, providing a laughable apology for service. According to Dougie, who frequents it for entirely satirical reasons, it's the haunt of British brokers and dealers (I mean those who work for purely British firms or deal in purely British commodities) and constitutes the maximum luxury allowed by their firms on expenses. As a result they take potential clients there and invariably fail to close deals, thus making everything worse. Dougie's firm, being mainly American but not a little Swiss, regard it as a slum where they take clients whose business they no longer need. Ironically enough, the food itself is good, as I've said, but the food seems to count for very little in these matters. Simon once took me to the place where his firm take their honoured clients, a very chic City spot; it's one of those Japanese places where they present you with a tray bearing tiny bowls of seaweed and rubber and a rather noxious looking orange thing that may well still be alive. Dougie tends to take me to the Leather Room because he knows I appreciate the cuisine. And as he once said, 'Obviously if you like that awful Magpie place, you like slumming.'

Across the aisle from us, four very earnest besuited men of about my own age sat. On all of them, clear signs of wear and tear were visible. One of them had a suit that was just too creased and whose lapels and general cut clearly denoted a year not altogether recent. Another had very thinned hair which lay around the outskirts of his head, while his jowls and heaviness of face indicated good times once, but no longer, enjoyed. Another had the opposite hair problem, too much of it but not well cut. The fourth just looked rather like me, dwindled and clapped out, though he didn't seem to have cultivated my range of fascinating skin diseases. The heavy-jowled one and the crumpled suit were having an intense discussion that looked pretty acrimonious. I cut another chunk of my steak and paused to admire it. Blood ran from the medium rare middle. Thought association took over, and once more Gray, complete with knife, appeared on the movie screen of my mind. I gave a very audible and visual shudder.

'Gordon. Are you all right?'

'Sorry. A heavy night last night. And suddenly I felt guilty about this poor cow. Still, too late now, isn't it?' I shoved the lump of dead animal into my mouth with fake zealous cheer. 'Anyway,' I rambled on with a full mouth, 'they'd eat us if they got the chance, wouldn't they?' I felt the juice running around my mouth and suddenly imagined I could sense the slightly rusty taste of blood. I think my face betrayed something.

'You're not all right. Is it the meat?'

'I think the meat's OK. Just give me a moment.' I picked up my wine glass to refresh my mouth, but guess what colour that was? Great help. 'I'm sorry, Doug, I think I'm turning drastically allergic to the colour red.' I gave what I think they call a rueful laugh. 'I must also confess that I wasn't really listening to what you were saying just now.'

Dougie laughed, his long large face opening to reveal a generous helping of teeth. Was it my imagination or were they somewhat red-stained? 'Just the usual,' he said. 'Trying to save you from yourself.'

'I'm the least of my worries at the moment.'

'Oh. I see. Did you go out with this boy again, then?'

'Aidan. Yes, I did. But Aidan's not the issue here. Well, he's an issue but not the issue.'

'Gordon, you aren't seriously getting involved with a rent boy, are you? I mean, be practical, you can't afford it.'

'We didn't do anything. Not just because I was too drunk, although I was, but because we both thought it would have spoiled everything. I don't think he thinks I'm just another punter. He even showed some signs of affection. I think.'

'And you were drunk, were you?' Dougie laid his eating irons aside for a moment and sat back. 'Well. Just don't let yourself get hurt. And don't let yourself get taken in.'

'Dougie?' I queried sweetly. 'Can I ask you something?' Dougie nodded. 'Do you think that I'm imagining everything I tell you? Or do you think I'm occasionally on the same planet as the rest of you?'

Dougie now hunched forward. Briefly, discreetly, he reached forward and laid one of his hands reassuringly on one of mine. 'I'm just very concerned about you. So is Horst. So are a lot of people.'

'You never answer the question, do you? Let me put it more simply. Do you think I'm crazy?' I removed his reassuring hand in the most indiscreet manner possible.

'Don't be silly.' He picked up his knife and fork and resumed an eating posture. 'What I think – and Horst agrees with me – is that after that terrible accident you were very brave. We were very impressed at the way you kept going. But obviously there's going to be a reaction and they say it's often about six months or a year. Between then. When all the immediate details have been cleared up. And, pardon me for saying this, but something as terrible as that is bound to affect the imagination in some way, particularly with someone as imaginative as you.'

'Imaginative? Me, a humble mathematician?'

'Now you know as well as I do that you're hardly a typical mathematician. Not with your achievements. Not with your interest in music and painting.'

Fucking arts graduates. They're all the same. Give a pillock an English degree because he managed to struggle through six books in three years and he thinks he's some kind of guardian of the sacred flame of our cultural heritage, equipped and qualified to patronise your taste and correct your English. People like Dougie just don't know what it's like at the working face of pure theory. There are moments in Maths – and you don't get them in English Literature to my knowledge – where you catch glimpses of the infinite, of the Ultimate Secret. And it's pure terror. Rather different from the nice safe world of the Wuthering Brontës and E. M. Woofter and that self-contained little crowd.

'My achievements are history, Douglas. Like me. No, that's not the point. The point is, I agree I have an odd mind. But I don't invent whole incidents. Particularly not when they involve knives and blood. My mind doesn't run that way. And what about that bit in the paper? I showed you that, didn't I?'

'I didn't say you invented things,' Dougie replied in a tediously parental tone. 'I just think you can't resist embroidering what you do see. Not because you want to deceive anyone, but because of what happened. It's natural when some awful violent act has hit you to start seeing similar things everywhere.' He paused to drink. I was too furious to speak. 'Look, you remember I had a brief thing with a policeman a few years ago? Before I met Horst? Well, he's currently stationed in the area where that man, the brewery rep, was killed. You see, we still keep in touch, just as friends. Obviously, being gay's a bit difficult in his job and it's hard for him to have much of a social life. Anyway, I rang him and asked him what he knew, if he knew anything. And honestly, Gordon, it turns out that it's

73

practically certain this chap killed himself. He was unmarried, no real friends, maybe even a closet queen, had had medical leave and treatment for depression. Several people have said he was very depressed recently. They didn't really need to bother with a post mortem.' Then he let out an inappropriate giggle. 'Actually, after the train hit him there wasn't much left intact to post mortem, it was going so fast.' He resumed his po-face. 'So there's not much doubt, do you see?'

Suddenly Darren's tablets had a genuinely beneficial effect. I began to think on my feet. 'All right. Maybe. But two things. Just because he was depressed doesn't mean that he wasn't killed. That's just hearsay and I wouldn't have said it was conclusive evidence. It isn't just cheerful optimists who get murdered, you know. But anyway, where has all this hearsay come from? Do you know what's going on here, Douglas? It's a conspiracy. A real conspiracy. I know it. So maybe someone's bribed the witnesses. Maybe someone's bribed the brewery.'

'Gordon, I really think you're getting a bit over – '

'Listen. Last night Gray tried to pay me off. He gave me money. This morning he rang me up at work and made a few veiled threats. Two more points for you. Where did he get the money from? And how did he get hold of my work number?' I smiled because I considered my evidence conclusive. 'This is conspiracy, Dougie.'

Dougie, his face set in a pondering expression, picked up the wine bottle and poured more into his glass. I noticed that he ignored mine. Ostentatiously, ignoring the colour which still disturbed me, I drained my glass, nearly making myself throw up in the process. Dougie did not recharge my glass. Instead, he reached into the inside breast pocket of his fine, expensive suit and pulled out a piece of paper. He laid it on the table in front of me. On it, in his own surprisingly childish scrawl, was an address and a name. Harley Street. I don't remember the name.

'I asked some people I know, some doctors, and they reckon this man's the best. If you needed any help with fees, Horst and I would be only too happy to help, really. A loan with no hassle, as long as you like.'

'Interest free?'

'Oh, Gordon, don't be silly. Of course.'

'Well, now, that's something.' I reached over, took the wine bottle, poured a brimful glass and drained it. Still disgusting. 'Dougie, in the ordinary way I'm very fond of you. And Horst. I'm very happy for you. But my God you've got a fucking

74

nerve. That's what this lunch is about, isn't it? We didn't have a bet. I know we didn't. It's just your way of softening me up, sweetening the bitter pill of telling me I'm bonkers. Is it just your idea? Or is Simon involved too? I think I can detect his delicate touch in all this somewhere.'

'Look, Simon and I did talk a bit, but really – '

'Well, ta.' I got up. Unfortunately I'm too short to aspire to dignity in such situations. I picked up the piece of paper, screwed it up and stuffed it in my empty glass. 'I haven't got any cash on me, so I can't give you my half of the bill. Maybe the insult pays that, however well meant it was.'

'Gordon, sit down and talk for a minute.'

'What about? Medical science and its application to the over-imaginative? No, Dougie. I'll be in touch. And soon, because the next time I talk to you I'm going to give you proof, real hard concrete proof that I saw what I said I did. Proof for the lot of you.'

I left the table, aware that my behaviour had been a bit self-advertising for the Leather Room. Dougie called my name softly once, but, this being the City, he felt he had a reputation to take care of, so he didn't do anything too demonstrative like coming after me. For which I was profoundly relieved.

The Westbound indicator laboriously spelt out a message. If no Wimbledon train is shown please take an Ealing or Richmond train and change at Earl's Court. Above this message it promised a Wimbledon train in one minute. Staggeringly typical. The journey back to work gave me a chance to review my bravado. Had I meant my parting shot? I rather thought that I had. The wisom of even saying it, let alone carrying it out, never entered my mind. Also I was furious with the lot of them. Not least Simon. He and I were supposed to be close friends; part of the reason I'd chosen to live in the area I did was that it was close to him. He'd never pretended to be that close to Dougie. Until fairly recently his contacts with Dougie had been exclusively through me. I was childishly peeved at the thought they'd gone behind my back. I had to prove to them now that I wasn't crazy. Well, I couldn't prove that in a general way and maybe in a general way they were right, but I didn't want them to think I imagined acts of random violence.

When I got back to the office, I tried to channel my fury into work, but the stuff in front of me was so idiotically simple that it proved a poor avenue for sublimation. I turned away from my work and looked out of the large window behind me, offering a vast prospect of London to the South-West. From my dungeon on the fifteenth floor I watched darkness fall over glass and concrete and thought about Aidan.

By the time I left to meet Toby, the main evening rush at the station nearest the office was on the decline, so the crowd on the platform was only about two deep. I sidled along to the far end, just past the stairs leading to the alternative exit. I felt in my pocket and found I still had some of Darren's pills in a box there. My body was flagging a bit now, so I slipped a couple into my mouth. I didn't want events catching up with me just yet. I knew I was being stupid, because my pulse hadn't actually slowed down at all and my heartbeats were practically audible. The pills, quite large, were difficult and unpleasant to swallow without liquid, but after the wine at the Leather Room they were child's play. I gulped them down and then I sensed the breeze of the incoming train in the near distance, arriving from my side of the station. I leaned forward slightly to get more of the wind, the nearest thing to ventilation on offer. And then someone pushed me.

A deliberate, firm shove in the small of the back. I felt my footing go and I went forward, flailing. A woman screamed. I, rather oddly, said, 'Stop him' and then, 'Fuck.' There was a noise behind me. Teetering on the edge, I saw the lights of the train I was going to fall in front of. Well, that was that and goodnight.

My body, though, didn't fancy co-operating with my brain's rather laid-back approach. It was just getting its latest speed charge and wanted to survive to enjoy it. As it happened I'd been standing sort of sideways to catch the wind. So when I thought I must fall my instincts noticed that a quick-witted, beefy commuter next to me at the edge had thrust out a hopeful arm, and because of the way I was facing I was at an angle where I could catch it. Because I'm a skinny runt he could take my weight for just that split second I needed to pull myself back and right myself on the platform. At which point the train arrived. I thanked the man who'd saved my life, but he was totally embarrassed and obviously in a hurry to get home. With typical British reserve, everyone around me shuffled away in case I got into the train and stood next to them. I didn't. I just stood there, shaking. And, it should be said, because I'm as typically British as anyone else, feeling intensely embarrassed too.

The train pulled away, leaving the platform about half empty and a spacious cordon sanitaire around me. An angry-looking guard came stonking down the stairs and swore at me.

'You daft cunt. I saw that.'

'Sorry?'

'I was over there. Stupid drunk pillock. If you can't handle it, don't drink it. Don't see why everyone else should be held up getting home 'cause you can't fucking handle your drink.'

'Sorry? Look, someone pushed me. Where'd he go?'

'Pushed you? I should fucking cocoa. It's this all day drinking and daft bastards like you ...' He continued in this vein. I looked over at the opposite platform. My vision wasn't entirely clear yet. But I was sure I could see something at the end of the other platform.

'Excuse me,' I said to the porter, dodging round him. I ran the length of the platform, bumping into people here and there. As I reached the other end I heard the train for that side approaching. But before it blocked my view I got a glimpse, long enough for it to be returned. Red baseball jacket, tight jeans. He gave me a grin, baring his feral teeth. Lewisham Jason. I ran up the stairs to cross over, but as I started down the stairs on the other side the train pulled away and I'd lost him.

Beneath the tall rococo arched ceiling with the gold leaf design a waiter showed me to a table for three booked in Toby's name. This intrigued me. Who was the third to be? Clive, I supposed. I ordered a large gin and small tonic. The waiter, with dyed black hair gelled back, swept camply away and returned in an inkling. I placed some coins on his tray and this seemed to suffice. Despite the attempt on my life I'd made sure I had more money. Amazingly, the bank machines were still catering for my endless appetite.

The Brasserie was crowded and the noise of conversation rebounded with that hollow sound echoes thrown back by a high roof seem to acquire. In the midst of all the tables a piano stood; I'd never, on my few visits here, heard it played before. But today my luck was in. Or do I mean out? A young man of medium height with curly blond hair and a round, slightly sulky face sat down and began to play rippling chords. He sang 'Just The Way You Are' followed by 'Hello', removing whatever slight differences between each other the two songs had ever possessed. I could tell I was in for a treat.

Fortunately, Toby came bursting through the crowd, almost tiptoeing, his tall thin frame looking awkward. He'd managed to sneak ahead of his guiding waiter. He put his briefcase down. 'Sorry. Late call for some meaningless figures about trade in Denmark.' He turned back to me again. 'Gordon. I want you to meet Michael Hamilton.'

I stood up. It was, of course, the polite thing to do, but even if politeness was normally meaningless to you, it's my opinion that Michael Hamilton's natural bearing would bring you to your feet in tribute. The world's most conventionally handsome man offered me his hand.

'I've heard a great deal about you, Gordon.' The handshake was cool and firm; the blue eyes held me seriously, as if to convince me that I was the most fascinating person in Michael Hamilton's life at that moment. Seeing my reflection briefly in one of the Brasserie's mirrors, I didn't think that this was actually very likely.

'Yes. So have I. About you, I mean.' The dark grey suit he was wearing had probably cost more than my flat. 'You were at Simon's on Tuesday, weren't you?'

'Simon's? Oh, Simon Green, yes. A friend of Katy's, really. I think he's still rather making his way, isn't he?' Michael made this sound like an inexcusable social faux pas. 'Shall we?' He gestured to our seats. Both Toby and I waited for him to sit before we dared to. Michael turned and waved a finger vaguely at the bar and immediately waiters leapt from all points of the compass to serve him. He ordered for the three of us. Then he resumed conversation. 'I gather you've turned your back on making your way,' he said to me with a smile.

'I doubt whether I'd be very suited to Simon's line of work. It would be nice to pretend it was a conscious decision, though. Rather than just a random cock-up.'

'Very Freudian choice of words, Gordon,' Toby said with a nervous laugh.

Michael seemed to ignore this. 'I actually asked Toby if we could meet, after he'd told me about your research. Of course, like all arts students he failed completely to give any explanation or real sense of what you'd actually done in anything other than terms verging on the mystical. But I gather it has to do with probabilities and beyond.'

'It started that way. It ended up in Chaos.' Toby laughed at this, but Michael nodded. 'Anyway, I'm not really anything now.'

'I've heard a bit about Chaos,' Michael said, 'but I don't follow what you mean about yourself.'

'The popular theory was that I reached burn-out. Which is why I failed to get an academic post. Apart from the fact that Chaos isn't highly thought of over here. But burn-out was the general view. It's thought, you see, that some mathematicians can go so far and no farther. Then – phfft.' I made a gesture with my hand.

'Burn-out?'

'Burn-out.' I nodded. 'After which you find it difficult to prove that $2+2=4$. Actually, I always did find that difficult. To me $2+2=3+1$, but that may just be me. The Chaos thing was taken as a symptom. I was given my doctorate and politely told to retire.'

Michael laughed, not unsympathetically. He opened the case he was carrying and pulled out some papers. 'I'm not going to bore Toby here with high-powered theory well above his level. And a bit above mine, probably,' he added modestly. 'So I'd be grateful if you could find your own way around these and give me your general impressions about any thoughts or anything that occurs to you in any way. I've put my office number at the top of the first page. I'll make sure this is worth your while. It may also lead further. But perhaps I shouldn't say too much now.' He gave me the papers. First glance indicated that they were some kind of forecast. I couldn't see what I'd have to say that would be of more use or interest than one of Michael's own experts. But if he was prepared to pay me, well then. I nodded.

'Of course, I shouldn't know anything about any of this,' Toby said, 'as an employee of another institution.'

'You don't expect me to believe that you believe that,' Michael said.

'Well, I know you don't,' Toby giggled. 'If you did, you'd still be earning the pittance I get.'

'Oh, Toby, I was never so poor. Sorry, Gordon, this talk of salaries must be a bit galling for you.'

'Not really,' I said. 'As I was just nearly killed, I'm taking a strange and unaccustomed pleasure in just not being dead at this moment.'

'Nearly killed? What happened?' Michael asked.

'It wasn't – ' Toby began and then obviously thought better of saying it in front of a third party.

'Tobes, I don't mind what you say. And yes, I think it was to do with what you were probably going to say.' I went on to give a brief, precise account of what had happened, adding for Michael's benefit the explanation that I was in danger because I had seen 'something incriminating in a lowlife pub'.

'You're sure what happened this evening was deliberate?' Toby asked.

'Those platforms do get very crowded,' Michael added.

'Yes. I'm absolutely sure.' I repeated the narrative very carefully. 'I mean,' I went on, 'a jostle or an accidental push is usually somewhere about shoulder level or on the arms. Most likely shoulder level if you're my height. This was a definite shove in the small of the back.' I laughed. 'The porter or whatever he was, guard, thought I was pissed. Typical London Transport excuse. If trains crash, stations burn down, or passengers fall on the line, then it's the passengers' own fault.' I shrugged. 'I should explain, Michael, that my friends, including Toby I suspect, believe that I have an over-vivid imagination.'

'Yes, well, you do,' Toby said.

'Dougie recommended a psychiatrist to me this lunchtime,' I said.

Toby laughed. 'Yes. Dougie told me all about lunchtime. He was very worried.'

'If you'll allow me,' Michael intervened, 'the odd people I've known have usually been scrupulously truthful. Of course, there are two types of habitual liar, the fantasist, doing it out of compulsion, and the deliberate liars, who usually do it for profit in some form or other. Fantasists are easily exposed because they're hopelessly inconsistent. Poor attention to detail, you see, never tell you the same thing twice, and if they're barmy then they're usually completely hopeless and incapable of fooling a babe in arms. No, to be a good liar, a convincing liar, you've got to get your details right and stick to them, with just that degree of flexibility that can be written off as human fallibility. That kind of liar has got to be more than usually sane to carry it off.'

'Very interesting theory,' Toby said, 'but what does it prove?'

'Well, I've just listened to Gordon here and it all leads me to the simple conclusion that if he is mad as your friend Dougie Simpson seems to think then he must be telling the truth. So we should take him seriously. On the other hand, if he's lying then you can stop worrying, because his grasp of detail is lucid, logical and consistent, ergo he's completely sane. I'm afraid, Gordon,' he smiled disarmingly at me, 'that I don't know you well enough to be certain which is the case.' He fixed me charmingly with his eyes and raised his glass to me and at that moment I realised that Toby's suspicion had been correct; Michael was gay. And he saw that I saw it. A gentle shrug of the shoulders told me.

'Brilliant,' I said, 'but rubbish.'

'Oh, I don't mind talking rubbish as long as it's plausible and someone believes it.' He thought for a moment. 'And as long as it makes me a great deal of money.' He gave an over-theatrical stretch and yawn. 'I'm fascinated as to why you should hang around "lowlife pubs" as you call them, Gordon.'

'Self-abasement,' I said.

'Rubbish,' he replied. 'I suspect it's something to do with the fauna and its aesthetic appeal.'

'He won't give you a sensible answer,' Toby said. 'In fact, I'm sure it's his sense of sin. All lapsed Catholics are the same – they have to wallow in it. Hence Gordon's preoccupation with the company of prostitutes.'

'Toby,' I said. 'Do you ever look at girls in the street?' Toby giggled. 'Well, of course you do. But do you ever look at girls and fancy them and know you can never meet them? Doesn't that give you an appalling pang of sadness? Do you ever feel that on the Tube, in pubs? It's always happening to me. Wherever I go, I see boys, boys outside my social range, boys too lovely for me to approach in the normal way of things, even in a run of the mill gay bar. But in that appalling pub it's different. I can try and approach anyone and the way I look isn't going to be what matters. And any boy I like the look of is probably going to stick with me for at least the duration of one free drink. It's his way of life. It's his job. Do you see? Probably not. How else am I going to get the company of handsome young men?'

'Interesting,' Michael said, grinning. 'Very persuasive, actually. But I'm a man of simple tastes and pleasures myself. And I don't like the sound of the ad hoc cabarets in these pubs of yours. Particularly not when they involve audience participation in Tube stations.'

Toby looked at me, as serious as he could ever be. 'Are you going to the Police now? I think perhaps you should, if only for your own safety.'

'You know how I feel about the cops, Tobes. I really don't think they'd be any use unless I knew a great deal more than I do anyway.'

'I'm sorry. I don't see what you mean.'

'I've witnessed one rent boy stabbing someone. Another's tried to push me under a train. I could report that and maybe – only maybe – get them put briefly out of circulation. But how many others are involved? And who's giving them their orders? And what exactly is going on anyway?'

Toby gave me his appraising look, which consisted of drawing back his head slowly. Then he laughed. 'Gordon McKenzie walks the mean streets,' he said in a perfectly dreadful American accent, 'in search of truth, justice – and rent boys.' He laughed. 'Are you really intending to do some Chandleresque detecting?'

'Hardly. I mean, I'm not cut out for it, am I? And I'm a marked man.' I drank, then smiled. 'I was thinking of asking a friend.'

'My advice,' Michael leaned over, 'is to steer well clear of this kind of situation.'

'Ah yes,' Toby said melodramatically, 'of course. You have – personal experience, don't you?'

'Of a kind. But don't imagine for a moment I'm going to talk about it. In any case, I was only peripherally involved. Two friends of mine were concerned, that was my only involvement. No, Gordon, I think your best bet is to find a hobby. A nice safe hobby like the Futures Market.' He looked at his watch. 'I really must move now. I'm looking forward to hearing from you, Gordon.' He picked up his case, but rather than standing immediately, he stayed seated. 'This meeting tomorrow,' he said to Toby, 'are your crowd really seriously expecting us to dabble?'

'There seems to be a view that you'll find our proposals interesting, yes.'

'Oh dear. I was afraid of that. Look. A word to the wise. All this diversification and small investment stuff. Let's save it for the party politicals, shall we? Small businesses are no use to us, Toby, they're about as helpful as an infestation of crabs. They're only useful as cover companies, and we've got quite enough of those already.'

'But surely the great strength of a market economy lies in diversification?'

'My dear Toby, great strength in a market economy lies in monopoly. Monopoly by any other name.' He rose to his feet and gave me another charming smile. 'Of course,' he added, 'I never said that.' He nodded and turned, making his way to the exit. I watched him go and then turned to Toby.

'I didn't think people like that really existed.'

'Michael wasn't always quite like that. It's a style he's acquired with age and success.'

'And money.'

'Oh, absolutely. He came very close to over-reaching himself a few years ago. But Michael's great accomplishment has always been escape. He invariably escapes. And profits from it. When he did it in the Crash last year, the City decided to stop doubting and just simply love and admire him.' He laughed.

'Any word on his political ambitions?'

'Yes. He's making definite moves and they're being

enthusiastically welcomed in significant quarters.' Toby shook his head. 'The man is not a Tory.'

'Well, he's hardly a Militant supporter, is he? Anyway, Margaret Thatcher's not a Tory. Not according to most traditional interpretations of the term "Tory".'

Toby gave me another appraising look. 'I shall ignore your – your blasphemy. Michael Hamilton is a corporatist – ' he spat the word with venom – 'an internationalist.' He dropped his parodic zeal. 'Are you going to follow up his offer? I think you should. You need something a little more – well, challenging.'

'It was kind of you to mention me, anyway.' I toyed with my empty glass. Toby looked round for a waiter. 'I could use a bigger salary, what with interest rates and so on. If a bigger salary is what all this is leading to.' The waiter arrived. We ordered several more drinks, just to be on the safe side.

'Do you want to eat?' Toby asked me after a brief essay in rubbishing the pre-Raphaelites, always an amusing way of passing the odd hour.

I looked at my watch. 'I have to meet someone later, so I'd better pass. Besides, I still feel a bit too shaky to eat, really.'

'Ah.' Toby raised his arm and gave a levelling gesture with his hand. 'Aidan is going to console you, is he?'

'A nice thought, but no. I have to meet someone else who's going to tell me something I need to know. Quite what I'm not sure.'

'How is Aidan?'

'We spent a very enjoyable evening together, thanks.'

'And a very enjoyable night?'

'No. Absolutely not.'

Toby raised his finger. 'In this particular context, what did you make of Michael?'

'Not a lot,' I lied. 'I didn't pick up any real sense of what you suggested. No "vibes", you might say.' Toby tried to probe a little further, but I erected a veil of impassivity. The conversation passed on to *Parsifal* and general matters operatic. I was enjoying myself greatly by this time and thought I was doing pretty well, particularly given my general condition, levels of consumption, complete lack of any form of sleep, the recent attempt on my life and so on. All in all it was a bloody shame when the time to meet Darren rolled around. I wondered whether I could reasonably be late for him, but I was feeling guilty and worried, to be honest, about having let his name slip out to Gray on the 'phone.

'You really must go?' Toby asked. 'If you're not going to that dreadful pub, perhaps I could come with you.'

'Actually, I'm not going to that dreadful pub. But I think I'd better meet this guy alone. I don't think you'd find much common ground with Darren.' Toby laughed at the name. 'He tends to get huffy and won't talk if he hasn't got my undivided attention.' This was a bit of a fib, but it was in a good cause.

'A shame. I've never met anyone called Darren before and it would be a thrilling new experience.' Toby sprang to his feet decisively and I followed suit. He felt in his pocket, pulled out a derisory amount of change and left it on the table as a tip. 'Don't forget to call Michael,' he reminded me. 'And of course next week we go in search of the Grail together.'

'I can hardly wait,' I said. 'Let's hope I live that long.'

At the door we stood for a moment, hit by the lights, the noise and the insistent clammy English drizzle. Toby gave me more or less a formal salute, then we parted; he entered the Tube station, I headed for Soho. Suddenly I was conscious of being very nervous again. There was so much traffic, and at this time of night it was going just fast enough to be damaging if one came into sudden contact with it. I stuck to Shaftesbury Avenue as far as I possibly could, until I reached the turning before the one where the Magpie could be found.

'You all right, Gordon?'

The voice came from just behind me. I swung round, alarmed.

'How you going, mate? Buy us a drink?'

'Paul. Right.'

'Who d'you think it was? You look fuckin' terrified, mate.'

'Sorry, I've – I've had a bit of a shock, that's all.'

'Gordon, you comin' to the Magpie? I mean, can you get us a drink? I don't like askin', but I'm skint.'

'I'm not actually, I mean, I'm not going there, but look, here's a couple of quid, I might see you later, but I've got to get to the Berkeley.'

'What, you meetin' Aidan or someone?'

'Actually, no, not tonight, I'm – ' I stopped.

Paul looked down at me and laughed. 'You seem terrified, mate.'

'Look, I must go, I'm late. I might see you later.'

'You goin' to the Adonis tonight?'

'Yes. Almost definitely. I'll see you there.'

'Good. That's good. Hey, Jason was askin' for you.'

'What? Which one? When?'

'Oh – about 'alf an hour ago. He asked where you was goin'

tonight. I mean, I didn't know, so – '

'Which Jason was it, though?'

'Oh, you know, red jacket, Lewisham, that one. What's he want with you, Gordon? You wouldn't do business with him, would you, 'cause you shouldn't, he's a bastard.'

'No. No, definitely not. Look, Paul.' I located my wallet and pulled out a fiver. 'I'll see you later. I want a word with you, actually. But just don't tell anyone where I'm going right now. OK?' I pushed the fiver into his hand. He looked at me with a smile.

'What's goin' on, Gord? Are you up to somethin' or somethin'?'

I wished I could have told him the answers. But I couldn't tell what I didn't know. I took to my heels and dashed around the corner to meet Darren.

5

Barmy Billy sat at the bar of the Adonis Club, talking quietly to his drink. In the half-light he almost looked tolerably attractive. You couldn't see the unshaven fluff on his childish pink cheeks, the tidemark on his neck, the grime and grease in his fair hair; you couldn't tell how filthy his revolting padded anorak was. You couldn't see these and other legacies of weeks of sleeping rough, interrupted only by the rare nights he struck lucky with a punter – and no punter ever took Barmy Billy home twice. When he looked up and saw me with Darren, he perked up and, guess what, asked me if I'd buy him a drink. His voice had a caricature West Country simpleton bumpkin twang. Darren gave me a warning look.

'Remember what I told you, Gordon,' he muttered. He leaned down and talked directly into Billy's ear. 'Gordon's not going to buy you a drink, so you can cut that out. He doesn't want to waste his money on a daft prat like you. So you can cut that out.'

'Darren – ' Billy essayed a plaintive tone. His pleading look was rather undermined by a slight cast in his eyes.

'Don't start all that. I'm still fucked off with you about Gareth and all that the other week.' I had been told the relevant story, but it was only an unremarkable tale of minor deceit. Billy wasn't capable of successfully pulling off even the smallest-time crookery.

'I didn't do nothing. Nothing what you wouldn't do anyway.'

Darren tutted. 'Come on, Gordon. We'll get a drink downstairs.' He turned away, stepping towards one of the club's two fruit machines. Each of these always had a little crowd, because of the vast hundred pound plus cash jackpot that was promised (and hardly ever won). The boys would often pass long evenings at these, spending nearly five times as much as they ever got out of the things, disconsolately pushing the buttons. I don't play them myself and I don't finance other people's addictions to them because the odds against the player tend to the hyper-astronomical.

As I turned to Darren, Billy caught my arm and began to stroke it. 'Stay here, Gordon. I ain't bad, not really. You've got to do what you has to, what else can you do? Take me home, I ha'n't got anywhere to go. You always said you'd take me back. If you can't do favours, what can you do? Take me home with you, I really need the money.'

This is a fair sample of Billy's style. Often he'll try and shove bits of his body up against you – what you might call the hard sell – but the content of his sales patter is usually along these lines. Strange gnomic pronouncements alternate with whingy demands and bare-faced requests. Of course, there is a long and honourable literary tradition of fools who are really wise and whose simple remarks accurately diagnose and expose the truth of the human condition. But do not be fooled. In my experience, simpletons talk meaningless bollocks and Barmy Billy was no exception. I smiled sweetly at him, removed his hand gently from my arm and walked away.

Darren had got stuck into one of the machines and was, as usual, having his small wins eaten by his huge losses. At the end of the rather late Chinese meal we'd just eaten, he had decided to chew a few tablets of various chemicals, so he was getting quite excited and loud. And unpredictable. 'God,' he said, 'I wish Aidan was here. I really wish he'd come down those stairs now.'

'As you've got your back to them it's a pretty pointless wish. Anyway, he doesn't come here. You know that.'

'That's what he told you. I've seen him in here.'

'And I haven't. Darren, Aidan is not the main issue here.'

Darren took his hands off the machine and grabbed my lapels over-eagerly. 'Yes he is. I don't want him to rip you off. You care about the little bastard and I don't want to see you get hurt.' He was obsessed with this line of argument and over the previous two or three hours had reverted to it over and over again. Despite the fact that I thought we'd established that there were more obvious threats to my safety and, if it came to that, to his.

As you can see, I've got rather ahead of myself. I usually do when telling stories, particularly this story. After so much speed and booze my memory rather abandoned the nice linear structure so beloved of other, more reliable narrators. Anyway, when I'd got to the Berkeley a few hours earlier, I'd told Darren about my experience with the train. He almost seemed pleased and jumped around in his seat in triumphant vindication.

'Well, what did I say the other night?' By this of course, he meant the night before, but Darren's temporal structure is as fucking haywire as mine. 'There's something going round about you, Gordon, but I can't quite work out what. Why won't you tell me what's happened?'

'How could anything be going round about me? Boring little me.' I'd looked round the Berkeley. I like the Berkeley. A simple wooden pub with few pretensions and no grandiose dimensions. A straight pub too, but I must say that generally I prefer straight pubs these days.

Darren leaned over the table. 'I've been asking people. All I know is you know something. Something you shouldn't. So what the fuck is it?'

'How do you know that much?'

'I asked Lewisham Jason when he was pissed. I said, "Why's pillock-face Gary talking to people about Gordon?"'

'And did he answer?'

'You know Jason.'

'Well, not too well, thankfully. He told you I knew something.' I kept remembering Aidan's warning. I thought I knew Darren, but such a belief begs an immortal question. 'Darren, what's going on in the Magpie?'

He shook his head. 'Some fucking heavy stuff.' He lowered his voice. 'Look, Gordon, you know I deal a bit. You see, if I deal a bit, I get a better price on the stuff I want meself. And I'm always happy to help mates out. You know, like those tabs I get for you.'

'OK. Fair enough. But please, Darren, don't pretend that drug dealing is altruistic. You do it for your own benefit. For your own drugs and for money for yourself. Slipping me the occasional amphetamine doesn't make you Mother Teresa.'

'I didn't fucking say it did, did I? Listen. The past couple of months, right, I've been having some trouble. Particularly in the Magpie.'

'What kind of trouble? Threats? Police?'

'Nothing as obvious as that. More like – well – getting frozen out. You know what I mean?'

'Well, not exactly. I've not sold a lot of drugs myself.'

'Look, what I think is that someone's trying to stitch it all up, take it all over. You know, like one firm or summat.'

'Darren. Do you watch a lot of television? What kind of firm? East End? Triads? Harrods?'

'Bollocks, Gordon. You just don't know, do you? I don't know either, come to that, not who's behind it. Some geezer at the end of a 'phone, that's all I know. Some geezer who's running Gary and Jason and fuck knows how many of the others.'

'Mmm.' I stopped suddenly. Wasn't this what Aidan had been saying?

Suddenly I felt very tired and frightened. I put my hand in my pocket and fortunately there was one tablet left. I pulled it out, stared at it, popped it in my mouth.

'How many of those have you had today?'

'Darren. This morning I had a 'phone call from Gray. Gary. At work. How did he get my work number? I never give that to anyone, not even you. And look – ' I held up my hand to stop him cutting in. 'I said I was meeting you tonight.'

'Thanks a fucking bunch. Did you say where?'

'No. The only person I told was Paul – you know, London Paul – about five, ten, fifteen minutes ago.'

'Not very clever. He's almost certainly in with them. What else did you tell him?'

'Not a lot. That we're going to the Adonis. But we can always give that a miss, can't we?'

Darren suddenly sparked up. 'No way. We're going there. If they're waiting for us, let's go and meet them. As long as we know they're waiting.'

'Darren. What's going on?' I sighed. 'I can't fight, you know. Is Aidan involved in all this?'

'Honest, Gordon, I really don't know. Unless you know what the hold Irish Paul has on him is?'

'How the fuck would I? Drugs, I suppose.'

'I don't like him, Gordon, I really don't. Are you really that concerned about him?'

'Oh God. Yes. Something about him – well, I can't explain.'

'You shouldn't fall in love with anyone, you. I fell for a bloke once. Older than me he was. I loved him like crazy. Then one night the Police turned up at our place and told me he'd been picked up for interfering with boys. Broke my fucking heart. Since then I've never let myself get involved. Not with anyone.'

'I don't think Aidan's likely to get picked up for boy bothering.'

'What about the massage parlour?'

'I know he did massage.'

'All his other names? Paul, Graham, Nick – you know them all, do you?'

'Come on, Trevor – you're in no position to slag anyone off for using false names.'

'Do you know his real name?'

'Yes,' I lied.

'And?'

'I haven't told him yours. Why should I tell you his?'

Darren laughed. 'Fair enough. Fair enough. Has he told you about his Stanley?'

'Doesn't sound like his kind of name, really.'

'Stanley's his mate on armed robberies. In fights. Nice little Stanley knife, understand?'

'Look, I know he's no saint. I know you're no saint, come to that. What are you trying to say, Darren?'

'He's a bastard.'

'Is he mixed up in this other business, though?'

'Fuck knows. Not as obviously as Gary and Jason and Jason and Paul. But Irish Paul's a dangerous friend to have.'

'Aidan doesn't like him very much, actually.'

'That's what he says.'

'The thing is, he's the only person I've talked to up to now who believes me.'

'Who believes you about what?'

'About that guy from the brewery. The one the papers say fell under a train. Gray, Gary, and some of his friends stabbed him in the cellar room or whatever you call it at the Magpie. Well, it was Gary who did the stabbing, actually.'

Darren sat back, visibly shaken. He let out a long whistle. 'So that's what you know.' He leaned over again, quite angry. 'Why didn't you tell me before? When did it happen? It was that night I came back, weren't it? Why didn't you fucking tell me? Why didn't you tell the fucking Police?'

I explained about the Police. 'And I tried to tell some of my friends. But they all thought I was making it up or something. They think I'm a bit mad.'

'So do I. So do I.' Darren took a packet of cigarettes from his black leather jacket pocket, along with a rather smart lighter. Aware I don't smoke, he saved himself the effort of offering and lit himself one. He coolly surveyed me. 'And you've told Aidan, have you?'

'Yes. But so what? He hates Gray.'

'That's what he says.'

'Anyway, Gray saw me. I told you. No, I didn't. So it doesn't really matter who I told. Anyway. Gray started giving me money. He tried to make Aidan do business with me at a cut price – '

'Did Aidan agree? That's very important.'

'We didn't do business. I'm not sure I could do business with him, Dar, I love him too much.'

'Can we just shove the sentimental stuff for a minute? Tell me about Gary and the money. And Aidan. That was last night, was it, before I saw you in the Parrot?'

'That's right.' I gave Darren a brief summary of the previous evening's events. 'How do I know you're not involved?' I laughed nervously.

'Well, you don't, do you? Face it, Gordon, you know fuck all.' He drew on his cigarette and tried to create a smoke ring. 'So yesterday they're giving you dosh, today they're trying to get rid of you. What's changed? Have you done owt? Said owt?'

'Well, apart from Gray ringing me at work, I've only seen old friends all day. Oh, and one guy who gave me this lot.' I waved Michael Hamilton's papers at him. 'Could be a job in it.'

Any other time, Darren would have pounced on a potential change in my financial circumstances. For himself and his friends that would be significant. But he didn't chase this point.

'And Gary's got your work number. Think about it, Gordon, you'll get there eventually.'

'That's what Aidan said. I'm not sure I want to get there, actually. No, I definitely don't.' It still didn't bear thinking about. 'Can we talk about something else now, please?'

'Gordon. Concentrate. Your fucking life's in danger. So's mine, possibly.'

'Unless you're mixed up in it. This could all be a trap.' I looked round hysterically. I couldn't see Gray or any Jasons or Paul or anyone, but that didn't mean they weren't there. 'Let's go. Let's eat. You must want to eat.'

'We're safe enough here. We're safe enough as long as other people are around.'

I just wanted to go home and bolt the door. But I wouldn't be safe even there. Which of them was it? It was hard to believe that one of my supposed close friends – and I was pretty sure which one – was mixed up in drugs and murder. Well, murder, anyway. We'd all had some experience of drugs at University; we'd all dabbled to some extent. I'd known a rather glamorous young man called Caspian Forrester (to whom Aidan bore a slight resemblance, now I came to think of it) who'd been able to procure anything for anyone. Dougie and Simon had both had their sources – I seemed to remember that Katy Goldsmith had originally exposed Simon to the dangers. Toby, of course, had been well acquainted with the upper crust drug set, including the daughter of that rather hopeless Tory Cabinet Minister who died of an overdose. But it was still very hard to believe that one of them wanted me dead. But the evidence spoke plain and clear.

'Mind you,' Darren went on, 'I wouldn't say no to a nice Chinese. I reckon you could do with some food as well, Gordon, you look thinner than you did yesterday.' He peered across the table. 'Actually, pardon my saying this, but you look terrible.'

'Yes, well, I haven't slept for a while. Have I? Food, yes, I'll happily get you a nice Chinese, even a meal as well, but I shan't eat much myself, I'm really not, well I did sort of eat earlier – funny that, the meat, the blood, it got to me a bit, I'm afraid, it upset me rather.'

'Gordon, you're starting to ramble a bit. How much have you had to drink today?'

'Oh – this and that. Here and there. Not enough.'

'I don't know where you put it all, I really don't.' He sat back. 'So what's this about a job?'

'Oh – all very up in the air at the moment.' I waved the papers and explained a little – a guarded little – about Michael Hamilton. I didn't see him being the type to want his name and attributes waved around the rent boy scene. 'I imagine nothing'll come of it in the end. He just wants some cheap consultancy work done, I suspect.'

'Still – it's all dosh. Fancy another drink?' I smiled and handed the cash over to him.

While Darren was at the bar, I looked briefly at Michael's forecasts. It was easy to see the primary error they made, from my personal viewpoint. As it occurred fairly early in the calculations, it rendered the whole lot invalid. I threw a few figures around my head. This was where I felt happier. Darren put some drinks down on the table. I started scribbling calculations on a beer mat.

'Gordon.'

'Sorry. Miles away.'

'You fancy going to eat after this one, then?'

'Oh – ah – yes.' I put the papers aside. 'Tell me then, what happened about America? You were full of it the other night.'

Darren began to talk about America and video arcade games. This was, again, more solid territory than the world of drug conspiracies. To be honest, by this time I'd had so much to drink that I didn't know what was solid and what wasn't. The great thing about getting Darren to go on about himself was that I didn't have to listen or think about what he was saying except to throw in the occasional word of encouragement so that he'd keep going. He kept this up all the way into Chinatown, into one of those small noisy Chinese restaurants laid out in old living rooms and up rickety stairs. Off-handedly the hostess slammed down a pot of tea, dishes, chopsticks, silver trays of food. Darren, still talking, piled his bowl high and started eating, wielding his chopsticks in an expert manner. I put a lot of rice in my bowl. I'd allowed Darren to order the food and with an uncanny knack for the totally inappropriate he'd landed us with an array of red and pink meat. I made a token stab at it, but with the same result as at lunchtime. It was no good. Vegetarianism looked inevitable.

I nibbled at some peppers and water chestnuts in a fairly colourless liquid. Darren was now telling me some lengthy story about what had happened when he'd first tried the drug Ecstasy. Apparently it was 'fucking amazing' and had enabled him to screw someone seven times in one night. 'Coming down was a total bummer. Can't stand that fucking acid music, though.'

'I don't think I'd call it music as such,' I said in best fogeyish manner. 'Have some more food.'

'No. You fucking eat something. I've been watching you and you've hardly touched it. You've got to eat, Gordon. You're going to need all the fucking strength you can get. I tell you that now. Because you and me, we're going to the Adonis Club. Then tomorrow morning you're going to the Police.'

'Oh, I can't do that. I've got work. I must go in. And I said I'd see Aidan tomorrow. I've got to see Aidan.'

'Not fucking Aidan again.'

'Look, what's it to you?'

'I've told you, one way or another you'll end up badly hurt. He's no good, Gordon. He's done some heavy stuff back up in

Manchester. Come down here on the run and for all I know still is. He's bad news, complete poison.'

'Look, he's told me a lot of this himself. It's different between him and me.'

'Well, remember what I said. About rent boys and punters.'

'That goes for you and me too, does it?'

'A bit, yeah. But we are different. We communicate. There's something between us.'

'God, you sound hopelessly Californian. So we're different, are we?' I paid the bill and looked Darren straight in the eyes. They were bulging with excitement and he obviously thought he was being totally honest, poor love.

It was time for the Adonis Club. I wondered why I was allowing myself to be taken there, knowing full well it would mean trouble. But I wanted to know what was going on. It was now clear that keeping my head down wasn't going to work. The game had changed and I hadn't got that option any more. Aidan had been right; the rules weren't of my making. But deeper than nervous curiosity lay a peculiar fatalism and a sense of an ordeal designed either to change my life or end it. After all that had happened, I wasn't sure which of those was the preferable outcome. Since the accident, I had felt that my lease had in any case been unnaturally and unfairly extended.

What no-one knew was that I had been supposed to be with them on that journey; in which case two cars would have been used, so that even if the accident had still happened, there'd have been a chance that half the family might have survived. And, of course, there'd have been a chance that I'd have been killed. At the root of my being I felt that it should have been me terminated on that February day. And now I believed that what I would face now in the Adonis Club, or soon on some deserted street or in some Tube station at the hands of Gray or one or more of the Jasons, was what I had managed to evade by catching 'flu back in February.

Darren and I made our way through soaking streets, jumping enormous puddles provoked by clogged drains it wouldn't have been cost-effective to unblock. The rain was beating down, turning a walk across two streets into an expedition through hostile terrain. As usual in Chinatown people tended to dawdle and stand still (even in torrential downpours) and large cars found their way into the narrowest crannies. Darren was also trying to be circumspect, checking who might be following or watching us. As we arrived at the doorway of the Adonis, at the top of the steps leading down to the club, he laughed to me.

'One good thing about weather like this. Fucking Gary and fucking Jason are too fucking lazy to hang around outside in it. Come on, Gordon.' And down the stairs we went. The imposing, bull-necked, but sweet-natured bouncer took my money and opened the door for us.

The Adonis Club has quite often been described in print, particularly following the various rent boy scandals zealously sought out by the fearless truth seekers of the Press. At this point in its history it had just changed hands again, and in an attempt to alter its image the new management had begun advertising it in the nightclubs section of a London listings magazine – that one that had reviewed a Disney film, the one about the dogs (but aren't all Disney films about dogs?), in terms of its relevance to the class struggle and the feminist movement. It had been a very unflattering review. I digress. The advert for the Adonis in this journal read 'Exciting club, two dance floors, lively young crowd.' I suppose there was a germ of truth in the bit about 'young crowd', but no-one had yet located the second dance floor. Still, you could hardly put in an advert saying 'Seedy rat hole full of rent boys and punters', could you, just for the sake of being truthful?

The Adonis is on two floors, one below ground level and one below that. At the very bottom is the (usually deserted) dance floor, which took on a sporadic lease of life during the Acid House craze, probably because it seemed like a good excuse for the boys to take a lot of drugs. Each floor has a bar, inadequately staffed and stocked. The barmen are mainly former or trainee rent boys, looking, where possible, to combine business with business. The decor is non-existent; if there were such a thing as used paint, it's what was put on the walls there. The chairs and tables were obviously obtained by hanging assiduously round the roughest down-market pubs when they were getting rid of furniture well beyond its natural lifespan. Still, given that the main use for the chairs and tables was to act as bludgeons or other weapons for three Geordie rent boys called Duane, Dean and Lee, I can understand the general reluctance of the management to go to any greater expense.

Duane, Dean and Lee were, of course, already there when we arrived; they were in the Adonis through its every open hour and I'd begun to wonder if they weren't just kept in cupboards there and put out at opening time. Duane was tall, blond, beefy and on acid; Dean was tall, dark, beefy and on dope; Lee was small, mouse-haired, shifty and on whatever he could lay his hands on. I should point out that they only ever used the furniture on each other. Still, it didn't give one a particularly favourable impression of them. They were completely baffled why they didn't get many punters.

As I've said, social life in the upper bar tended to revolve around the two fruit machines. There was very little space by the bar, just room enough for a few stools and it was hell to get past them when the place was full and you needed to go to the loo. At the far side of each bar was an exit into the outside 'well' of the whole six- or seven-floor building, an iron jungle of fire escapes, electrical equipment and pointless steel things. Ou.. here you could escape to look through iron at the moon, up and down the steep ladders supposed to take you to safety. On fine nights the boys often took punters out there to finalise details privately, or else they'd go out there in gangs of three and four to smoke dope. Some of them would go out to do that even on monsoon nights like this one.

The place was still relatively tranquil. Apart from Barmy Billy, Duane, Dean and Lee, there were only three or four elderly punters and some boys whose names I didn't know in the first bar. After our brief interlude with Billy, which I have already described to you in such moving terms, Darren and I descended further. Two boys I knew vaguely hung around the edge of the dance floor, which covered about half the floor space on a token raised platform; they listened to a rather dreary voice enjoining them to stand up for their love rights, but it didn't move them to any kind of political protest. At the bar, smaller than its counterpart above, sat two more punters, discreetly wealthy men in early middle-age, one of whom I knew to chat to. Generally I found chatting with the punters heavier going than with even Barmy Billy.

We made our way to the bar. I ordered our drinks and Darren excused himself to the loo (there was another one on this floor). I smiled at my vague acquaintance. He smiled back and returned to the conversation he was having with his friend.

'Well, as I was saying, if it doesn't liven up soon, I shall have to return to my virgin couch. I mean, I've had all the ones I want here.'

'Yes, this place really does need some new stock, doesn't it? One really doesn't want to end up like the BBC, forever resorting to repeats.'

'Quite. I'm a Tory voter. I demand value for money.'

'You'd think they'd be stocking up for Christmas, wouldn't

you?'

'Definitely more Santa's Grotty than Santa's Grotto.'

'What happened to that French piece? I thought he was quite sweet. I was rather hoping he'd be here.'

'Don't bother. Big cock, but won't do anything with it. Went on and on about his girlfriend and some modelling job he was after.'

'Oh. How disappointing. Oh God, that awful Kraut's here.' A tall blond boy with an incipient moustache and clad in tight leather trousers had appeared at the foot of the stairs.

'Yes. Been there, seen it, had it.'

'And who hasn't? I think it's going to be early beddy-byes for me.'

'Me too.' He turned to me. 'Boring, isn't it? Where's darling Darren gone?'

'Ah yes, Darren,' the other said, 'he can usually provide entertainment one way or another.'

'If not in person then he always nominates a decent proxy. By the way,' he returned to me, 'I saw you in the Blue Parrot yesterday. You looked straight through me, my dear, but I'll forgive you. After all, you were engrossed in that beautiful creature from Manchester.'

'Oh which one's that?' his friend asked.

'Paul — with the ears and the innocent smile. Tall, fairish, quite nice cock. Not much bum, though.'

'Oh yes, him. Couldn't understand a word he said myself.'

'Yes, that's definitely the one.'

'Bit on the pricey side in my view. For what you get.'

'Yes, well, isn't that true of all of them?'

'Not if you catch them young, if you take my meaning.'

'My dear, why don't you just hang round King's Cross and meet the trains?' He raised a finger. 'Now there's a thought. Definitely be cheaper than here.'

'And a better atmosphere too.'

'Could hardly be worse. I think I might go to the Parrot, actually. Is Paul around tonight?' he asked me.

'I — er — think he's meeting someone, he told me. Said he might be there later, though, at the Parrot.'

Darren reappeared in time to catch this. 'Who're we talking about? No, no, let me guess — it's Aid- '

'Paul,' I squeezed in quickly.

'Oh, Paul,' Darren sneered significantly. He looked at the chap I knew (whose name totally eluded me). 'If you need fixing up, Peter, I'll be happy to help you out a bit later.' He moved over to Peter and they talked quietly. The noise of the music was loud enough to drown their chat, as some woman warned us never to trust a stranger, a song the gay community seemed to have taken to its heart in a bout of sexual and medical irony. The German boy drifted by and fondled my bum. I smiled and shook my head. He smiled too. He'd tried this before, but I knew I couldn't trust him. At the bottom of the stairs a thin, very smartly dressed, dark-haired boy appeared. He saw me and waved.

'Hello there. Long time no see.' It was an indefinable, slightly London accent. 'You remember me – Kevin.'

'Yes,' I sort of lied. I vaguely remembered somebody like him. 'You're the ex-Army man, aren't you?' That's quite a safe-ish bet, actually.

'Ex-regular, certainly,' he said. 'Buy us a drink?' Darren, obviously lip-reading, kicked me as a deterrent, but I decided to stage a rebellion over an issue so palpably trivial. Kevin was another improbable lager merchant, and presented with the peculiar bottle, he flicked the cap off with chilling military precision. Taking a swig, he rooted inside his designer jacket with his free hand and pulled out two photographs. 'What do you think of these?'

Expecting some wearisome pornography, I glanced politely. What the pictures actually showed was Kevin in army fatigues in a very sedate domestic room (probably a dining room, I'd have guessed) surrounded by lots of modern and sophisticated looking weaponry, toting some gun-like thing.

'Impressive, isn't it?'

'I remember you now. Lee Harvey Oswald. So you got away.'

He snatched the photos back. 'There's no need to be like that.'

'Well, what about it? Are you some kind of hitman?'

'Shut the fuck up,' he said, turned on his heel and stalked off. Darren, who was now free again and watching, laughed loudly.

'Very good, Gordon. That put the bullshitting little bastard in his place. You shouldn't have bought him a drink, though.'

'Oh, it was worth it just to see the pictures.'

'Yeah, I only got a quick look at them.' Darren, who was now well into speeding, collapsed in laughter. 'Maybe you should get him to help sort out your problems.'

'I don't see him successfully smuggling a mortar and bazooka in here.'

'Don't know. It'd liven the place up a bit.' Darren started jiggling about. If he'd been serious about 'helping' me in some mysterious way, that little dose of drugs he'd taken wasn't going to be to our advantage. 'I've got to get some dope tonight, I really have. You couldn't do us a favour, could you, Gordon?'

'Why not wait until the boys have got me? Then you can loot my corpse.' I think this probably sounded petulant.

'Now what's got into you? You did say you'd do me a favour.'

'No, I didn't actually. If you remember, I came here with you because of that other business. You were supposed to be helping me.' I looked round the bar anxiously.

'Yes, yes, I know that.' He placed his hands on my shoulders. 'Relax. There's nothing to worry about.'

'Darren, I really wish you could control your drug habits. I really do. You're making about as much sense as Billy at the moment. Those guys could kill me if they find me, and you've brought me to the one place they'll definitely look. And after promising to look after me, suddenly you're going to run off.' I pulled away from him. 'You're in it too, aren't you?'

'Don't be a daft bastard, Gordon, you know me better than that – '

'Know you? I don't fucking know you at all, do I?' I closed in on him again, furious now. 'I mean, take this evening. You've sat there bad-mouthing Aidan, going on about what a dangerous scrounger he is – and when's your hand dipped in your capacious pocket at all? You've never even treated me to a bag of crisps. And then you bring me here. You're going to help me, you tell me. So you drop acid or whatever it was and as soon as we're here you start crapping on about dope. If you didn't bring me here to set me up, then you just hadn't the faintest fucking idea what you were doing.'

Darren's face assumed a kind of furious concentration and he grabbed me again, this time by the arms. 'Is that it? You finished? Or do I belt you one? I'll help you deal with them bastards later. But I've got to get some dope. I've got my needs as well, Gordon. All right?' He let go of my arms, but kept his stare on me.

'All right for you, maybe.' I shook my head. 'Oh, all right, just piss off and get your dope if that's what you want.'

'And I promised Peter there I'd do him a little favour, too, so I'll have to go off for a few minutes anyway.'

'Oh yes, sorry. Super-Pimp strikes again.'

'Gordon, I've always done right by you, you know that. But I've got my living to earn.'

'Far be it from me to interrupt the steady smooth flow of

commerce.' I stood back and bowed ironically.

'Look, I'll be back before they get here. Anyway, I tell you what,' he went on brightly and my heart sank, expecting that he was going to offer to do me some 'favour' for a small fee, 'I'll probably see bastard features Aidan where I'm off to. Do you want me to tell him you're here? I mean, if he's not doing anything. From my point of view it'd make an interesting test for him.'

'Do what you want,' I said. My body was so chemically confused I no longer knew what I could feel or hardly whether I was awake or asleep. I just resigned myself to letting it all happen. Maybe I could get away, maybe I couldn't. It was too late to care. 'Do what you fucking well want.'

Darren clapped me matily on the shoulder and then kissed me on the mouth. 'I'll be back. And I'll send Aidan to see you, 'cause I know that's what you want. Why don't you read them papers that bloke gave you?'

'Papers? Oh yes.' Shoved in my pocket a century ago were Michael's forecasts. Great. Just the stuff for a light read in a club full of rent boys. Darren dashed off up the stairs. Bored, nursing a seven-eighths empty glass, I drifted after him. So melancholy and out of it did I feel that I even bought Billy a drink. As a result, he tried to grope my cock, which remained resolutely flaccid.

'Take me home, Gordon. I ain't got nowhere to go. We could go now. You need it, I bet you do, I bet you need to go home too. I really need the money.' Well, this is stupid stuff, I thought, and I wandered along the bar, past the fruit machines to the place where the theoretical second dance floor ought to have been. And what a treat awaited me there.

While Darren and I had been downstairs, someone had set up and plugged in a portable Yamaha keyboard and sitting behind it now was the fair-haired gnome last seen accompanying Norma Jean Bakelite at the Blue Parrot. He was setting off on a dash through a selection of songs from the shows and related items – 'Oh, What A Beautiful Morning', 'Button Up Your Overcoat', 'Cabaret', 'If I Was A Rich Man' and, for some bizarre reason best known to himself, 'Hava Nagila'. Presumably some obscure anti-Palestinian gesture, that. Apart from me, no-one was taking the slightest notice of his efforts, so he decided to try for audience involvement. This started very promisingly as one of the drunks from the Magpie and a good-looking Glaswegian boy called Neil (whose only recorded utterance to me had been a less than sensitive 'fuck off' delivered at the 'Dilly Coffee/Kebab Shop) sang 'I Belong To Glasgow' without bothering with technicalities like the words or even the tune. Then Neil gave 'Danny Boy' the same treatment.

By this time a few of Neil's mates had gathered round for a laugh, drawing a few interested punters with them. The gnome at the keyboard made eye signals at one of them, a strange little man in thick, heavy-framed glasses with the physiognomy of an elderly frog. He clutched a fat cigar and what looked like a champagne glass. I looked along the bar and, yes, at one of the tables – and how could I have missed it, even in my stupor? – was perched a bucket with a bottle of Moët peeping out. What kind of man comes to the Adonis to drink champagne, I asked myself. Slumped next to the bucket was an elderly man looking rather like Karl Marx after a heavy night's capitalism; he wasn't at all dissimilar either from a wino who'd once haunted the streets of Tooting. In fact, I became more and more convinced that it was the wino from Tooting.

'And now,' the keyboard gnome said, once Neil had floated off on the Londonderry Air, 'I'd like you to put your hands together for a real character with a great voice – Jack.' The frog-man stepped forward. The rent boys began clapping enthusiastically. Jack was their ideal man. If he drank champagne, then he must have, as Mile End Jason would have put it, 'plenty of handbag'. Keeping champagne glass and cigar together in one hand, Jack took the microphone. Neil had handled this as though it were a live, pinless grenade. By the way Jack took it, you could tell you were watching a pro. First he murmured to the gnome. Then he put the mike close to his lips, almost French kissing it.

'I'd like to sing this song,' he said in an amplified transatlantic murmur, 'for the gentleman over there –' he gestured at the Tooting Wino with his glass and cigar and all heads turned – 'who once conducted an international tour of the show from which this number comes.' And then he sang.

You know those American TV shows where dead old gits in toupees pay tributes to each other? Some elderly bastard with a cigar wanders out and says, 'I'm ninety-two years old' and gets a fourteen-minute standing ovation. Bob Hope comes on and tells anti-Liberal jokes and forgets the words of 'Thanks For The Memory'. Gene Kelly creaks through a few arthritic steps and flees to his oxygen tent. And there's always some guy you've never heard of who sings in a quavering voice to show he's full of emotion. That last guy was obviously Jack's major influence.

'If ever I should leeeeeeve yoo – oo – oo,' he quavered, 'it wurdurnt be – ee un sprungti – i – me, knuring how in sprung I – i – i – m burwutched by – y yoo sew – ew – ew.' Et cetera, et cetera. I can't do it justice here. I started to giggle and, realising this was rude, to control it by drinking. No good. I was giggling more and more. Boys started looking at me crossly. Jack didn't seem to notice, however. He romped on through the song, his face more screwed up than ought to have been physically possible given his starting point, and paused only for the briefest of puffs on his cigar before launching into another fab emotional classic. 'Memreez, luk the caw – aw – aw – awnuz urf muh mi – i – i – ind...' This time I tried biting my cheeks on the inside. I'd used up all my booze, so I backed through the crowd, thinking it more tactful than overtly turning away. Backing through, I bumped into someone, said, 'Sorry', and turned. He didn't move. It was Jason.

In fact it was Jasons, both Lewisham and Mile End, with Paul just behind them. I gulped. Then I gawped.

'Hello, Gordon,' Lewisham Jason said, baring his teeth, 'we didn't get the chance to have a chat at the station.'

'Shame that,' Mile End Jason took up. 'Mates should always have a chat with each other.' His slow sly smile appalled me.

'I – ah – I don't suppose you'd like a drink, would you?' I asked.

'We already 'ad one,' Paul said, 'with that dosh you gave us earlier.'

'Yes, Gordon, thanks. Now we just wants a word.'

Behind me Jack reached his dramatic climax. 'Ha – ha,' he declaimed. 'Curn urt bee thurt urt wuz aw – aw – awl so surmple thur – ur –urn, awaw hurz ti – i – ime rerurttun urvuree li – i – ine?' he asked. Involuntarily I laughed.

'You amused, Gords?' Mile End Jason asked. 'Wanna tell us a joke?' He put his hand out and pinched my cheek. 'Skin and fucking bone. What you reckon, boys? Reckon what they say's true?'

'Losing weight, bad skin, funny eyes,' Lewisham Jason replied. 'Must be true.'

'That's bad,' his namesake said, 'he might be infectious.'

'Well,' Paul laughed, 'we'll have to be careful, won't we?'

'Look at it this way,' Lewisham Jason said, 'we'll be doing him a favour. Saving him a lot of pain later on. Right, Gordon, we're going outside. Out the back.'

'But it's raining,' I objected weakly. 'And I can't miss the rest

101

of Jack's act. He's so funny.'

'Business before pleasure,' Mile End Jason replied firmly.

'Well, he doesn't do business, the mean get,' his namesake added, prodding me in the tummy. 'Bit late now to start, I'm afraid, Gordon, old mate.' He articulated these last two words to emphasise their total insincerity. He and the other Jason took up a position directly on either side of me. The Mile End edition had his right hand in his jacket pocket; he pressed this against my side.

'All right, let's move, shall we?' he said, as if I were being tiresome. I started to move and then stopped. Something sharp briefly jabbed me.

'Look,' I said very loudly, 'if you're going to kill me anyway outside, why should I feel particularly threatened by that knife, if that's what it is? I mean, I could call your bluff and make you kill me here in front of witnesses, couldn't I?' I laughed. This was crazy – but, well, what would you have done? I waved at Billy. 'Hello, Billy,' I said, 'they're trying to kill me.'

'Trust Gordon,' Paul said, 'he has to ask the fuckin' village idiot to help him.'

'Hello everyone,' I shouted, 'they want to kill me. Hello Mister Bouncer, hello – '

I shut up as Lewisham Jason smacked my face and nose with the heavily-ringed back of his right hand. I put my hand to my face and felt liquid. I'm no good with human blood, I'm really not, particularly not my own. I whimpered.

'Get outfuckinside,' he said. 'I'm not telling you again.'

The bouncer, though, had been drawn towards all this. 'If you lot want to get rough, you can fuck off somewhere else,' he said.

'Don't worry, Dave,' Paul said, 'Gordon here's just had a bit too much. He gets a bit out of order. Needs a firm hand. Likes it, too, if you know what I mean. We're trying to get him out the back, help him sober up.'

'Don't fucking bother. Get out the fucking lot of you. For good.'

'Please,' I whimpered, 'they want to kill me.' The three rent boys erupted with laughter.

'He's a scream when he's pissed,' Paul said. 'That's why we love him. We're only trying to look after him.'

'Oh – take him out the fucking back then,' the bouncer said. 'Keep him quiet.'

'Please,' I whispered, falling to the floor, clutching at his fat legs. Dignified behaviour, this.

The bouncer shook his legs, kicking me a bit. 'Geroff.' He prised me away and hands began to drag me. People were laughing now. I was hauled up and Lewisham Jason began whispering savagely in my ear.

'Oh dear, Gordon, suppose you had an accident now. You easily could, the state you're in. And you've made such a fool of yourself. Suppose you did something stupid. Couldn't live with yourself. Oh dear, Gordon.' We had gone round the bar now. Although I was still dizzy from Jason's blow, still drunk, still drugged, I still felt the rain as it hit me, coming through the perforated iron of the fire escape platforms above. I was pulled upright. We stood on the platform. Paul closed the door to the bar. Lewisham Jason pushed me to the edge of the steep flight down to the bottom of the well.

'Right Gordon,' he said. 'Jump. You never know. You might survive. For a minute or two, anyway. Till we get down there and kick you a bit. And if that don't work, we can have a repeat performance. Until you get it right.'

I sighed. I couldn't look him in the face. 'Spare me the details.' I clung to an iron bar. 'Just give me a minute.'

'What you fuckin' expectin'?' Mile End Jason asked. 'No fuckin' cavalry on their way 'ere.'

I thought of my family. Maybe I was going to get a chance to see them again. Maybe not. Here was my chance to find out. And did it matter? Here I was, barely scratching an existence, slumming, usually drunk, in love with a rent boy. Not much to give up. But suddenly it mattered like I'd never thought it could. Aidan. That brought tears to my eyes. I pictured his rubber-necked smile, my beautiful, worthless darling. And then that picture was crowded out by earlier loves, family scenes and words of prayers. Lighting candles. Flowers for Our Lady. Innocence.

'Right, Gordon. That's it. Jump.'

'Actually, Gordo, I'd just walk down if I was you,' called a voice from below. At the bottom of the flight a slender figure stepped forward into half light from the lower bar. And then the upper door opened and uniformed figures appeared.

'Gordo, down here, quick,' called Aidan. Lewisham Jason aimed a punch at me; I swerved, nearly fell and then took Aidan's advice. Dashing down, I clung to him for dear life. He gave me a sheepish grin. 'Dead exciting that, weren't it?' He put an arm round my shoulders. By now I was crying quite a lot.

'What are you doing here?' I asked him.

He recoiled. 'Well, that's nice. Shall I go away again?'

'Oh, Aidan, I do love you. I'm so glad to see you. I think I'm going to be sick.'

'It gets better and better. You say the nicest things.'

And then I threw up, quite a lot. After which I felt very much better. Aidan murmured some consoling words during all this. Then some policemen came out and joined us.

'Christ, sir, you look done in,' said one, a cheerful moustachioed sergeant. 'Do you want a doctor?'

I shook my head. 'I suppose you'll want to interrogate me.'

'Well – we'd like to ask you a few questions, yes. But I think we've got the general picture. Your friend here explained it to us.' I shot Aidan a look. He gave a sheepish smile. 'And we don't need your word to hold those three for a day at least.' He shook his head in mock sadness. 'The knives they was carrying. Very nasty. And the substances in their pockets. Very careless.' Aidan laughed. 'So if you'll just tell us a few simple things, give us your names and addresses, we'll be in touch tomorrow. You sure you don't want a doctor?' I nodded.

In no time at all really, after a little paperwork, we were out standing in Leicester Square.

'I should invite you back, really,' Aidan said.

'I was hoping you might.'

'Only I think I've got a punter. Something Darren said.'

'Oh God. Darren. Yes. You must have seen him?'

'Yeah. He told me where you were. Said you was in a bad way. I just got there when you was on the floor, so I ran off for the cops. Lucky that. Normally you can't get one when you want one, let alone three or four.'

I reached into my pocket. There were papers there. Oh yes, the papers. I tore the bottom off the back page, found a pen and wrote down my address and 'phone numbers and the name of a pub. 'Tomorrow night,' I said, 'we're supposed to meet.'

'You can' tell me you're off to fucking work, Gordo. I don't believe you.'

I shook my head. 'No. But I do want to see you. Thank you properly. We can't meet in the Magpie. Not now. Come down South.' I told him which station. 'That's the name of the pub opposite the Tube. I could see you there at – what? Six? Seven?'

'Seven.' Aidan laughed. 'I might just have got up by then.' He patted my arm. We were in Charing Cross Road. 'You got any money left, Gordo?'

'Oh – yes, how much do you want?'

He laughed again. 'I meant, can you afford a cab? For yourself? 'Cause there's one here.' He stuck out his arm. He looked at my address and repeated it to the driver, who went through the usual act of looking dubious. South of the River, you see. Aidan reached his hand into the cab, and I'll swear he slipped the driver a note. Then he opened the door for me. 'Seven o'clock,' he said, 'the pub opposite the Tube. I'll be there.' He shut me in. The cab swung round through one hundred and eighty degrees.

'You been in a ruck, mate?' the cabby asked. I laughed dutifully, but didn't answer. Too much melodrama tends to be bad for my conversational abilities. Well, that was enough for one night. Back home, I paid the cabby some exorbitant fare, got out and let myself into my little flat. It hadn't been ransacked in my absence. No booby traps. Nothing very Hollywood. I crawled onto my bed and fell asleep.

My first thought was that I'd forgotten not to set the alarm, but my clock told me it was only 4.30. Pitch black. What the fuck was the noise? The doorbell. Terror seized me. I was still half dressed. Grabbing my keys, I crept down into the hall of the building and looked through the communal front door. Two neutral looking men, smartly dressed. I opened the door an inch.

'Mister Gordon McKenzie?'

'Yes, do you know what time – ?' An identity card was pushed at my nose. 'Detective Sergeant Stuart Morgan,' it said.

'May we come in, sir?'

'Oh – er –' I let them both in and led them up to my first floor matchbox. Turning the light full on hurt my eyes. They sat down on my functional, comfortless sofa.

'Well, what can I do for you? The chaps in uniform seemed to think they wouldn't need to talk to me 'til tomorrow, but I suppose the CID never sleeps, is that it?'

'Sorry, sir?' The one with the card looked puzzled. 'If I could explain, I'm Detective Sergeant Morgan, this is Detective Constable Bowen.' I looked at the other and nodded. A handsome brute, probably joined the Police for the violence. He looked as though he could have got on well with Duane, Dean and Lee and I suspected that thousands of lurid tattoos lay beneath his dark suit and expensive shirt. The Sergeant, a discreetly dressed, presentable, unexceptional type, not handsome, not ugly, cleared his throat. 'I see you're still partly dressed, sir.'

'Very late night,' I explained. 'I've not been back long.'

'I wonder if you could tell us where you were at around one o'clock this morning,' he said.

'Actually, yes,' I said. 'So could your uniformed branch. I was in the Adonis Club in Soho playing the role of victim in a murder attempt. Well, it was some time around then, not far off. Anyway, I was definitely in the Adonis from midnight.'

'You can corroborate this, I take it?'

'I think so. Well, people saw me there. And I was with a friend before that, so –'

'Ah. Yes. That would be one Trevor Greenhalgh, would it?' He looked at me uneasily. The use of Darren's real name brought me up short.

'Well, yes, although everyone calls him Darren – '

'Yes, sir, we know all about that. Right.'

Up to this point I had stayed standing. But now I sat down. 'You'd better tell me what this is about,' I said. Pray God, I thought, he's only been pulled in for drugs.

'Mister McKenzie. I'm afraid I have to tell you that Trevor – Darren – was killed this morning. Stabbed. It's rather unpleasant, I'm afraid. Were you and he close friends?' I thought I heard a snort from the other one, but he got a sharp look from the Sergeant.

'Well, yes, I suppose we were,' I said. 'Yes, we were.' And at that moment I realised how close we had been. Darren had died on my behalf. Because of me. I started to cry. The Sergeant tried to come over all sympathetic. 'Oh God,' I said, 'the stupid bastard. The stupid, stupid bastard.'

6

Aidan tried to cheer me up by telling me a ghost story. He lounged on my hideous furniture, giving it the most decorative appearance it had ever had, and started in on something that had happened up in Manchester when he'd been staying at one of his girlfriends' homes.

Although I was befuddled and wearied by my apparently endless day, I was not too tired to marvel at his ability both to change the subject and be simply inconsistent. When we'd been left on our own that evening, he'd been particularly harsh on the somewhat meandering style of my rambling account of the hours since he'd put me in the cab. 'What's that got to do with the price of fish, Gordon?' he'd kept on saying in his driest

Mancunian. And now, when the two most pressing things on my mind were 'We're in terrible danger, let's get going' and the perhaps apparently contradictory 'I want to go to bed with you', he started telling me a ghost story – to cheer me up and 'make me think'.

'It must have been about five in the morning or summat, I woke up and there was this woman standing by the bed, so I thought it was Karen's mum, checking up on us and that.' Was this his way of impressing his heterosexual prowess on me? Was this a response to any sexual signals I was putting out, a reminder? If so, it rather contradicted his perpetual response to my repeated avowals of faith in his straightness, offered every time so far in the evening that he'd tried to convince me he was either bi or gay. 'Why do you want to put me in a box?' he kept saying, almost petulantly. No comment, you notice, on whether or not I was right. He probably didn't understand that by insisting to him, and thereby to myself, that he was straight – like most boys of his calling – I'd simply been trying to find a simple, easily digestible fact to hold on to. There weren't too many of those left around now. I'd had a bizarre day, to say the least. Anyway, let Aidan continue his story.

'So when we went down to breakfast – well, dinner really – next morning, I asked Karen's mum if she'd come in our room, and she looked at me kind of funny and one of Karen's sisters asked me what this woman'd been wearing and that and I told her and, anyway, it turned out that was the way their nan always used to dress, honest to God, Gordon, I swear on me mam's life that's what they said –'

'Fancy anyone bothering to come back from beyond the grave to watch you fuck her grand-daughter.'

'You shouldn't make fun, Gordon, there really are ghosts. A poltergeist tried to kill me once.'

'Yes, and several more substantial figures might very well have a go if we don't sort out some plan of action.'

'Jason and that lot's locked up now, you know. We won't be seeing them for a bit.'

'There's still Gray. And whoever gave him my work number, whichever one of my sweet friends it was, will have given him my home address as sure as eggs is eggs.'

'As sure as what?'

'Eggs is eggs. It used to be a – look, how come I always get told off for being irrelevant when you're just as bad yourself?'

Aidan smiled. 'That's easy. You see, when you go off the point, I can't understand what you're on about, when it's music and that, or that painter you're always on about, that Umbrella, or all that stuff about disasters and how the world got going. At least when I go off the point I talk English.'

'Not always. Some of those phrases you used in that charming story about how you got paid for pushing your best friend's girlfriend into bed with some other bloke were a bit beyond my understanding of the language.'

'What, you mean like "selling her arse on tick"? I wouldn't have thought that took much figuring out for a brainbox like you.' He laughed. 'Did that shock you, that, Gordo? It shouldn't. I mean, my mate used to do it himself anyway. She's a tart, after all and he's a con man.' He reached forward to light a cigarette, putting his can of Australian lager down on my cheap and nasty table. 'That's why I left Manchester really. If I'd stayed there, I'd have been in prison by now what with Johnny – that's me mate – and Bren, our kid. Then I'd really have gone bad. Our kid's a real hard bastard, you know. I don't think you'd get on with him. You wouldn't worry about a soft cunt like Gary once you'd met our kid.'

'So you came to London and went on the game to avoid a life of crime?' I asked gently, but the irony was lost.

Aidan nodded earnestly. 'Yeah.' Then he grinned. 'Well – and Patsy, Johnny's girl, she got up the stick, and it could have been mine, so I thought I'd better make meself scarce. Mind you, I don't think it was mine,' he added, after a moment's reflection. He perked up suddenly. 'Gordon, can we go out for a bit?'

'At last. What have I been saying – ?'

'Only I know a pub not far from here where I think I can get some dope. I was down here once with a mate. There's lots of blacks round here, aren't there?' I tried to interrupt at this point, but the flow was unstoppable. 'I mean, you'll give me the money for some dope, won't you? I'd much rather have dope than dinner, you know.'

'Hang on. Our lives are in danger and you want to chase after dope.' I'd had this conversation before, of course. 'You do realise this is how Darren was going on last night? He went running after dope, and look how he ended up.'

'Yeah, well, Darren was a daft pillock. Sorry, Gordon, but he was. Well, he obviously was last night.' Aidan seemed to have a healthy disregard for superstitions about speaking ill of the dead. 'Do the cops know who it was did that?'

'It's obvious, isn't it? I mean, if I hadn't been so shit scared and dead beat after all that in the Adonis, I might have given some thought to where darling Gray had got to.' I laughed mirthlessly. 'He's a great one for knives, after all. Unless the big boss hired another of the lads. Your mate Irish Paul, for instance.'

'He's not my mate. Anyway, he's inside. They picked him up yesterday for possession – he's on remand.' Aidan's information was definite, authoritative. 'Thank God for that. I can't stand him, honest to God, Gordon. And he's got this idea that I owe him favours, just 'cause he helped me a lot when I first come down here.'

'Ah. I did wonder what his hold on you was, after that night I first met you.'

'It's the Irish connection, you see. Some of his people are Travellers, so they know some of my people. And we always try to help each other out. Except he wanted me to keep doing him favours.'

'The obvious favours?'

The rubber-necked smile came out. 'He didn't get owt a customer wouldn't. I've told you that.'

'I always thought he was quite good-looking, actually.'

'Not my type. A bit flat-chested, really.'

'In short, a man. So not your type at all.'

'You're at it again, Gordo. I'm not getting in your box.' He stood up. 'Where's your toilet? I'll just go, then we can be off.' I pointed – you really can't get lost in my flat – and he went. I got to my feet and wandered around. I flicked a switch on the television.

' – tape-recording taken by a police motorcyclist escorting the motorcade. Playing the recording from the time the procession entered Dealey Plaza, we can actually hear five shots in rapid succession, and with stereophonic enhancement it becomes clear that those shots emanated from different sides of the Plaza – '

At any other time I would have been transfixed, but now I was too full of jumpy fear. I'd brought Aidan back to my place after only one drink at the pub on the theory that an Englishman's home is his castle. Then I realised the obvious, that Gray, or his controller, or whoever, was more likely to try and find me at home, which was a definite and easy to locate address, rather than going on a mystery off-chance tour of the pubs in a grey patch of South London which I was bound to know better than they did.

Wanting to do something decisive, I picked up the 'phone and rang Simon. This was all part of the provocative guerrilla campaign I'd been waging all day to try and baffle all my friends and my adversary. Sally answered the call, full of concern. I'd already had one rather sticky conversation with Simon earlier in the day, so perhaps it was just as well she answered. I asked her to tell him that I – carefully avoiding the use of the first person plural – was going out now, and might come round later. She seemed puzzled, and, as Simon must have told her about our riotously amusing lunch together, I'm not surprised she was puzzled. I put the 'phone down. Then I rang Dougie's number and got Horst. He treated me to a chillingly polite dose of correct English usage. I told him to remind Dougie what I'd said earlier and then said I was going out. Very exciting, all this. Toby wasn't in, doubtless he was out somewhere playing Aristocrats. Lucky him. Still, I knew he'd had a lousy morning, because Michael Hamilton had told me about it. Not that I'd had a great morning myself. Mind you, my eventual meeting with the Police, the one I'd been trying to avoid all week, hadn't been at all terrible. 'The great irony,' I'd said to Michael, 'is that in the end the cops were charm itself.'

I think I'd better pause. You may detect that coherent chronology has broken down completely. However, by the Friday evening I'd been on the go for nearly three days without sleep, continually on the piss and the tabs. So you can understand that there are bits that resolutely refuse to fit in their correct place in the structure, even now, bits that never quite got properly filled out or filed away. The Friday is, taken all in all, something of a blur. Boring bits and horrible bits jostle together in a random way. I tend to remember the bits with Michael and Aidan best, because they were both the least and the most eventful and definitely the most important. And some of those bits are things I want to remember. I suspect that somewhere in there it's all carelessly stored away, every vivid, horrid or mundane detail and one day I'll have to sit down and put it all in the right order. Starting from the moment that Morgan and his handsome Constable Gorilla took me to identify Darren's body.

It turned out I'd actually been in his diary as an appointment for that evening, which was why they came to me first and I got lumbered with all the formal stuff, even though enough members of the Police knew him anyway. Darren – Trevor – was not, to them, an unknown quantity. I don't think I was a serious suspect once they'd actually met and seen me, although the Murder Squad didn't know about the business at the Adonis at all when they first called on me. Once they found out about that, they took it over and incorporated it into their enquiries. Unfortunately, it's not uncommon for one part of the Met to have no idea what another part's up to until it's all down on disc drive and floating around behind one of their green screens. This fact proved to have rather serious ramifications for me later.

In my experience, dead people who are all in one piece look like waxworks. Darren hadn't been mutilated – I always think of him as Darren, which is marginally preferable to Trevor as names go – at least not facially, although I was given to understand there was some nasty, gratuitous wounding lower down. But I didn't have to identify him by any other part of his body.

'The actual killing was pretty swift, at any rate,' the Sergeant said. 'One swift blow. The killer knew what he was doing. All the blows but one came after death. Well, either he knew what he was doing or he struck very lucky with his first blow.'

'The odds against that kind of luck are quite high,' I said. 'That's why they usually go to the trouble of training surgeons.'

Morgan regarded me oddly. 'You know about anatomy, do you, sir?'

'In fact, I do. But only really when I'm dealing with pre-dead specimens. I haven't got the bottle to hit the right spot on a living target of any species.' I rubbed my eyes for a moment. 'I'm sorry, I don't mean to seem flippant. I just can't quite believe all this. And I've had a hell of a week. I suppose I'd better tell you all about it.'

'Well, I'm not sure how much we need – '

'I think you need to hear all of it.' And afterwards, I thought, you'll charge me with all kinds of things from obstructing the course of justice to assault on minors, and I probably deserve it. But, of course, the hyper-reasonable Sergeant wouldn't do a thing like that. He seemed vaguely concerned, rather in the manner I've always associated (for no tangible reason) with social workers, that I hadn't come straight to the Police. But, again like my hypothetical social worker, he seemed anxious to find deeply-rooted causes to excuse me this lapse. He sent his handsome assistant away, scrupulously ensuring that at least one fellow officer remained as a chaperone, to check out the brewery rep's demise. When the report came through, he shook his head.

'I'm surprised this wasn't picked up on before now, sir. So many glaring questions, in my view. Still, it's not for me to criticise the work of my fellow officers, is it?'

Unfortunately, as I didn't have the remotest idea what

Gray's surname was, there wasn't much could be done about tracing him. The Sergeant seemed disinclined to make me wade through albums and albums of photographs.

'It all looks good on television, sir,' he said, 'the drama of the sudden recognition. But on telly they can cut down the time a bit. We do have rather a lot of photographs, you see. Even if we tried to cut it down just to pictures of young men under thirty called Gary, well, we'd still be talking about hours. And to be honest Mister McKenzie, I'm not sure how reliable your powers of concentration are likely to be at the moment. Another cup of tea, perhaps? We shan't keep you much longer now.'

'Perhaps you should,' I said with a quiet laugh. 'If my adversaries, known and unknown, get their way, it might be your last chance.'

Morgan looked vaguely embarrassed. 'Yes, I see what you mean.' He picked up a pencil from the table in front of him, fondled it and let it fall. 'Unfortunately, I'm not in a position to order surveillance or a bodyguard or whatever. And – ' he grimaced – 'there isn't anyone around here right now who is. My chief, you see – well, he values his kip, to put not too fine a point on it. Some time tomorrow – ' he paused.

'With a bit of luck,' I chipped in. 'Oh, it's not your fault. I'll try and keep out of harm's way, then. I suppose my enemies will need time to regroup a bit, anyway.'

'I suppose I should commend your spirit,' Morgan said, 'this being the era of the Active Citizen and all that.'

'Spare me that. Remember me when you come into your Privatisation.' He laughed dutifully. 'I must say,' I went on rather daftly, 'you've been remarkably restrained in certain areas of your – questioning. If that isn't too strong a word.'

'This is a murder enquiry, sir. Your private arrangements are between you, the other parties involved and your respective consciences.' He said this with a practised air. But I still almost believed him.

Despite his concern not to overstretch my faltering powers of concentration, we were still more or less into daylight by the time Morgan had finished with me. I had to admire his style; a charming, concerned way of asking the same question twice without actually seeming to; no reprimands if I appeared to wander off the point. And as a result I suppose I told him more or less everything I reasonably could. Well, I didn't tell him anything about Aidan, except as the anonymous 'friend' who'd brought the Police to rescue me the previous evening. And I couldn't quite bring myself to be completely honest about my second visit of the week to the Magpie. It wasn't just that I'd taken the money from Gray, although that was part of it; it was also part and parcel of not bringing Aidan any further into it, of trying to protect him. I knew he'd seen Darren after me, you see, but as far as I was concerned it was up to Aidan to reveal that. I was already frightened that his decisive intrusion into my little difficulty had put his life in danger. I'd already managed to get Darren killed. That was another death on my conscience. Too many, too many.

I declined an offer to see me home. 'The Active Citizen must be responsible for himself,' I said to Morgan.

'We'll do what we can as quickly as we can,' he promised earnestly. 'And I'll get onto the uniformed officers you saw last night. I think you've probably earned a rest for today. And from what you said, I imagine we can let the Drugs Squad loose on all your Jasons for a couple of days.'

'Do you think there's a collective noun for Jasons?' I asked. So many emotions and physical demands were playing on me that I'd averaged out at whimsical. 'A rent of Jasons, perhaps.'

Morgan laughed dutifully again. 'I believe these things are usually alliterative,' he observed. 'How about a jamboree of Jasons?'

'Yes. I like that.'

To my surprise, one thing I definitely was was hungry. I still didn't feel up to any kind of meat, so bacon was out of the question, but an overwhelming urge for egg and chips seized me. I also definitely didn't want a drink, apart from tea. Positive signs, after all this time. I felt strangely secure, wandering those early morning streets. A break in the rain had given the early morning sun a chance and the pavements shone despite the rubbish of the previous day still lying around. I stood on a street corner and watched some cleaners. Deliveries were well under way; the capital stretching and yawning. Despite everything a stubborn bedrock of optimism was making its presence felt for the first time in over a year. I should have felt even worse. It was my fault Darren was dead. Yet here I was thinking about breakfast. And Aidan. Oh yes, I was thinking about Aidan.

Breakfast, anyway, was easily dealt with. I had been going to buy a paper to read, but the news looked unappealingly dreary, full of analyses of forthcoming summits. The geriatric meeting the bald. Sneaking a look at a paper in a shop, it seemed that even the book pages were crammed with glasnost and perestroika. Then I jammed my hand into my jacket pocket, and realised I'd put on the same jacket I'd worn the night before – presumably the first thing to hand at 4.30 a.m. After all its adventures, it had taken on a rather odd and not altogether pleasant smell. I must have presented a peculiar picture to anyone bothering to give me a casual glance. Fortunately, the bruise and marks from Jason's blow to my face just blended in with all the usual skin complaints. But it occurred to me that perhaps I should start caring about clothes, about appearance generally. Out of my pocket I pulled the battered Hamilton forecasts. Well, now was an ideal time to look at them properly. Dripping egg, chip, vinegar, sugar and tea on them I annotated every calculation until the original was indecipherable.

My excuse to the office was greeted with what sounded, even on a poor 'phone line, like scorn. I suppose the old tummy problem excuse was wearing a bit thin, rather like the tummy itself. While I was near a 'phone I made a few more calls. First to Michael, telling him I'd read his stuff and asking him to pass on my regards to Toby (oddly enough, I'd remembered that they were due to meet that morning). He greeted me with surprising keenness, and strong-armed me into agreeing to visit him at his office in the late afternoon. Flattered to be wanted so badly, I quickly gave way.

'After all, it is Friday,' he said. 'Let's discuss a few things over a quiet drink. One of the perks of being exalted is being able to arrange total privacy in one's own office. Come and enjoy it.'

'I'd love to. But I need to be in South London by seven. I'm meeting a friend.'

'No problem. I'll drive you down.'

'You can't. It would be miles out of your way –'

'I haven't been in South London for ages. You must let me.' What was he after? I decided to give him a run for his money. I could always introduce him to Aidan, which would be a thrill for both of them. And I was, let's be honest, probably going to be safer in Michael's car than in the Tube. He told me where his bank was, but I already knew. It was that famous.

The next call was to Dougie. 'Oh Gordon, thank God,' he oozed, 'I was so worried –'

'Now why should that be, I wonder?' I asked coolly. 'I'm fine, Douglas, rarely better. Now tell me you're glad.'

'Gordon? What do you mean?' I'll swear he almost laughed.

'Death is everywhere, Dougie boy, but I walk through. I stride on.' I decided to push it. 'Me and Aidan. He saved my life last night, you know.'

'Gordon, what are you talking about? I can't possibly talk here, there are lots of people around. Look, can we meet, let me buy you a proper lunch, we should talk properly – '

'Lunch two days running? How could you possibly afford that? No, no, I really will have to say no. Anyway, I'm not at work. God, you fucking lying hypocritical bastard, you really – '

'If you're going to get abusive, I'm just going to put the 'phone down. You're very ill, Gordon, you know as well as I do, you drink too much, and don't think we haven't noticed those pills you take, and Horst agrees with me, in fact, he's tried to stop me having anything to do with you, and do you know, I think he may – '

I seized the initiative and put the 'phone down. Then I snatched it up again. Dougie's next move might have been to ring Simon and I wanted to get there first. After all, I told myself childishly and pathetically, Simon was my friend first.

Simon didn't come on all concerned from the word go, anyway. If anything, he was guarded. We'd made an arrangement the last time we talked, you see, and normally we didn't contact one another once an arrangement had been made unless one of us had to break it. 'Is everything OK?' he asked suspiciously.

'Fine,' I said. 'I'm very well. I've just been taunting Dougie, actually. Great fun.'

'What's all this with giving Dougie a hard time all of a sudden?'

'I like to share my experience out. Give the over-privileged little glimpses of how their deprived lives could be.'

'Are you sure you're all right? I must say you don't sound all right.'

'It's a beautiful morning, the sun is streaming through the decorative perspex of this public telephone cubicle, all is well – '

'You're not at work, then?'

'I don't need work. I've just survived two attempts on my life. One of the boys I actually genuinely liked has got himself stabbed dead. Aidan saved my life. I've spent hours telling it all to the Police – '

'Well, that proves you're making it all up. You almost had me fooled. So you're not at work. Have you been drinking?'

'Nearly all night.'

'Anything apart from that?'

'Would I?'

'Yes.' He sighed. 'Oh dear, sometimes I almost give up hope. Well, seeing you're not at work, and seeing I'm having a lazy afternoon, do you fancy a late lunch up this end?'

'On one condition.'

'No, you can't bring Aidan.'

'I promise you'll feel differently about him when you meet him. No, my condition is very simple. Don't tell anyone you're meeting me. Least of all Dougie. That's all. The one favour I ask.'

Simon laughed. 'All right.'

'Promise.'

'All right. I promise,' he said with heavy irony. 'I'm not that fond of Dougie, you know.'

'No, well – shall I come to your multinational Corporation or whatever it is?'

'Two o'clock. If you remember to put a suit on, we can pretend you're a client.'

Yes, that was a good idea. But it meant going home, and I wasn't sure if that was a good idea. Still, I agreed. Then I tried to ring Toby, but he'd gone off to get snubbed by Michael. So I left him a message, put down my marker, as it were.

The bout of 'phoning had been exhilarating, but now it was over I felt a bit nervous. Time was getting on and obviously the thing to do was to go home, have a bath, put on fresh clothes, perhaps even declare war on a few zits. But actually descending into the Underground made the butterflies perform aerial here, acrobatics. Gliding down, I watched the endless pizza parlour adverts reverse their logical sequence, epicene models wearing trashy pretentious clothes glowered out at me, endless exhortations to runaways reminded me of Darren. Darren was dead, it was my fault, and I was going out to lunch. Well, I'd eaten since my family had been wiped out, hadn't I? Death doesn't stop the world of those left behind, I knew that only too well. Anyway, what had Darren been to me? But again came the sense of responsibility. Fortunately, at the foot of the escalator, absurdity butted in, disguised as a West Indian playing Chopin waltzes on a steel drum. After a moment's thought I decided that Chopin and the steel drum deserved each other.

Nobody tried to push me under any trains. There was no sign of Gray anywhere. I was adopting my best circumspect invisibility act. Perhaps the Police had got him by now. The train rushed South. By the time I emerged again, the sunlight had been stopped by some much more fittingly British cloud cover. The grey sky lurked decoratively behind the enormous brown phallic building slap bang outside my station.

The part of London I live in isn't really a place at all. It's just a convenient enough distance between the two stations on

116

either side to merit its own stopping point, so once they'd done that they had to give it a name of its own. All it really is is a slab of the main road between Tooting and the sea. There's nothing that gives it any character, except possibly the hideous brown phallic building. There are several roads going to other places, but who wants to live on an elongated traffic island? I think its lack of identity was what had originally attracted me, but that had recently begun to pall. It's also disturbingly close to several major loony bins, a fact the estate agent had neglected to use as a selling point. I had never seen any evidence to contradict my theory that I was the youngest resident of my street (a street which went absolutely nowhere, like all the other residential streets of the area, but just hung off the main road pointlessly). That Friday morning I made a vow to move out of the place if I survived the ordeal ahead, but even as I swore this silently to myself, I did wonder how the hell I'd find anyone to sell my flat to. Who'd move there of their own free will?

Clean, spruce, besuited, uncharacteristic attention paid to such things as hair, though there's not a lot you can do with limp straw like mine, even a facial wash (more for the effect on the morale than on what met the naked eye), I presented myself at Simon's office. As modern(ish) City buildings go it's dazzling only in its dreariness. No ornamental fountains or courtyards inside it, just lifts and offices. Not even glass lifts. Boring. A guard led me up to Simon's fifth floor playpen. He shares a terminal and about six 'phones with two others, but neither were there. Well, of course, they were all in the pub boasting about the past week in futures. Simon was pressing some buttons on his terminal with one hand, writing with the other, the 'phone receiver pressed under his chin at the same time. What a caricature.

'No, not now,' I heard him say. 'Later. Definitely. Very definitely.' He paused and then continued, obviously interrupting, using his ratty tone of voice, 'Well, that was then. Markets change. Just do it.' He dropped his pen, grabbed the receiver and slammed it down. 'For God's sake,' he said, staring at the hopeless instrument.

'Brilliant,' I said. 'Was that caricature for my benefit?'

Simon shook his head. 'Just some bond dealer fart-arsing around. Nothing major.' He stood up and pulled his jacket from the back of his chair. 'Shall we go?' Then he surveyed me properly. 'Very good,' he laughed. 'Is this caricature for my benefit?'

'No,' I said, 'for mine. Where are we going?'

117

'There's rather a good wine bar I think you might like.' My heart sank. That was a contradiction in terms.

I knew that Simon was going to be sceptical if I tried to tell him about the previous night. Or I knew, I should say, that he was going to appear to be sceptical. What he was actually thinking was a sixty-four million dollar question. And I knew Simon well enough to know that getting him to tell me what he was really thinking would be impossible if I kept on at him like a manic sledgehammer. Particularly if he was really thinking what didn't bear thinking about. Anyway, I managed to wrongfoot him at the outset by asking for mineral water.

'Have they discovered unsuspected alcohol content in mineral water?' He was genuinely puzzled. 'No, I know, you just want it on the table for appearance's sake. Very high-powered. Well, don't worry. No-one's looking. Anyway, no-one can see a thing in here.' It was one of those wine bars that goes to town on pretending to be a cellar. Lots of bare stone, barrels, straw, no lighting you'd notice. I was surprised they hadn't gone the whole hog and thrown in a few rats.

'No, no and no. I've decided it's time to give up. That's all.'

'You're not going religious on me, are you?'

'What if I am?' Actually, it hadn't crossed my mind, but Simon is such a proselytizing atheist it can be fun to taunt him. And I hadn't forgotten my thoughts on the fire escape. Remember, I'm the man who meets angels. 'You wouldn't be so shocked, would you?'

'Well, anyway. I know one thing. After what you said to Dougie on the 'phone this morning, you can't be taking the love thy neighbour bit to extremes.'

'Mortal men are doomed to sin, Simon. Inevitably and tragically.'

'Well, show me where in the Good Book it says that mortal men are doomed to ring up their friends and give them an earful of choice abuse.'

'The Book of Job.'

'Oh no, you're wrong there, Gordon, I'm pretty certain. There's no mention anywhere of Job having a 'phone. And if he had, the chances are he'd have got cut off.' He laughed at his own wit.

'Job's comforters. They got an earful, remember. There's Job sitting around the wreck of his real estate saying, "This is fucking unfair, why me?" and his mates roll up and start suggesting that he must have done something to deserve it and he's kidding himself if he says he hasn't. So he gives them an earful.' I poured out a glass of Italian mineral water. 'The parallel's not exact, but it's there.'

'I see.' Simon nodded, with mock seriousness. 'So you're Job, are you? And Dougie and I are comforters?'

'Only in a way. I'm not claiming any special moral privileges here. But you certainly take the view that I brought it all on myself.'

'Now, that's absurd. I never said that about – well, anyway. But going to the Magpie was bound to lead to trouble. As is hanging around with this Aidan.'

' "This Aidan" saved my life last night.'

'So you said this morning. What did he do, buy you a drink? Pat you on the back when you were choking? Relieve you of some cash the weight of which would have placed an undue strain on your heart? Agree just to rob you and not stab you as well?'

'You're not going to wind me up, Simon. You really aren't. You know I'm telling the truth.'

'I do? Gordon, I don't know what I know any more. Christ, Dougie Simpson isn't someone I especially love – he's a useful contact and I always see him as your friend rather than mine, anyway – but I have to say he's making a bit more sense than you at the moment.'

'So you think I ought to see a doctor?' I raised my glass to my lips in a calculated manner.

'I'm not such a great fan of doctors,' Simon replied quietly.

'Simon, everything I've told you is the truth. As truly as I'm sitting here. As truly as I'm going to see Michael Hamilton at half past four.'

'Oh, come on, that's the battiest yet – '

This amazed me. 'Why the fuck should I make that up?'

'Michael Hamilton's a very important banker desperate to get into politics. What the hell would he want with – you?' But the perceptible pause had been fatal.

'I wish,' I said in a cheerfully furious manner, 'you'd actually finished that sentence. "Clapped out drunk"? "Pathetic old wreck"? "Mad old queer who chases after rent boys"? Some mellifluous combination of the three? Oh Simon, Simon, we've been such good friends and despite everything you've betrayed I still love you dearly. I'm even prepared to put up with you saying things which provoked me into walking out on Dougie. I wouldn't walk out on you. But. But, but, but. If you believe what you're saying, then you and I are finished as friends. And if you don't believe it – ' I smiled at him.

119

'And if I don't believe it?'

'Then you know I'm telling the truth. And you don't want me to know that you know. And you're probably trying to have me killed.'

Simon slammed his knife and fork down viciously on his plate. 'Now I know you're mad. I'm sorry, Gordon, that's it. Go and see a doctor.' He got up, reached inside his jacket for his wallet, decased some cash and threw it down. 'That should cover my share. You can stay and drop this pretence with the mineral water and drink yourself into a stupor. If you want to. But if I were you, I'd ring Dougie, apologise, and ask him for that doctor's address. Anyway I'm not you, and I can't sit and listen to your paranoid delusions.' He stared down as if waiting for an apology.

'Fine,' I said. 'I think you're probably right.'

He softened a little. 'So you'll ring Dougie? Or do you want me to – ?'

'No. I think you're right that you aren't me and you can't sit and listen to what I'm saying.' I peered over to the money he'd thrown down. 'I think that should be enough.'

Simon shook his head. 'You're being very stupid, Gordon. Really you are.'

'Is that an observation or a threat?' I raised my glass of acqua minerale frizzante and smiled. 'To the future.'

Simon sighed, turned and left. Well, this was all very interesting improvisation. What a pity I couldn't have a go at Toby as well. Mind you, it would have been difficult to have a go at Toby along the same lines. As you may have noticed, he was possessed of a more anarchic sense of humour than Dougie and Simon, and was also infinitely less publicly pious than either of them. Therefore he was harder to wind up. I reflected on this as I ordered a pudding and more mineral water. I was really rather enjoying the stuff, ashamed though I was to admit it.

In fact, I was enjoying it so much that I was rather less than circumspect when I left the wine bar. Some rather groundless confidence in my ability to get through had surfaced, and instead of drowning it again, I rather buoyantly floated through bits of the City. I always tend to get lost there anyway, because all the streets look alike. Enormous buildings lowering on every side, cancelling the climate, all looking identical. I had thought I might walk to Michael's bank, but after passing the same sandwich shop for the third time I decided to chuck that idea and get the Tube. A sense of general direction only really works if you can see the horizon.

This left the problem of finding a Tube, and working out where to change trains when I did find one, because Sod's Law dictated that the first one I found would be on the wrong line. It was. Central and I wanted District. Being proved right was a small consolation. Down in the ticket hall, I stopped to look at the map. Something prompted me, at that moment, to look back. At the foot of the stairs I'd just come down stood a tall, handsome, devilish figure in a rather sloppy anorak and faded jeans. He gave me a brief smile and then disappeared. The smile was disturbing. It was always disturbing when Gray smiled.

So, he was following me. Well, at least I knew and could do something about it. It also rather suggested that his master didn't know where I was going. That, in retrospect, was good news. But all this dodging and hiding, ducking and weaving, was rather a nuisance, particularly in view of the fact that the Police should have been relieving me of the need for some of it. I ran down onto the wrong platform. A train was due in two minutes. That would give him enough time, as it wasn't a station where any other lines intersected. Standing very conspicuously in the centre of the not too crowded platform, I looked towards the stairs. After about ninety seconds Gray cagily advanced down them.

The train was due in two minutes. Sometimes London Underground's elastic concept of the minute was more than the mind could cope with. Gray did not advance towards me; well, he knew I knew he was there, so he couldn't push me by surprise. And there were just enough people around to make his life awkward. After another two minutes (and I know because I kept an assiduous check on the second hand of my watch), the breeze from the train could be felt. Gray began to walk towards me now. I guessed that he wanted to be in the same carriage as me, to be sure where I got off. Fine. It was just a question now of whether he'd seen the same films as me. If he had, I was sunk.

The train arrived and, after a perceptible reluctant pause, opened its doors. I didn't get on immediately. Neither did Gray. The lights above the doors went out and I leapt on. So did Gray. The doors hissed, showing they were about to close. I jumped out. So did Gray. The doors began to close and, when they were half shut, I threw myself on again. The advantages of being a skinny runt told again. I got through clear, and before Gray could react and try and jam a limb in to hold them open, the doors were fast shut. My one dread was that they would open again for no good reason like they do so often, but that fear proved unfounded for once. The train lurched off. I waved, notionally, in his general direction.

Of course, I was going the wrong way, but I'd cross that bridge when I came to it. In my head I planned a strange circuitous journey involving three changes. The advantage of the confusion quotient easily outweighed the inevitable delays. If I didn't do the obvious things – reverse direction at the next station, or get off at the first interchange (which was with only one other line anyway) – he'd never fathom out where I'd gone.

'I really think you should give up travelling by Tube,' Michael Hamilton said. 'I'd say there were plenty of more orthodox reasons for giving it up, anyway, but you do seem to have introduced a new element of chance and hazard to one of London's more uncertain methods of transport.' He handed me a glass of sparkling water, French this time. 'Are you sure you won't have a real drink?'

'Actually, I am.'

'Then you belie your reputation. Or vice-versa.' He poured himself what looked like a gin and tonic. Then he sat down behind his desk. 'Excuse the formality of the seating. We could go over there – ' he waved an arm towards some sofas and armchairs obviously designed for 'hospitality' – 'but this is the most comfortable chair in the room and, anyway, I like posing. It is my office, after all.' He compensated for this confessed egoism with a thoroughly charming smile. 'Anyway, we are here to discuss business, aren't we?'

We discussed business. I explained my objections to his forecasts, which I won't bore you with to any major extent. Suffice to say that they revolved around the question of random event quantification. These institutions are all the same – they fondly imagine that some kind of average of any previous 'blips' over a given number of years will give some realistic 'impersonation' of likely future quirks. The whole point, of course, is that while you can reduce random events to some form of pattern, you can't do it by medians and quartiles. It all fits fairly neatly into elementary chaos theory.

'So these expensive, highly streamlined forecasts are, in fact, wrong?' Michael asked after I'd waxed lyrical for a bit.

'Not exactly "wrong", not in their own terms. It's just that those terms are pretty pointless. Probably. Unless everything trundles along amiably and nothing much happens. But I assume you don't take the view that it will. What you have to remember is that any stock market strategy is doomed if it assumes that a stock falling from sixty to ten will necessarily sell at fifty along the way. That's not an original line, by the way.'

'Right.' Michael pressed his fingertips together. Then he tapped his nose with his index fingers a few times. 'You see, given the situation here and in the States, it's very unlikely that things will trundle along amiably.' He dropped his hands, sat back in his chair and began playing with a distinctly tacky looking knife-like thing, presumably a letter opener. 'Words like "stagflation" are starting to drift back into the financial vocabulary, so in one way it's like the '60s and early '70s, but in other ways it very much isn't. Given the rest of the world picture, those old models won't work. All kinds of random factors are coming into play, not least the scars left from last year's crash. Then there's this new American administration, which looks like being appallingly weak from our point of view – a fiscal catastrophe – and bankrupt of ideas. There's the interest rate. But there are other imponderables, like the sheer speed of events, the implications of High-Tech markets, new technology, things you didn't have fifteen or twenty years ago. Last year's crash was partly a result of world-wide technological link-ups.' He dropped his toy with a clatter. 'Does all this make sense to you?'

'In a way. I catch the general drift. I don't see why you're telling me, though.'

'Well, you've confirmed my gut feeling, you see. That this kind of forecasting is a waste of time. We need – well what would you say we need?'

I laughed. 'The occasional quantum jump?'

'And that's where you come in. This Chaos science, didn't part of it grow out of a study of the money markets?' I nodded, surprised that he was aware of this. 'Well, there you are. I want this bank ahead of the competition, I want someone who knows about it, but someone who isn't the kind of traditional money man born and bred on this crap.' He waved a copy of the forecasts in the air. 'I want you, Gordon. You'll do it well. And appointing you, an obscure academic, that'll be worth some publicity that will make it look as though we're ahead of the others again. That's always good for morale and better for business. In fact, a couple of banks in the States are already employing people from your line of research, but we'll definitely steal the march over here. Anyway, from everything I've heard, and I've done a lot of listening and a lot of research about this, you're able to the point of criminality and

123

thoroughly wasted doing what you're doing.'

'Are you offering me a job?' I said cautiously.

'If you want one. My assumption is rather that you do.'

'You must have some other motives. It wouldn't make sense otherwise.'

Michael laughed. 'And what other motives do you think I might have?'

'Perhaps you want the spotlight in the City that plays on this bank to fall on someone other than yourself. You might be up to something.'

He smiled. 'Not bad. Not bad at all, Gordon. Yes, I might be. There is something else you might as well know too. My personal plans may be leading to my having to be absent from this place as often as I'm present, maybe more often if all goes according to plan. With this in mind, I'm in the process of making several key appointments which lie in my gift. And I'm giving these jobs to people I know I can trust. People who have to be loyal to me because they owe everything to me. People I have created.'

'Yes-men, in other words.'

Michael glared at me. 'Really, Gordon, how uncharacteristically crass. Far from it. This bank's full of yes-men. Look, the worst mistake anyone can make when building an empire is to fill it full of incompetent time-servers. All my appointments will be – must be – talented. I'd like you to be one of them because I think you're likely to be very good at the job.'

'If you've heard so much about me, you must have heard about my – well – drawbacks.'

'Oh yes. Unstable, hyperactive imagination. The kind of lines dullards tend to use quite often. That business about your family – well, that was totally appalling and I won't embarrass you with any banal platitudes. I'll leave that to those rather amateur friends of yours. Then there's the rent boys. Well, who gives a fuck about all that? As long as you don't hurt yourself, that is.' He smiled again and fixed me with his blue eyes. 'I think you're aware that we've a certain understanding on that side of life.'

'Yes. I had realised. Toby hasn't, though. I doubt whether Simon or Dougie have either. Surprising about Dougie, but there we are. And they won't find anything out from me.'

'Good. I thought as much. I'm pleased to hear Toby doesn't know. Who's this Dougie character? Oh yes, Dougie Simpson, the minor consultant who drones on to all and sundry about his wedded bliss. Bit of a third-rater. In my opinion,' he added, merely stressing that his opinion was the only one which mattered. 'Anyway, I shall be getting married soon. At the right moment.'

'Congratulations. Any idea who to?'

'Oh yes. It's all settled. The young lady I was with the other night, Katy Goldsmith. I thought you knew each other, actually. She's well aware of what's what. Some rather decent financial settlements won her heart. Such an emotional girl, our Katy.' Michael smiled. Then he mentioned a job title, which didn't immediately signify a great deal to me, and a starting salary, which immediately meant rather a lot.

'You can't be serious.'

'I don't see why not. I must say, I like your suit. Don't take this the wrong way, but I wouldn't have guessed you'd have had such a tasteful one from our two previous encounters.'

'We didn't actually meet at Simon's.'

'No. But you were pointed out to me. Do you want more of that absurd fizzy water?'

'Actually, I prefer the Italian variety. Is that perverse of me?'

'God knows. I never touch the stuff. Aren't I taking you to South London? Who are you meeting – one of your Dougie and Simon crew? If I were you, Gordon, I'd think seriously about getting rid of that lot. Toby's all very well in his way, but –' he gestured expressively.

'I'm not meeting any of them. I'm meeting a young man called Aidan, who isn't, I'd guess, the kind of person you'd normally encounter socially.'

'Really?' Michael's face lit up. 'Can I meet him?' He became almost childishly excited. 'That sounds like fun.'

'Sure.' I thought I'd try a joke. 'Is pimping going to be part of my job description?'

Michael didn't laugh, but he didn't look annoyed. He just looked thoughtful. Eventually he smiled and said, 'One can't always predict every eventuality, Gordon, as you ought to be aware. But I do find the fact that you have – well – a different circle of friends quite an interesting facet of your personality.' It took me a while to fathom that one out, but when I thought I had I was rather taken aback.

'I was thinking of giving all that up,' I explained. 'But I'll certainly have to give up Dougie, Simon and even Toby.'

'Really? Is this all to do with that murky business you were talking about last night? I think you really should take my advice. Don't get involved.'

'A bit late, really.' I explained, succinctly everything that had happened, including Darren's death and my encounter with the Police. 'Irony of ironies,' I said of the Police interview. 'They couldn't have been nicer. No reference to my little trouble whatsoever. In fact, I was the one who brought the subject up and the civilised sergeant just dismissed it. "Doubtless an oversight by some overzealous junior officer." His very words. Nice to know that now.'

'This civilised sergeant.' Michael looked at me sharply. 'What was his name?'

'Oh – something Welsh. Morgan, I think. Yes. Why – a friend of yours? Same Lodge and all that?'

Michael smiled. 'Not a friend. I have encountered him. Can't say I took to him greatly, but I'm sure he's – decent.' The way he said this showed what he thought of 'decency' as a concept; unquestionably it was second-rate. I was sorely tempted to ask Michael how he knew Morgan, but I suspected, remembering the brush-off Toby had had the previous night, that it might be tactless.

'Carry on, tell me more while we go South,' Michael said. 'Explain how Dougie, Simon and Toby fit into all this.'

'Well, one of them does. I don't know which, but I have my suspicions. One of them must be behind it.' We were now heading out of Michael's office towards a lift. But my assertion made Michael halt.

'Is that the famed McKenzie imagination at work? Or can you prove it?'

'Not tangibly. But how did Gray get my work number? And it's odd that the attempts to kill me started after I told Dougie that I was going to find out what was going on so I could prove I wasn't making it all up.'

'So you think it's Dougie? No, let's go this way.' He led me along another corridor, to what seemed to be the edge of the building, apparently just an enormous window. He pressed a button in the wall. 'This will be fun,' Michael promised.

'No,' I said, answering his question. 'Dougie always gets straight on the 'phone and blabs to everyone else. Simon doesn't usually, but they've definitely been in cahoots over this business of trying to get me to see a doctor. As for Toby, God knows. He seems to believe me, but that could mean anything.'

Michael nodded. A glass lift arrived, it's only non-transparent part being the richly carpeted floor. We got in. Michael pressed the button for the highest floor. The lift set off at what seemed to me to be an indecent speed and took us from the tenth floor to the seventeenth. I'm not good at heights. I started to feel very sick and moved back against the door. Way beneath us was the sumptuous courtyard of Michael's bank, complete with trees, fountains and little people crawling around. Out in front of us was a prospect of the City, the Nat-West Tower, the Lloyd's Building and sunshine against massive and threatening grey clouds.

'Isn't that glorious?' Michael said.

'And the Devil took him up into a high place,' I commented, not feeling any better just because the lift had stopped.

'Don't you think it's remarkable?'

'I think I feel sick.'

'I'm sorry. Do heights give you vertigo? I am sorry.' He pressed the down button. Unfortunately, he pressed the express down button, which may have been a good idea from his point of view, but gave me a few problems with food retention and stomach control. Michael laughed. 'You're perfectly safe, you know. I won't let anything happen to you, Gordon. You're one of my men now.'

'I don't doubt you can control the lift. I'm not so sure about Gray.'

'Gray? Oh, the thug who's chasing you. It is a bit poor about the Police, you know. Still, if I remember Morgan's boss correctly, he's probably slumped in a bar somewhere, pissed.' The lift stopped. I felt very unsteady and wobbled out behind Michael's firm step.

Michael's car was everything you'd expect. It had probably cost more than the entire national debt of Mexico. It seemed almost wasted on London traffic. I rather feared for its safety if he proposed parking it in my dreary little non-place. As he negotiated us through a series of endless lines of traffic, he took up the story of my adventures again. He asked a few questions about chronological sequence (never my strong point, as you'll be only too well aware by now), showed a polite interest in Darren and a slightly more than polite interest in Aidan. Or was that just my jealous mind? I tried to explain everything as simply as I could. Probably more simply than I have here, but Michael wanted factual details and not much more. I wondered if perhaps he had a Sherlock Holmes streak, so I asked him if he'd come to any startling conclusions.

He laughed. 'Not really. I'm hopeless at mystery stories. Never did manage to guess whodunnit. I was just seeing if your theory was borne out by the basic facts or whether it was just intuition.' I looked at him quizzically. 'Having heard it all, I'd say six of one et cetera.'

'You don't think I'm making it all up, then?'

'We've been through this one, I seem to remember. Last night.'

'So we have. God, that seems about a century ago.' I asked Michael a question about politics. We began a series of slight arguments, with Michael alternating a standard textbook Tory view and the attitudes of a real maverick roaming the full range of the political spectrum. I suspected that one set of views was merely being rehearsed for practice, the other to show what he actually thought. I, as usual, was hopelessly inconsistent in a typically wet middle-class liberal sort of way and thus no match for him whichever persona he was adopting. This all led on to his meeting with Toby and others from his organization that morning.

'Toby was pretty furious, I think,' Michael said. 'Tragic. Truly tragic. But he's really swallowed all that small business stuff. I thought once he had more about him than that.' The car came to rest in another long line. He looked at me again. 'So what do you suppose all these murders of yours are about?'

'From something Darren said, I would imagine it has to do with drugs. I don't know where the brewery rep fits in, though. He was doing some kind of inspection of the pub's books. Maybe he came across something that shouldn't have been there.'

'Unlikely anyone would put it in books which will be inspected if it wasn't supposed to be seen. And that would mean the landlord of the Magpie would have to be involved.'

'Well, yes. To some extent. But I can't think he's roaming the streets trying to terminate me with extreme prejudice. And I don't think he's the mastermind.'

'No. It wouldn't be likely. But I don't suppose the Police will have erred on the side of caution and picked him up yet, do you?'

'Of course. They'll have everyone under lock and key and I'm perfectly safe.'

We were almost there by this time, and a quick debate about the Police saw us there. Michael's views were very much an attempt to have his cake and eat it, his 'public statement' face being very pro, but his personal attitude shone out as violently anti. I suspected that this had something to do with his previous acquaintance with Sergeant Morgan, which made me even keener to ask, but he managed to make it impossible to do so. We found a place to park his car and made our way into the pub.

It was a desolate place. No carpet, a dartboard, a long bar with one disconsolate elderly barmaid, a fruit machine so elderly it was a surprise it didn't have an arm, furniture obviously at its last staging post before the Adonis Club. At the bar sat two elderly shabby customers. There was another bar, but it was less smart. Aidan hadn't yet arrived. I asked Michael what he wanted to drink.

'I think asking for anything other than beer might prove a bit beyond the barmaid's capacity. Gordon, this place is amazing. Straight out of some hideous sociological experiment to recreate the '30s.'

'Like the Government's, you mean?'

'Oh, ha ha. Very amusing.' I smiled sweetly and ordered a pint of bitter and an orange juice and lemonade. 'So where's this charming young friend of yours?'

'He's only a bit late. I doubt whether he's that remarkable a timekeeper. Most of them in his profession aren't.'

'Most people aren't, Gordon. I'm certainly not.'

'I thought time was money and all that.'

Michael laughed uncontrollably. 'Do people really still say that? How funny. No, Gordon, timing is money – speed, quick-thinking.' The door opened and Aidan drifted hesitantly in. 'I deduce from your change of manner that this is your young man.'

'Thought you weren't any good at the Sherlock Holmes bit.' I waved. Aidan gave a rubber-necked smile.

'Hello, Gordon. This one of your friends?'

'Michael Hamilton.' He introduced himself, turning all his piercing personality traits on Aidan. 'I'm going to be Gordon's boss very soon.'

'New job, Gordo? Very nice.' I bought him a lager. 'You heard about Darren?'

'I identified the body.'

Aidan tutted sympathetically. 'That's really terrible, that.' I wasn't sure whether he meant Darren's death or me having to identify the body.

'You knew this boy then?' Michael asked. 'I suppose in your circles – if you don't mind me saying this – you all know each other.'

Aidan smiled. 'I can tell you've never been down the Magpie. Yes, I knew Darren. Didn't like him much, though. Sorry and that, but we didn't get on.'

'Well, you're not likely to now, are you?' Michael said.

'Gordon liked him, though, didn't you, Gordo?'

'Darren was fairly good to me, all things considered.' I didn't want to go into the guilt question here.

'Anyway, are you all right now? After last night, I mean,' Aidan said, as though I'd had a slight cold or something.

'Well, Gray's been chasing me around a bit again, but I managed to give him the slip. Anyway, since I saw you there's been all the business about Darren.'

'Oh yeah, you said. What's this job, then? Are you sure you can put up with him?' he asked Michael.

Michael made some polite comment. He was giving Aidan a peculiar look, and Aidan was aware of his own effect. He asked a few polite and totally uncharacteristic questions about Michael's firm. This politeness, to this extent, was a new act. Aidan's nose had obviously picked up what, for him, was the most interesting point about Michael. I listened to their anodyne, really dreary conversation. It seemed to last amiably enough while I went to the loo. But I sensed, when I arrived back, that something had passed between them of much more import than all the surface stuff they seemed to be talking about. Or was I being paranoid again? Michael decided to bring me into the conversation again.

'Oh, Toby sent his further regards. Reminded you to give him a ring about *Parsifal*.'

'Right. Thanks.'

'I must say, I think you're incredibly brave to face Wagner in any form. Is that the one where all the people are called things like Clingfilm? Of course, he did write his own words so that probably explains it. I'm sure it's just a weakness of mine, not liking it all.' He smiled at Aidan, to emphasise that, of course, it was anything but a weakness. He stood up. 'Right. I must be off.' He offered Aidan his hand. 'Pleased to meet you. Get Gordon to invite you to lunch in the City or something.' He let go of Aidan's hand, turned and offered me the same privilege. 'I assume you'll need to give a month's notice, Gordon. I'll be writing to you on Monday. You can rely on that. And I'll send the offer and contract round to your place by messenger.' Then he stepped closer, so that only I could hear him clearly. 'And don't worry about the other matter. I'll try and put some pressure on the Police.' He relinquished my hand, stood back, smiled and left.

'A very impressive guy, Gordon,' Aidan said. A smile crept slowly across his face. 'And very well off too.'

'Extremely.'

'I think he fancied me.'

'He's getting married soon.'

'So? He's very handsome.'

'You're straight. Why should you care?'

'Why do you want to put me in a box, Gordo?'

And there was the opening of this subsequently endless reference. 'Well,' I said, 'you were extremely polite, I thought. One of your little acts, was it?'

The rubber-necked smile. 'It's a good'un, isn't it? Not as good as the sad one.' He banished all smiles from his face, took on a little boy lost air, looked sadly at his drink and began to light a cigarette in a forlorn way. He looked, for all the world, like an innocent waif adrift in a wicked, cruel world. 'You see,' he went on, not altering his expression, 'I'll notice someone looking at me, and I won't look back. I can tell when they're looking. That's a really good one when you've got a bag next to you. Makes them think you don't know what's what. Like if you start reading the "A to Z".' He resumed his normal posture and expression. 'Hey,' he said, 'I might've been the last person to talk to Darren. What do you think? You know, when he told me where you were. Did you tell the Police?'

'I left you out of it more or less altogether. Except about what happened at the Adonis, because they'd have heard about you from the other cops anyway. But I didn't mention you at all in connection with Darren, and I didn't tell them I was talking to you the night the other guy got stabbed.'

'You told them about that, then?'

'It's gone too far not to, now.'

Aidan nodded. 'If you get that Michael to have dinner with us,' he said, 'you could do yourself some good. I bet he'd pay you extra for fixing him up with me.'

'I don't think he does business with rent boys.'

'He wants to do business with this rent boy. I bet he'd pay well, too. He could be a regular. You could cover for him. Think about it, Gordo, it's a good chance.'

I felt annoyed and jealous. 'I don't think I ought to encourage this, quite frankly.'

'So you can get a new job, but you grudge me a chance to make some decent money. Ta very much.'

'Decent money?' I laughed. Then I shuddered. Without Michael there, I didn't feel so safe. 'Shall we go back to my flat?' Aidan drained his glass. Outside it had finally started raining again, rather heavily. We got over-wet. Back in my flat, I felt no safer. While Aidan prowled around looking at the pictures on the wall, I rang the Police. Morgan and Bowen were out. I left a message, but the man taking it seemed dubious about how soon they'd be back.

'Christ, this Umbrella guy's a rotten drawer, Gordo. Since when have horses had square legs?'

'It's a perspective device,' I explained, 'a realism based on a trick of the eye rather than an achievement of what we'd call photographic replication.' I rambled on in this vein. I tried putting some music on, but that wasn't successful. Aidan gave a fairly scathing verdict on my decor, comparing it with houses he'd burgled in Manchester.

'I mean, Christ, honest to God, Gordo, on me mam's life, if we came across a place like this, we just used to smash it up for a lark. 'Cause it's fucking annoying to break in somewhere and find it's a tip with nowt in it. There's lots of places look really nice from the outside, turns out they've got fuck all in them.'

'I'm not sure I want to know all this.' I looked at him. He was very smart this evening. 'God, you're lovely,' I said.

'Thank you.' He smiled. 'And you know my situation, kind sir.'

That seemed to be a kind of code. Suddenly exhausted, I slumped. And he told me his ghost story. Which, of course, is where we came in.

So you may remember that Aidan thought he knew a pub where he could buy some dope. To get there we had to head North. This meant braving the rain both before and after the Tube journey. Aidan managed to convince me that I should buy him a two quid Travelcard rather than a single ticket, using some ingenious explanation about what we might do later. I didn't follow entirely, but as usual I was putty in his hands. Through the journey he regaled me with stories of how he and 'our kid' had lured innocent stooges into games of pool for large bets. Aidan would play the inept innocent, softening the prey until 'our kid' innocently challenged the now cocky victim. Then, one way or another, 'our kid' would take all the dupe's money, usually by winning the game, although sometimes this didn't happen and then he and Aidan would mug the man later that night. From this little tale, Aidan went on to fill me in on the details of 'our kid's' career. We were about halfway through a list of 'our kid's' convictions (criminal, not religious, political or philosophical) and drenched to the skin, when Aidan suddenly said ,'I think this is it.'

'This' was a peculiarly grimy pub, complete with shabby, near-black, ruched net curtains and misspelt posters in the window advertising Irish folk bands. Ah, well, that explained how Aidan knew the pub. The Irish Traveller connection, one assumed. We went in and I bravely sauntered to the bar and ordered our drinks. Rather like a horror film, the bar fell completely silent when 'the strangers' came in. The barman looked particularly unimpressed when one of the drinks I ordered was an orange juice and lemonade. Aidan affected not to notice all this. 'I think we need the back bar,' he said. 'I'll just go and look.'

He dashed off through a door leaving me alone, still fairly closely surveyed by the clientele. I'd said nothing apart from ordering the drinks; but I can't help my accent. Not knowing either tune or words to 'The Wearing Of The Green', I cast around for something to hum, but the only tunes that came to mind were 'Nessun Dorma' and 'Danny Boy', and neither seemed quite appropriate somehow. In an attempt to appear nonchalant, I strolled over to the juke box, which was beyond a pool table. Two diminutive, hard-faced men were potting balls there savagely. As I came within cueshot, one dashed round and suddenly I found the cue being backed into my chest.

'Mind yer fuckin' self,' snarled the player.

'I'm terribly sorry,' I said. This didn't seem to go down well. I reached the juke box and was examining its contents (thirteen different versions of 'The Old Rugged Cross' and the complete oeuvre of Brendan Shine), when suddenly a cue hit my buttocks.

'Get out the fuckin' way.' I think it was the other one, fortunately.

'I'm very sorry.' I moved. In another minute, the cue jogged my arm and managed to spill some of my drink. 'Hey,' I said.

'Aw, shut the fuck up.'

'I do apologise.'

Aidan drifted over. 'About five minutes,' he said.

'You put your name on a waiting list?'

'Well, sort of. But it might be a bit of a wind-up. This bloke says he can get me –' A cue jabbed into him.

'You fuckin' move or what?'

'Go fuck yourself,' Aidan said. My heart sank. Not a fight. I just can't fight. But instead, the man just laughed, clapped Aidan on the arm and moved himself to make his shot from another angle.

'How did you do that?'

'I've a right to stand here.'

'Yes, but when I –'

'You didn't say sorry, Gordon, did you? Yes, you would. You

133

don't apologise. If you say sorry, you're soft.'

'Ah. Not polite. I have these old-fashioned ideas.'

'You've got a lot of principles, Gordo. That's good. But they don't really work in places like this. The people here have principles too, you see. Different principles.' He gestured. 'Let's go back over there. Do you play pool?'

'No. Can't cope with it.'

'That's a pity. I don't want to play either of these. They're far too good.' We moved away again. 'You see, they take their frustrations out on their pool game. Work hard and play hard.'

'What's your excuse?'

'I work hard, Gordo.' A sheepish grin. 'You might find out one day. Can I have the cash for the stuff?'

'How much?'

'Fifteen. Well, call it twenty.'

I laughed mirthlessly. 'Yes, let's. After all, it's only my dead family's money.'

'They left you all right, did they?'

'I'll ignore that crass question.'

'I didn't mean it like that. You know I didn't.' He held my arm for a moment. 'Come on, cheer up.' He put his drink down. 'Look after that. I'll be back.' He went into the other bar again. I looked round uneasily. This wasn't a pub I'd been in before and I wasn't looking for an early return. Actually, it wasn't far from Simon and Sally's flat. But the days of wandering up for nights in front of their TV were well and truly lost now.

Aidan came back. He didn't look particularly happy, so I assumed the deal hadn't happened. 'No go?' I asked.

'Yeah. Got it,' he said quietly.

'Good. Can we go?'

'Where?'

'Somewhere else.'

'I like it here. Let's stay here a bit. Then we can go back to your place and I can have a smoke.'

'I can't?'

'You don't smoke, Gordon. And you know you don't approve really.'

'I gave you the money.'

'I know. Thank you very much.'

'Aidan.' I was getting impatient. 'What is going on here?' As I said this, the door opened and Gray came in. 'Fuck,' I screamed quietly, 'how the fuck did he know where we were? Unless —' I turned to Aidan. 'You didn't.'

'You can't think that, Gordon, you can't. You know I hate the bastard, I really do.'

'So what do we do now?' Gray was still standing at the door. He was drenched too, but seemed totally unaffected by the rain. His devil's smile was completely in place.

'Hang on. Just don't move. I've got an idea.'

'Yes, but can I trust you?'

'Gordon. What about last night? I saw you right. Now listen. I'm going to take him on, when he comes over here. And he'll come over in a minute. Just wait. I'm going to wind him up, you get out and run like hell. We'll meet up again later. Where? Your place? A pub?'

'God – I – well – hang on. A friend of mine. His flat. It's the third street on the right from here – out of the door, turn right – then second left. Number 15d. If that's no good, there's a pub at the end of that road. The Roebuck.'

'Out, turn right, third right, second left. Number 15d. Or the Roebuck. Right. Here he comes.'

Gray stood before us, blocking any exit. 'Hey there, man. Aidan baby. You two boys having a quiet night together, eh? What a shame I'm gonna have to bust it up. What a shame.'

'What's it to you, you fucking ape?' Aidan asked. He adopted an aggressive posture but still looked slight next to Gray.

'Button it, little boy. Nasty things happening to Gordon's friends these days, I hear.'

'Fucking soft daft Jock. Why don't you just fuck off out of it before you get hurt?'

Gray laughed unpleasantly. 'I'll deal with you in a minute. Come on, Gordon, outside, man.'

'You deal with me first, nancy boy.' He thumped Gray hard in the chest. Gray's smile vanished.

'Fuckin' queer fuckin' rent boy. Just you listen.' He moved towards Aidan and grabbed the lapels of his leather jacket. Aidan kicked me. There was daylight now. I ran. As I bolted through the door, I heard uproar start. God, would Aidan be all right? Or had I landed myself with another death on my conscience?

I didn't look back. Pounding up the high street, I turned at the third right, then at the second left. Where had this speed of mine come from? Fear, trembling and panic, probably. The rain was driving down. Drenched, I slammed almost my whole body against the bell of 15d. I hoped that Gray would have lost me. The streets are badly lit round there. Number 15 has no porch, so I continued to soak. A female voice crackled over the intercom.

'Hello?' Sally said.

'Sal. It's Gordon. Please. Emergency.'

'Hang on,' she said. I waited, but the buzzer didn't go, the front door didn't unlock. I thought I heard distant, fast splashing footsteps. Or was that cars on the main road? Come on, I fretted. Then the door opened manually. Simon stood there, wearing a very trendy tracksuit.

'You've got a nerve,' he said.

'Simon. Please. Out of breath. After me. Gray.'

'Where? Just show me. Or did I send him? Well?' He surveyed me distastefully. 'You're drenched.'

'Simon. Please. He'll kill me.'

'I've said all I've got to say to you, Gordon. Go and see a doctor. Go to a hospital.'

I took a deep breath. 'Simon. I'm as sane as you are.'

'That's not what you usually say.'

'Simon.' I cut a ridiculous dripping figure, but I was trying to retain some dignity. 'I said. I'm as sane as you are. Please let me in, or I'll get killed.'

'According to you, I'm behind it all. I'm sorry, Gordon. You've had it.' He slammed the door shut.

'Simon!' I yelled. Well, that was that. I sank to my knees on the doorstep, careless of the soaking downpour. I began to cry. Then I felt a hand on the back of my neck.

'Hey, man. Your friend let you down, did he?' Squeezing my neck hard, Gray pulled me to my feet and, somehow, turned me round to face him. 'Nice weather, man. Nice for what I want to do, 'cause nobody goes out when it's like this.' He let go briefly, then put both hands around my neck, his thumbs on my windpipe. 'Start praying, Gordon baby. Just remember next time round, don't stick your nose in where it isn't wanted.'

'Aidan,' I croaked.

'He's got a broken nose and he's sleeping it off on the floor of that pub, man. Forget him. Forget it.' He applied the pressure. 'Christ, you stuck-up bastard, you pompous fuckin' tourist, I've always hated you. I'm gonna enjoy this.' I couldn't feel the rain on my face any more. Vision went double and then cut out. The only senses left to me were the feel of the intolerable pressure at my throat and the sound of laughter in my ears.

The astute amongst you will by now have leapt to the obvious, and correct, conclusion. If I'm telling the story, I'm highly unlikely to be dead. Dead men tell no tales. Actually, you get that kind of trick more and more these days, but let's be honest, it is a bit of a strain on the average credulity. It's quite a neat device on film. That's my opinion. As a literary device, it's usually there to draw attention to the artificial nature of narrative, or so my literary friends tell me. Good. Well, I may have ruined your suspense by going on about all this, but let me tell you that if someone had popped up to go on in a similar vein while Gray was throttling me, I'd have been very relieved – always assuming I'd have been able to hear them. Conversely, if anyone had turned up to tell me I was about to die in order to make a statement about the role of the narrator, I don't think it would have been much of a comfort.

As I lost consciousness, I really thought I'd had it. Again, it was my family who came to mind, along with early, iconic images and flickering candles. But then – and it can only have been a second or two later – I felt the wet pavement seeping through my sodden suit. I was lying down. Looking up, I could see, blurred, unclear, dripping wet but still Satanic, Gray standing there and laughing.

The fact he was a sadist saved my life. That and the fact he hated me so much. If I'd just been someone he didn't know, like the brewery rep had been, I'm sure he'd have finished me off quickly. Fortunately for me, he wanted to enjoy himself and he wanted me to feel it. Perhaps he was on something. God knows. I didn't give it a great deal of thought, neither then nor later. 'You fuckin' little cunt,' I heard him say, 'your fuckin' mother won't recognise you when I'm through.' As I wasn't getting much visual information from all this, I shut my eyes. Simon wasn't going to come out and rescue me. There weren't any passers-by; even if there had been, a convenient hedge was protecting us from the public gaze. I wasn't properly conscious. I just waited for all things to pass.

Instead, I heard a groan, followed by a thud. The groan wasn't mine, the thud didn't land on me. However, curiosity doesn't rush to make itself known when injury and death are high on the agenda. There was another, pretty indescribable, quiet sound, a bit like a cough not quite starting. Then I felt a gentle hand on my shoulder.

'Come on, Gordo. You'll catch your death of cold lying down there.' I tried to open my eyes, but being conscious was still a bit of a difficult concept. Both of my shoulders were grabbed firmly and I felt myself pulled upward. I sort of opened my eyes. Then I smiled stupidly.

'Aidan. You're all right.' I feebly stuck my arms out. Aidan let me hold him, and gently dragged me to my feet. His fine hair was plastered by the rain to his head. Traces of dried blood still clung to the end of his nose. There was a distinct swelling beneath his left eye. I gave a weak laugh. 'He did hit you. He said he hit you.'

'Yeah. My fucking nose hurts like hell. Fucking sucker punch as well. Our kid'd kill me for letting anyone land one like that on me.' He tentatively let go of me. I started to fall and he grabbed me at the waist. 'Come on Gordon. You're safe now. Concentrate.'

'Don't want to. Like standing here, you holding me.'

'One more minute.' He smiled. 'Then the meter goes on.'

I laughed. 'Don't you ever have a holiday?' I blinked and proper focus swam back. I drew back from Aidan's hold and took some unaided steps. 'Hey. Thanks. Twice in one day.'

' 'S all right.' He could still do his smile.'You reckon you'll live then? Wasn't your mate in, or what?'

'My mate? Oh yes, he was in all right. He wouldn't let me in.' I gave the briefest possible explanation.

'He didn't believe you? Or something else? If he's one of the ones who might be out to get you – '

'I really can't believe it's Simon. It just can't be. He's the least likely person ever.'

'Gordon. There's nobody in the world who can't do it. Not even you. And you know it's always the ones you don't think who do that sort of thing.'

'Not Simon.' I looked down at Gray. 'He seems rather quiet.'

'Yeah well – ' Aidan pulled a face. 'He'd got his knife out, Gordon. So I didn't really think. I hit him from behind. He tried to turn round and knife me, but I'd surprised him, so I knocked the knife out of his hand. Then I got to it before he did. Then he jumped on me. And now I don't think he's all that healthy.' My jaw dropped. Literally. I think it hit the pavement. 'Honest to God, Gordon, on me mam's life, he ran straight onto it. What was I supposed to do? Anyway,' he shrugged, 'what do you think the bastard would've done to you? He hadn't got that knife for a kids' game, Gordo. He's a fucking psycho.'

138

'You were always saying how soft he was.'

'Doesn't stop him being a psycho.'

'Well. I suppose we'd better get the Police.'

'Er, Gordon. I'm not sure that's a good idea at the moment. We don't want to get mixed up with the Plods round here, 'cause it'll take them years to catch up with what's really going on. Honest, they won't be very happy if you walk in the local nick and say, "Excuse me, my mate here's just killed this guy who was working for someone else flogging drugs and killing people and the guys at the Yard know all about it." They'll play daft buggers before they'll get in touch with your pals on the Murder Squad.'

'Are you sure?'

'Gordo, which of us two has had more to do with the Filth? Anyway, look – Christ, look at us both, like a couple of drowned fucking rats – we could wrap this up ourselves and then get your mates from the Yard in.'

'They're not exactly my mates. And I'm not sure where they're from.' I thought. Aidan might be right. And the chance of sorting it out, bringing it to an end, was very tempting.

'They'll be the Yard.' Aidan stooped down over Gray's body. He started searching the pockets, pulling out everything he could find. Amazingly enough, Gray actually possessed a wallet. Aidan opened it. 'Thirty quid. That'll come in handy.' He pocketed it. Then he handed the wallet over. 'Anything interesting in that?'

'Are you sure you should do that?'

'Oh come on, Gordo, it's probably not his anyway. Who's going to know or care? Look in the wallet.'

I looked. A Tube Travelcard of another day's date. Club tickets of varying ages. A photograph of himself. Something from a North London police station about a drunk and disorderly charge. A receipt from the same police station. And a plain card giving an address in Docklands. A date and time. Ten o'clock that day. I stared. 'Aidan,' I said quietly. I handed him the card.

Aidan looked at the card, then at his watch. 'It's gone nine. Do you know how to get to this place?'

'Not a fucking clue.'

'We'll get a cab then.'

'Don't rely too much on the famous Knowledge. Most of these Docklands places are brand new and unsignposted.'

'You don't recognise the address, then?'

'Not remotely. Don't even know if it's relevant.'

'It's got to be. I mean, everyone knows he doesn't get punters any more. Anyway, Gordo, after all the cock-ups, he'd have to report straight back, wouldn't he? I mean, if you were his boss, you'd want to know he'd got it right at last, wouldn't you?'

'Yes, but – don't you think it's a bit obvious carrying an address with a date and time on it around the place? A bit convenient for us? I'm afraid it worries me. Let's give it to the Police. They can handle it. I can't. I want a bath and a change of clothes.'

'Gordon, listen. You know what pratface Gary was like, always on hard stuff and that. That crap fucks your memory up, so if you ever wanted Gary to get anywhere, you'd have to write it down for him.'

'OK. I accept that. Brilliant logic, Aidan. So let's give the card to the Police.'

'Look, Gordon, the Police'll take too fucking long to get anything done. And the guy who's behind it all, he's not going to rest now. It's going to be like a matter of pride for him.'

'This guy may very well be behind that door.' I gestured at the door of number 15. 'And anyway, whoever it is can't do much now. Half his people are under lock and key and his main knifeman is dead.'

'Gordon. Do you want to get it sorted out or not? I mean, you might be right. It might be nothing. So we waste a bit of time –'

'And I waste the cab fare.' I shrugged. 'Oh, come on. I'm sick of getting wet.' I looked down at Gray. 'Are we just leaving him there as a present for the residents of number 15?'

'Hang on.' Aidan dragged Gray's body round the far side of a darkened bay window. 'No-one'll go round there on a night like this. Right, let's get cracking.'

We set off through the rain, tracing our steps back to the main road. I whinged on about the sanity of the enterprise and Aidan kept telling me not to worry. It being a rainy night, and South London to boot, taxis weren't exactly plentiful, so Aidan pushed me into the doorway of a minicab firm. He was very astute at dealing with them; they, for their part, didn't seem to worry about our being bedraggled or Aidan looking as though he'd been in a brawl (which he had). His left eye was swelling up nicely. He made them fix a price for us before the journey, a price Aidan seemed to think was reasonable. I wasn't quite so sure, but then I was paying. Aidan gestured at his watch when I moaned.

All through the journey I kept up this whining. Dark suspicion was cantering through my mind. Rain, streetlights and shadows combined to create strange illusory figures. This line of thought was out of order, surely. After all, Aidan had saved my life twice now. If it hadn't been for that, I'd have been even more dubious.

Oddly enough, the cab driver knew where he was going and even had an idea where the relevant road was. It was about five past ten when the car pulled up in front of a new, light brown stone block facing onto the road. I could make out the right name etched into the grey stone above the ghastly portico. Six or seven floors of desirable residences towered up, all with discreet neo-Georgian windows. Just the kind of building to gladden the hearts of the Royal Family. This was a first for me, as I didn't know anyone who lived in this part of the world. Or so I'd thought. Of course, it may have proved that I was wrong. Maybe no-one I knew was involved. I paid the cabbie. I'd suggested asking him to wait, but Aidan dismissed this firmly. The cab drove away.

The rain seemed easier now. 'Well, mastermind,' I said. 'How do we get in?'

'Ring the bell. It's easy. Watch.' Aidan pressed the button next to the number shown on Gray's card. The intercom next to the buttons crackled, but no voice came out. 'Hey, man, it's pissin' down. Open the fuckin' door.' It was a near flawless impression in the open air, so it must have been fairly convincing over an imperfect intercom. A buzz sounded in the front door. Aidan pushed the door open. 'After you,' he said softly in his own voice. I entered the plushly carpeted hall. A small plaque on the wall told us who the architects were (some firm whose name sounded like a cybernetic experiment) and which floors contained which apartments.

'Fourth floor,' I murmured. 'Now where are the stairs?'

'There's a lift, look.' Aidan pointed. At first I thought it was just a cupboard door. 'It's got them numbers on top of it.' And it had. A rather charming oaken panel with plastic numbers one to seven incongruously stuck to it. I found a button and pressed it. The door slid back.

The lift had mirrors on all three sides. This created a bizarre effect, as each reflection was reflected somewhere else, often at odd angles. Aidan and I receded on all sides into eternity. Aidan examined himself. 'Fuck,' he said, 'I'll kill that – '

'I think you already have.'

He giggled nervously. Then he took out a comb and tried to rectify the damage the rain had done to his hair. Water splashed on to the mirror. I rather regretted the mess made of my suit, but otherwise I looked like shit as usual.

'Suppose it is a punter,' I suggested.

'I'll think of something.' Aidan smiled. 'You can watch me work.'

'Doubt whether that'd please the punter much.' The lift door opened. Well, this was it. I felt very sick again. The acrobatic butterflies were putting on another display. I suspected – rightly – that I was trembling visibly. Creeping nervously along the beautifully laid out corridor with its royal blue wallpaper, its ornate gilt mirrors, we found the door with the right number. I was about to knock, when Aidan pointed out that the door was ajar.

'Let's give him a surprise,' he said.

'It could be a trap,' I whispered. Aidan pushed the door open. Nothing happened. I stepped cautiously in. Laid out before me was a large, split-level apartment. The large ground floor was a few steps down from where we stood. Half way across this, a set of steps led to an upper half-floor. Doors led off the lower floor to both left and right. The upper part was in darkness. Subdued, discreet lighting illuminated the lower part, sufficiently low for the lights of the boats and the Northern shore to twinkle picturesquely through the enormous picture window at the far end of the flat. The place was elegant, but very sparsely furnished, with no sign of any dominant personality, no sign of personal possessions. It was distinctly unlived in. I felt very uneasy, to give an understatement of monumental proportions.

'Go on,' Aidan said.

'Yes, do come in,' a very familiar voice said. A figure emerged from the shadows of the upper floor and advanced down the steps. 'You see where a preoccupation with sin leads you, Gordon.' He gave his customary manic laugh.

'The Wages of Sin is Docklands,' I murmured. I was shocked. 'Hello, Tobes.' I sort of laughed. 'OK, Aidan,' I said, not quite turning round, 'can I call the Police now?' He didn't say anything so I turned right round.

'Sorry, Gordo,' Aidan said, giving me his rubber-necked smile and waving his right hand so I didn't miss the gun he was holding in it. I gasped. 'Well, Mr Castle,' he said over my head, 'here we are as promised.'

'Oh, it's you, Aidan. I thought it was that idiot Scot on the intercom.' Toby laughed. 'I suppose that was for Gordon's benefit.'

'All right, Gordo. Down there.' Aidan prodded me with the

gun. I staggered down into the lounge. 'Sit down. Please.' I did as I was told. Aidan resumed his business chat. 'No, Gary's out of the way, Mr Castle.'

'Just as well. He had the competence of a boiled banana. Early retirement, but no tedious pension payments. Well, Aidan, I'm very impressed. You said you could handle it all. I wasn't entirely convinced when you said so, but now – the job is yours.'

'Ta very much.'

'Just this one loose end left then.' Toby sat down opposite me in an armchair. Aidan stayed on his feet, the gun levelled, roughly, at my head. Maybe my neck. I wasn't in the mood for any geometrical ballistic calculations at that precise moment. 'I can't tell you,' Toby said, 'how sorry I am about all this, Gordon. It's really been most distressing for me. I can't think of anyone I'd less rather have in this position. And I'm really annoyed you're not going to be able to come with me to *Parsifal*. But it is all your own fault, isn't it, really? I mean, I tried to give you hints, make it easy for you. I never thought you'd be so persistent. I have to say that I really rather admire you, in a way. You really are basically incorruptible, aren't you? You really do see yourself as on the side of Good, don't you?'

I shook my head. 'Far from it. But shove the flannel, Tobes. Aren't you supposed to give me a bit of a megalomaniac rant here and tell me how clever you've been, not try and flatter me? Anyway, I'm not going to apologise for putting you out. I'm a bit mystified why you didn't let Aidan let those other thugs finish me off last night.'

'Ah. Nothing to do with you, really. An internal power struggle. What you might call a staff purge. When that Irish boy who was looking after things for me was so carelessly arrested yesterday, a vacuum opened up. That ghastly Scot thought he should take over, but then I met Aidan here – thanks to you, of course – and he told me he could outwit the lot of them singlehanded. So I told him that if he could, a commensurate reward, along with an executive position, would be forthcoming. You were the chosen battleground, given that you were the most pressing business to hand. I just sat back and allowed the free play of market forces. Incentives, you see, competition. It all ensures a healthier, fitter organization, clears out the dead wood. And the Irish boy's personnel selection was not exactly masterly. What a shame you hadn't met Aidan when you first took me into that ghastly pub. Or, I should say, when I got you to take me in there.'

143

'Did you?' I laughed. As Aidan now had the gun pointing straight into my eyes, I thought this was quite an achievement. 'Do you mind if I say something, Toby? Every villainous mastermind I've ever read about or seen on the screen has always had one major basic flaw, namely the desire to explain the plot to the hero in the last chapter or reel or episode or whatever. I still have enough respect for you to hope you aren't quite that crass, Tobes.'

Toby fell back in his seat laughing. 'Extraordinary. I think I may have underestimated you. What a shame you're not prepared to be accommodated.'

'I think I rather underestimated you. Or overestimated you. It depends on your point of view, really. I hadn't twigged. I really hadn't. Can I ask a couple of questions, though? Out of genuine interest and not simply a desire to play for time.'

'I think I owe you that much.'

'Why the brewery rep? That's the first.'

'Ah.' Toby raised a declamatory hand in that gesture I knew so well from conversations about opera and art. 'The perfect example of how great a liability that Scot was. He and those tedious little henchmen of his, the ones with the common names, had found a way of getting into the cellar room at the Magpie from outside, and they'd go down there to do a little sorting out of commodities. The brewery man decided to go for a look around, why I'm not sure. I suppose the landlord was cooking the books a little too obviously. He caught them and dear Gary decided that drastic action was called for. He shouldn't have done that; I'd distinctly told Murphy that if any of his people got caught they were to lie down and take it quietly. Fuss was the last thing we needed; an atmosphere of panic and fuss is not very helpful to the conduct of useful business.'

An expression of near-Messianic seriousness lit up Toby's face; then he relaxed. 'Mind you, if it hadn't have been for you, they'd have got away with it. The business with the railway line was clever, I must give the young men their due; and they managed to get him there without anyone suspecting anything, which for those idiots was quite remarkable. And all that stuff Dougie told you about the man's depressions was quite true. He did have a record of suicide attempts, quite coincidentally. Well, that's one question. What's the second?'

'How do you stop the Jasons and the other kids naming you? The ones in prison, I mean.'

'They can't. They don't know who I am. Paul Murphy

knows, but he's on full pay until he's released and then he's Aidan's problem. Gary knew, but Aidan seems to have settled that satisfactorily. I must say, your meeting Aidan was a stroke of luck.'

'Yes,' I said. 'Well done, Aidan. A superb performance all round. You certainly had me fooled most of the time.'

'That's because you are a fool, Gordo,' he said, looking down at me with a calm expression of contempt. 'A fucking stupid fool. All that talk about art and that and you imagine you can swan around a place like the Magpie, handling the goods and never actually fucking paying. Me and our kid ran a stall for a bit, knock-off stuff, up in Manchester, and we had one rule. Touch it, you've bought it, you fucking pay for it. I'd watched you before we ever met, seen you at it there, window shopping. That's no fucking use to a boy like me, Gordo. Boys like me, Gordo, we don't want intelligent chats. And we don't want nice meals in nice restaurants. Well, we don't want them with fucking punters anyway. Nice meals in nice restaurants is for people like you anyway, you can sit there and talk about fucking opera and that. It's not my world and I don't fucking want it. I want drugs, I want girls, booze, fags, TV, video, a car, a place like this. I want cash, I want flash. Not fucking nice chats in restaurants. No, I'm past all that. Everything's past all that. This country isn't about all that any more. And take you and me, Gordo. You know my situation. You met me in the Magpie. What am I doing there? You fucking know. You want me. Do you just make a fucking offer, do you just do business, no nonsense? No, you fucking talk about it. I know what you're thinking all the time. You think if you talk long enough about love and that, buy me a fucking pizza, buy me some dope, then you'll get me on the cheap. Well, you're fucking wrong.' He jabbed the gun into my forehead. 'I've got my principles. Mr Castle here understands that. But you – you're from a different fucking planet. Planet of the Morons.'

This was all said quietly, calmly with not a trace of viciousness; he even had a peculiar smile on his face most of the time. I shook my head sadly.

'You're wrong about that, Aidan. About me. And I think you're wrong about you as well.' But I wasn't up to saying any more. My complete mistake about Aidan had gutted me and this tirade just about finished me off. This time I was a dead man. 'All right,' I said, looking over to Toby, 'what happens now?'

'Do you want to end our chat?' Toby asked. 'I must say, I

thought you'd have a few more questions. I really don't mind telling you what you want to know.'

'Sorry, Tobes. I'm doing you a favour here, I'm stopping you talking too much. Anyway, I really don't want to know. I just don't care.' Aidan had knocked the resilient bravado out of me, to tell the truth.

'I must say, that's rather unfair of you,' Toby said, evidently piqued. 'I was looking forward to boasting to someone whose intellect I respect.' I think he meant it. 'All right. What happens is that I go. I have an appointment to see a close friend on a perfectly legitimate matter. Once I'm clear away, and my alibi is established, then it's up to Aidan. The less I know, the better. The first I'll hear about it will be from Dougie or Simon. I must say, their assiduous concern was much more helpful at tracking you down than that imbecile Scot and his cretinous crew.' He stood up, reached in his pocket and pulled out a set of keys which he handed over to Aidan. 'Don't forget to lock up when you go,' he said.

Aidan, not loosening his hold on the gun, took the keys. Toby looked down at me.

'Goodbye Gordon,' he said. 'I am sorry. But business is business. I can't afford any further blips.'

'Is this your idea of diversification?' I asked, trying a smile.

'In a way. A small, lucrative corner of Soho is all I ask. And now that I have such a competent senior executive – ' he made a liberal gesture towards Aidan.

'Thank you very much,' Aidan said. Toby took an envelope, stuffed very full, from his pocket and handed it over.

'Call me tomorrow,' he said. Aidan nodded. Toby walked to the door and left.

So it was just me, Aidan and the gun. Aidan sighed and shook his head at me. 'I suppose you're going to try and talk me out of it now, Gordo.'

'What's the point?'

'Well, if you start on about art, fuck all. You know my situation. So make us an offer, and see where it gets you.'

I marvelled. 'Is there anyone you won't sell out on?'

'Meself. Me mam. Our kid.'

'You've spent years selling yourself out.'

'Only my arse, Gordo. Least important bit, really.'

'You reckon you've still got your integrity, do you?'

'There you go, Gordo, that's typical of you. Pulling out a dictionary word when it's fuck all use.'

'Look, Aidan. It's very tempting to beg for my life. Really

146

beg, humiliate myself, offer you everything. I never knew before quite how high a value I placed on life. It's only today that I've realised that I do care about it. But I'm not going to get involved in some ludicrous auction for your loyalty. Quite apart from the fact that it's such an unpredictable, fluctuating commodity, this kind of buying people, whether it's for sex or for more important things – well, even the little bit I've ever done has upset me. And you're right about one thing. Selling your arse is nothing compared with what you're selling out now. Well, if you want an offer, I've got one. Let me go now and I'll tell enough lies to cover for you with the Police. That's my one and only offer. But remember this. There are one or two people who might kick up a fuss when something happens to me. And your name has been much on my lips recently. And after last night the Police have a connection between us. As does Michael Hamilton. Listen, Aidan, you can kill Gray and call it an accident – '

'Honest to God, on me mother's life, it was an accident.'

'That's not the impression you were giving to Toby just now.'

'Yeah, well, I want Mr Castle to think well of me, don't I?'

'I'm sure you do. Come on, Aidan, let's get it over with. Are you going to shoot me? Stab me? Make me jump out of the window? Which is it to be?'

Suddenly I'd talked myself into believing I really did have the upper hand. All in all my logic was pretty good, except for the fact that Aidan had the gun. Evidently I'd got through to him, because he hesitated. I even thought I detected a droop in the angle of the gun.

'Make me an offer, Gordo. I'm open to offers. I can think of one offer you could make right now.'

'Nothing to compare with the senior executive position in the drug world of South East Soho. Nothing to compete with whatever's in that envelope Toby gave you. You've had my only offer.'

'Don't be thick. Think about it. Michael Hamilton.'

'You want to be the kept boy of the City as well as the drug baron of Soho?'

'We could make a fortune out of him and his friends.'

'We could? We?'

'Yeah, think about it. Not just the rent, though there's that. I could fix them up with boys and that. But even if Mister Castle got caught and went down, I'd still be able to get the stuff. I know where he gets it from. I know where Darren used to get it from. And our kid knows people who could get me as much stuff again. Those City types, they're really into drugs and that –'

'Aidan. I don't think I'd have been keen on this when I still had illusions about you.'

He shrugged. 'At least you've shut up with all that love crap.'

'Oh, I think I probably still love you. I mean, I'm gutted, I can't believe what a lying deceitful little bastard you are. But I still love you. Probably. And it's because of that I'm prepared to lie for you. Prepared to let you off. But I've got my integrity too. My principles.' I was amazed here at my own dignity. After all, he still had the gun, and so far the only person who'd ever come to my rescue in moments of peril had been Aidan himself. But I thought that if I kept firm, then it put him under pressure.

'Come on, Gordo. We've had some good times, you and me.'

'Not what you said in front of Toby.'

'Yeah, well, that was a little show for his benefit.'

'Very good.' I looked up at him again. 'Doesn't it occur to you that Toby may still have people who'll deal with you if he goes down and you don't?'

'No – he doesn't. Anyone who's working for him now'll work for me if he goes away.'

'And who is working for him that you haven't dealt with?' A thought struck me. 'It was you that got rid of Paul Murphy, wasn't it? You set him up for the drugs thing, didn't you? You tipped off the Police?'

Aidan gave a rubber-necked smile, which looked very weird from so far below. 'I hear they're charging him with dealing now. Tragic, isn't it? It's his own fault. He shouldn't have tried to screw me that night.' He looked quite pleased with himself. 'None of the boys you know are in it, Gordo. Look, are you going to do some business here? You've got one more minute to make your mind up.' He raised his watch so he could see the sixty seconds elapse. I wondered if I could wrest the gun from him. On balance I probably couldn't. Still, it would be worth a go. 'Thirty seconds,' he announced. I prepared to leap.

Then there came a thunderous knocking at the door. 'Mr McKenzie! Mr McKenzie! Are you all right? It's Detective Sergeant Morgan here.'

I smiled at Aidan. 'My offer's still open,' I said, 'for as long as it takes me to get to the door.'

Aidan gave me another rubber-necked smile. 'You're a lucky sod,' he said, handing me the gun carefully by its handle. 'I reckon I'd better stick with you.'

148

'Right. See that 'phone? Disconnect it and smash the plug. Quickly and quietly. That's our alibi.' Aidan moved over to do as he was told. I got up and walked slowly, very unsteadily to the door, but before I was halfway there, the banging started again. I shouted calming words of reassurance, which seemed to get through. Slowly, keeping my eye on Aidan, I turned the latch. Aidan gave me a thumbs up. I opened the door, and there stood the reasonable sergeant with some uniformed henchmen. 'Sorry,' I said. 'Do come in. Well, I'm making free with someone else's flat.'

The Sergeant laughed dutifully. 'We've got Toby Castle in custody, sir. Er – what's that you're holding?'

I looked down. It was the gun. I laughed. 'Oh yes. Toby gave this to my friend here under the mistaken impression he'd do something violent with it.'

'Ah. Mister Castle did say that your life might be in danger. Quite concerned, he was, in fact.'

'Not a bit of it. Aidan and I were just discussing our next move. I know we should have got in touch with you straight away, but – well, the 'phone was out of order, as you can see, and Aidan's like me. A bit Police-shy. And we needed a bit of a rest after our harrowing evening.' I explained about Gray, glossing it a little, to make Aidan sound braver and much more like a man acting in self-defence. 'Toby will tell you all about Gray, if he hasn't already.'

'Not yet, sir. But he does seem prepared to be co-operative. Showed no resistance at all. And once he'd had a word with Mr Hamilton's solicitor, who's agreed to act for him – '

'Hang on.' I dropped my carefully prepared act. Clearly I still didn't know what the hell was going on. 'Do you mean Michael Hamilton? Where does he fit into all this?'

'Ah.' Morgan looked rather shamefaced. 'Mr Hamilton and I go back a few years. Anyway, earlier this evening, he rang one of our Assistant Commissioners and played hell about the fact you weren't being properly protected. Dropped a lot of names that made a lot of noise, so to speak. Then sweetly offers to talk to me personally. End result was I was kicked out with a flea in my ear to talk to Mr Hamilton. Apparently you tried to get in touch with me ten minutes later. Sod's Law, I'm afraid, sir.'

I closed my eyes and swooned a bit. This was absurd. 'Sergeant, could you do me a favour? Just call me Gordon. I can't bear being called "sir". Or "Mr McKenzie". They both sound appallingly official. So how did you know where to find Toby? And how did you know it was Toby you needed to find?'

'Well.' Morgan swallowed uncomfortably. 'You'll have to thank your friend in a very high place again. Apparently he got some of his employees – despatch riders – to follow a few people. Three, I think. So we knew that Mr Castle had come here. We arrived about five minutes before he emerged. And picked him up.'

'Yes, but supposing he'd been completely innocent?'

'Well – Mr Hamilton seemed fairly sure he wasn't. Anyway – er – all's well that ends well, isn't it?' I gave him a look intended to be lethal. 'Oh yes, I've got a message for you from Mr Hamilton. I wrote it down because it didn't mean much to me.' He took out a notebook. 'Message reads: "Told you I'd look after you. Contract on Monday as arranged. There are plenty of high places I can take you up into and I can promise you won't get vertigo." Does that make any sense, sir, er, Gordon?'

I laughed. 'Yes. Quite a lot. Well, shall we go and wrap this up?' I turned to Aidan and gave him a reassuring smile. He looked rather nervous. Well, tough. He deserved to sweat a bit. But I was going to keep my side of the bargain. And so I did. Toby, apparently, was singing like a bird. For me, the question was covering for Aidan, which turned out not to be too hard. I just kept saying that I knew he was basically honest and that he'd told me all along about him and Toby, that the whole thing had been a rather rash hoax designed to catch Toby out and, yes, it had been foolhardy, but we couldn't get through to the Police at the crucial moment. Our spirit was commended, but we were warned about taking unnecessary risks.

It also turned out that Gray's body had been found. This caused a delay while the South London Plods proved as obstinate about handing the matter over as Aidan had predicted. Gary Cruickshank. That turned out to be his real name. I'd never thought to check that when flicking through his wallet. In fact, there were several things I'd not thought to check there. None of which seemed to matter until about three in the morning when we were allowed to go home. Because just as we were leaving a uniformed Sergeant, who'd been running a check on Gary Cruickshank's impressive record, showed me something which mattered rather a lot. In fact, what he showed me would have changed the course of events rather dramatically if I'd known about it twenty-four hours earlier.

Epilog(ue)

One strange, almost touching thing was that Toby sent me the two tickets for *Parsifal*. It was supposed to be an apology. But I had apologies to offer too, so I sent them on to Dougie and Horst with a carefully worded note. I knew that neither that friendship nor the one with Simon would survive, but I felt I owed a gesture or two in either direction. The Simon question would have to wait; but I knew that Dougie was keen on Wagner – much keener than I am, in fact. *Parsifal* always reminds me of the taste of fish, a taste I'm not fond of. My mother, you see, was a great Good Friday traditionalist; she never let me or my brother watch TV until at least half past five, always telling us that when she'd been young the only pub-lic entertainment you'd get on Good Friday would be *Parsifal* on the radio (after half past five naturally). So it was the only music Ian and I were ever allowed to listen to on that day and then only after we'd undergone the purgatorially long Good Friday Liturgy. Our own records were banned – all that flip-pant Mozart, Beethoven, Mahler, T Rex (Ian's not mine, that was). And the only food we ever got was, naturally, fish. Hot Cross Buns were a flippant pagan luxury in her view. Mind you, I never liked them when I experienced them in later life, so I can't say she deprived me of much. But as you can see, fish and *Parsifal* were inevitably intermingled for me.

So, rather than spend an evening in Covent Garden imagin-ing that I could taste fish, I sent the tickets on to Dougie and Horst. In any case, who could I have taken with me? I was going to miss Toby. Ironically, I was going to miss him much more than I'd miss Dougie or Simon. I somehow felt much closer to him. Of course, this was something of a self-indulgence, I realised that. Whatever specious reasoning I came up with, neither Dougie nor Simon had tried to kill me. Toby had.

Those of you with a structural turn of mind may, I suppose, be wondering about my use and spelling of the word 'Epilog(ue)'. I would refer you to those ludicrous old American TV detective shows featuring clean cut men in blue suits. They'd always have a two minute last section in which Efrem Zimbalist or whoever would draw a moral from the dastardly crime and its solution. This was always called 'Epilog'. Later, this degenerated into the scene where all the sycophants would

151

gather round the cop in the wheelchair/bald cop/blind cop/fat cop and fall about at some non-joke, usually at the expense of the show's token black character. Whether this part of the story is quite in the same spirit of either of those two archetypes of the 'Epilog', I leave entirely to your judgement.

Michael Hamilton was as good as his word. A letter offering me a job at a ludicrous salary with very generous conditions and a corresponding contract was delivered to my office by messenger on the Monday afternoon. Michael had given the messenger strict instructions not to leave until I'd signed the contract and entrusted it to him for a swift return. I suppose this was to put me under pressure to sign immediately and not allow strange scruples or reservations to creep in. He needn't have worried. True, I had a moment's qualm before I signed. I knew full well that I was selling myself. Wasn't I doing exactly what I'd berated Aidan for doing, and wasn't I doing it with a seriousness of intent that Aidan had never had? Yes, I was, but so fucking what. I was bored with scratching around. Being owned by Michael would give me more freedom than my so-called independence. The messenger was on his way again pretty speedily. In celebration, I submitted my notice on a piece of lavatory paper. My immediate boss, relieved at the thought I was going, laughed.

Michael also sent a personal letter, by way of explanation. It was something of an eye-opener, and reinforced my view of myself as a naive idiot.

'You're probably wondering' (it read at the crucial point, after a few pleasantries) 'how I was so sure that Toby was behind your little predicament. Well, from what little I knew of the other two, they seemed rather unlikely suspects. Dougie Simpson, with his model domesticity, boring everyone to death with his so daring upfront tales of his blissful home and hearth with heavenly Horst – ludicrous Kraut – didn't strike me as a very likely part-time drug baron. Simon Green has no imagination. So Katy says, anyway, rather uncharitably adding "Look at his taste in women." Well, chacun à son gout. Katy looks forward to renewing your acquaintance by the way.

'To the point, though. Toby seemed the most likely of your trio to me. Surprised you didn't think so too. I suspect that affection blinded you, as it certainly must have done with Aidan. I'm afraid, though, that I had an unfair advantage over you regarding Aidan. While you were in the loo in that charming pub, I showed Aidan a few facts of life, told him a few comparative incomes, dropped a few names. Some cash changed hands. But above all, I used sheer force of personality. Aidan is, you may have gathered, a snob and a sucker for rich blokes with posh accents. Don't underestimate your own appeal here. Whatever he may have said, he rather likes all that posh talk he can't understand. But Toby is a lot posher than either of us. Luckily, I'm much richer than Toby than Toby is posher than me, if you follow my logic. And my offer was much better – at least, on the surface. So Aidan told me the bare bones of what was going on. I didn't ask him to give too much away although I think he'd have told me anything for the right price. So I had to tell the Police without giving too much away. Fortunately, I have advantages over Sergeant Gorgon I didn't enjoy at the time of our previous encounter, so I could get any tale I liked (within reason) swallowed. And I did get one of our despatch riders to shadow Toby. You were always safe, you see. I knew nothing could happen to you while Toby was still around. He could never pull the trigger himself, or even watch the trigger being pulled.

'Let me say, I have no intention of honouring any deal I may seem to have made with Aidan. Nor should you. Don't let affection blind you. I'm aware that you must have covered for him thus far. My advice – and it causes me a certain amount of regret, if I'm honest – is that you should clear him out with the rest of the rubbish. You doubtless have other friends in those quarters. And if you think that that is a hint, then that's up to you. Remember – you're my man now.

'I'm away for the rest of the week. I'll call you at the weekend.'

Well, at least I'd been right about something passing between them in that pub. Of course, all this ought to have made a material difference to my view of Aidan. But it didn't.

It was the Thursday following, and I was waiting in my flat for Aidan, who was due to arrive around nine. I'd just watched a documentary called 'Do You Believe In Magic Bullets?' tracing impossible trajectories through JFK's neck and Connally's wrist via Jackie's bra buckle. Or something. Like all these documentaries, it was extremely convincing until about five minutes after it had finished. They really had to go the same way as alcohol and meat, both of which seemed to have made a permanent exit from the McKenzie regime. All very healthy. I'd even managed to put on a few pounds. Next stop the dermatologist.

Aidan was dressed a bit down market that night, and it was rather fetching. I sighed a little to myself as I sat him down. 'You are so attractive,' I said.

'Thank you very much.'

'But I know your situation.' I went to my fridge and took out a can of lager. He opened it adeptly. 'You know,' I went on, 'some men in my position would be using their knowledge to exploit you. That's your situation.'

Aidan grinned. 'But you won't, Gordo. You've got principles. So have I. And my principles say fifty quid, as you know.'

'Fifty? I thought it was thirty.'

'That was a special introductory offer. The time limit on that ran out last week.' He rubber-necked. 'I don't see why you can't let your principles slip now and again, though, Gordo. It'd be worth it. You'd enjoy it. I bet you need it, too.'

'I thought you made sure it was always over quickly.'

'Depends on the customer.' He composed himself and went thoughtful. 'Gordon?'

'Aidan.'

'Laurence is coming back from America next week. He'll want his flat back. Well, he'll let me stay, but only if I – well, I'm not going to sleep with him, not even once. Not for nowt, anyway.'

'Your principles again.'

'Of course. So I was wondering – ' he fingered the top of his can of lager – 'would you put us up here for a bit? Till I get sorted out?'

'I've only got one bedroom.'

'You've got this settee.'

'Hasn't Laurence got a settee?'

'Yes. But he hasn't got principles. He'll just go on about me owing him something for the use of his flat and getting a proper job and that.'

'And I won't?'

'No.' Aidan grinned.

'Well, don't worry. I'll see you all right.'

'Ta very much.'

'So – tell me – how did you come to meet Toby?'

'What? Toby? Oh, Mr Castle. Well. You remember that night we arranged to meet in the Magpie? You remember bastard Gary came over to me to tell me to be nice to you and slipped us a score? Well, he told me someone wanted to meet us, dinnertime the day after. Someone posh in the City. I thought he was on about a punter. I wasn't going to turn up, but after you and me had that talk, right, I knew Gary was working for someone and I thought I'd go and see what was up. So I met Mr Castle. I was very impressed. You know some very impressive people, Gordon. I'm looking forward to meeting a few more. Anyway, he told me Irish Paul was in trouble – that didn't come as much of a surprise – and like he didn't trust Gary to shit out of the right end. I told him to look no further, and he told me about the trouble you might give him, so I offered to take care of it. Then we made this deal that if I could look after you better than the other pillocks – well, you know all about that. He seemed to like me, any road.'

'Jolly good.'

'Oh, Gordo, don't go all sulky on us. It's all right now, isn't it? It's turned out right for you and me. Hey, when's that Michael coming back? You said he was off somewhere.'

'The weekend, I think. Yes. So you weren't involved with the business about the brewery man?'

'Honest to God, Gordon, on me mam's life, I wasn't. No way. That was nasty, that. I mean, it were just an accident the way I heard. Irish Paul was dead narked – he said he wouldn't have gone out if he knew owt like that was going to happen. I mean, he knew that bloke was out to cause trouble for Bob and Doreen 'cause of the books being bent, but that had fuck all to do with him. It were just bad luck that bloke decided to have a nose round when he did. If he'd done it half an hour before or after it wouldn't have mattered.'

'And three people would still be alive.'

'Yeah, well, Darren and Gary are no great loss.'

'Ah yes. Darren and Gary. Gary stabbed Darren, didn't he?'

'That's what everyone says. That's what you think. Isn't it?'

'Aidan. Darren was stabbed about one or one thirty in the morning, the night between Thursday and Friday.'

'Yes. So? Gary doesn't usually go to bed with a cup of cocoa at ten o'clock, does he?'

'He did that night. He was picked up on a drunk and disorderly charge in Camden Town at about ten fifteen. They let him out again at about midday on the Friday. One of the Sergeants at the police station told me that last Friday night. He showed it to me on a computer print-out. I hadn't known Gary's real name before then, you see, so no-one could check.

And anyway, even if they could have done, there's so many different divisions, so much data to be entered on the computer. So no-one could make the connection. Not until later. Not until too late, maybe.'

'But now you have.'

'It doesn't take a genius, Aidan. Darren had to go, anyway. This was your big break. You were there, I think you sent him a fake message about drugs. I'm not sure. He was looking for you in any case, just to tell you where I was. Sweet of him, seeing he didn't like you at all. But he found you, you told him you had some stuff. So you go up a back alley, two boys in the same business with the same sideline. He thought he could trust you that far. He thought he had you sussed. But he hadn't, the silly bastard. Christ, he warned me about your Stanley, he told me you carried a knife quite often. But, you know, I honestly think that he thought that if I liked you then you must have some redeeming feature somewhere. So he took the risk. Poor, sweet, stupid Darren. And you killed him. One swift, well-aimed blow. Just like you did Gary. Though with Darren you had time to stick in a few more afterwards, just for fun. You killed them both, Aidan, in cold blood. For your own advantage and for your own amusement.'

Aidan laughed. 'Don't worry, Gordo. I won't tell the cops you lied to cover up for me. Anyway, you promised you would.' He gave me a knowing look.

'Oh yes. I promised to cover up for you about Gary. And about me and about Toby. But Darren doesn't come into it. Darren's another matter altogether. I didn't make any promises about Darren.' I got up, walked over to the window and looked through the curtains. 'I can't forgive you for that one, Aidan. I really want to. I mean, I still have this appalling feeling I love you, but really –' and I turned and spat at him – 'you are no fucking good. You are evil.

Aidan shrugged. 'Darren was a nosy bastard. He shouldn't have slagged me off like that. I enjoyed sticking him, the pop-eyed little bastard. I wish I'd cut his face up as well while I was at it.' He laughed. 'God, he looked surprised when I stuck him. I loved it.'

He put down his can of lager and reached into his pocket. Guess what he pulled out. It was the famous Stanley knife – a small, plastic-handled thing. 'I normally keep this down my sock,' he explained. 'That's what our kid always does. In case of emergencies and that. God, Gordo, what did you want to bring all this up for? You after some of the same, are you? I thought

156

we'd finished with it all.'

The door to my flat opened. Aidan leapt to his feet. He made a lunge towards me, but I darted away, hurling at him a hefty biology book I'd kept handy for that express purpose. It caught him a blow on the head and he staggered. Detective Sergeant Morgan and his junior, the handsome brute, stood in the doorway of my sitting room. Morgan applauded my throw; the other made a swift grab at Aidan's hand and easily disarmed him. Two uniformed policemen came in and took hold of my best beloved. Morgan began to caution him. Aidan looked at me with disgust.

'You bastard,' he shouted. That was the first time I'd ever heard him really shout. 'You fucking bastard. I thought I could trust you. All that shit you fed me. I'll get you. I'll fucking get you – '

An element of the absurd was injected by the sight of one of the uniformed policemen scrupulously writing down Aidan's every expletive. But then he stopped his shouting as quickly as he'd started. A broad, sexy grin crept over his face. He gave one more rubber-necking smile. I looked at him properly and my heart nearly broke.

'It's all right, Gordon,' he said. 'I reckon you done pretty good, actually. That night I met you, I never guessed you'd got what it takes.' I shook my head and gave a wincing smile. 'No, really,' he went on. I looked at him – oh, those ears. 'Listen, Gordo, you're a real dark horse. You really are. Do us one favour. Come and see us. Write to us or summat. Keep in touch. If you don't – I'll set our kid on you.'

I laughed. 'I wouldn't want that. He's a hard bastard, our kid.' We both laughed. The Police were baffled. 'All right. I give you my word.'

'That's good enough.' I started to laugh. 'No, really, honest to God, Gordon, it's good enough.' And he laughed. 'You fucking dark horse.'

Morgan coughed. 'Well, if you two have finished – perhaps we could make a move – ' He broke off. Aidan and I stood and grinned at each other. It was all worth it. In that moment he admired and respected me.

'Your fucking principles,' he said, as they turned him to lead him away. 'Brilliant,' he called back. They took him away. A tear came into one of my eyes and I let it fall. Morgan gave me a peculiar look.

'I don't know how you do it,' he said. 'They seem to love you when we've arrested them. Toby Castle gives you theatre tickets, this one pays you compliments. I wish we knew your secret.'

I smiled. What could I say to this? It meant nothing from him. But from Aidan – well, it meant everything.

'Shall we go?' I said to Morgan. 'Let's get this business finished.'

also by Jeremy Beadle:

DEATH SCENE

When Guy Latimer's mutilated body is found in an alleyway outside one of London's leading gay nightclubs, at first glance it seems the work of muggers or a maniac. But circumstances suggest his assailant was known to him; and suspicion quickly falls on his circle of gay friends, who find themselves obliged to join forces in an attempt to solve the killing if they are to escape the consequences of a murder charge.

'This impressive murder mystery marks an impressive debut by this talented new writer. The book works on several levels - as an exciting and compulsive whodunit and as an acutely observed commentary on gay life in a post-AIDS world. Ends with an ingenious twist (which cannot be anticipated) which cleverly frustrates all expectations. Definitely worth investigating' - *Time Out*

'Grabbing the reader's attention and keeping them hooked until the last page' - *Gay Times*

'A narrative to keep you guessing, cutting through a slice of gay life in the 1980s. You don't have to be gay to relish picking up the clues or catching the red herrings, although if you are gay and familiar with the scene in question there's an additional pleasure in identifying the recognisable backgrounds and typical characters' - *Seven Days*

ISBN 0 85449 088 4
UK £4.95/US $8.95

GMP books can be ordered from any bookshop in the UK, and from specialised bookshops overseas. If you prefer to order by mail, please send full retail price plus £1.50 for postage and packing to:

GMP Publishers Ltd (GB),
P O Box 247, London N17 9QR.
For payment by Access/Eurocard/Mastercard/American Express/Visa, please give number and signature.
A comprehensive mail-order catalogue is also available.

In North America order from Alyson Publications Inc.,
40 Plympton St, Boston, MA 02118, USA.

In Australia order from Stilone Pty Ltd,
P O Box 155, Broadway, NSW 2007, Australia.

Name and Address in block letters please:

Name _____

Address _____

_____

_____